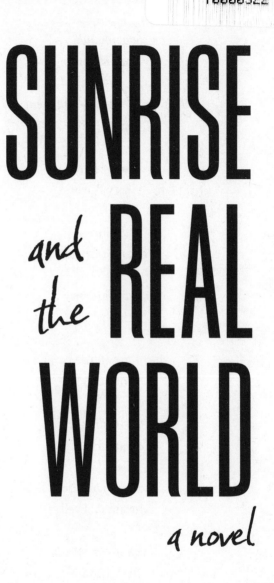

SUNRISE
and the
the REAL
WORLD

a novel

Fiction from Islandport Press

Spoonhandle
Ruth Moore

This Time Might Be Different
Elaine Ford

Robbed Blind
Gerry Boyle

Silence
William Carpenter

Blue Summer
Jim Nichols

Just East of Nowhere
Scot Lehigh

Pink Chimneys
Ardeana Hamlin

Contentment Cove
Miriam Colwell

Speak to the Winds
Ruth Moore

SUNRISE

and the

REAL

the

WORLD

a novel

Martha Tod Dudman

ISLANDPORT PRESS

ISLANDPORT PRESS

Islandport Press
P.O. Box 10
Yarmouth, Maine 04096
www.islandportpress.com
info@islandportpress.com

First Edition: November 2023
Printed in the United States of America.

ISBN: 978-1-952143-68-7
Ebook ISBN: 978-1-952143-80-9
Library of Congress Control Number: 2023939962

Dean L. Lunt | Editor-in-Chief, Publisher
Genevieve A. Morgan | Editor
Shannon M. Butler | Vice President
Emily A. Lunt | Book Designer

Before

The sun's not up, but I've been awake since three a.m., alone in my tiny room.

Might as well get up.

The room is chilly; I pull on my clothes in a hurry, then go out into the dimly lit hallway, a long corridor of closed doors where other residents—painters and poets and novelists—are dreaming their dreams. I hear them sigh in their sleep as I pass, and then I am out the door and into the cold air of the early morning.

The moon's nearly full, lighting the broad dirt path. My studio's far at the back, beyond all the others, and I have to cross the damp grass, where it's darker, to get to my studio door.

Every time that I come out early like this, and alone, I'm afraid that somebody's waiting in there, sitting where I won't see him until I put on the light.

There's no one this morning, of course, just a room with a glaring, unflattering light, a desk, a daybed, a chair: the bare bones of creation provided to every resident at Caledonia, the artists' colony where I am staying.

I sit down at the desk and open my laptop. Dive in, as I have every day since I came here to Caledonia. I'm trying to get the story right, at least on the page. Trying to explain what happened thirty years ago, when I worked at Sunrise Academy.

Begin with the body, my friend Alan always tells me; somehow, that doesn't seem right. I should start where it all began and zigzag my way through the wilderness of events, like I'm following a path through the trees.

Begin at Sunrise Academy, after the bodies were discovered, after the shouting was over, by the lake on a hot summer day.

"You realize, don't you, that nothing's ever going to be the same?" Elliot asked me.

He was standing quite close to me, but I didn't touch him. I didn't want to. Not after what happened.

"We're never going to go back to the way it was," he said.

He was right. We never did. All the violence and near-violence had erased everything else at Sunrise Academy—all memory of how things used to be—and I was an entirely different person from the naive young girl who'd come down that dirt driveway a year ago.

Sunrise

ONE

On a chilly day in late April 1980, I drove out to Sunrise Academy for the first time. I'd gotten directions over the phone, written them on a piece of notebook paper that lay on the seat beside me. *Take a left at the corner store just north of Ellsworth*, the instructions read. Right away, it was country the way it only can be in Maine: old barn with a sagging roof, a couple of cows in a field, white ranch house with a black asphalt drive, two dogs tied up in the yard going crazy barking.

There was the sign: SUNRISE ACADEMY, then a dirt drive, unpaved and rutty. The land was wild and uninviting—tangled woods on the left; a bunchy, overgrown field on the right. Everything felt like an omen.

A few more turns, then there was the lake, so big you could hardly see the far side, just a vague line of trees and a few scattered houses. Years later, I'd go to dinner at one of those faraway houses and, looking across the water, see a desolate clump of buildings on the opposite shore.

"What's that string of lights over there?"

My host, making supper, glanced over: "Oh, that's Port in a Storm. You know, where they have that residential treatment center for troubled teens."

"Did it used to be called Sunrise Academy?"

"Yeah, I guess so. A long time ago."

"I worked there for a while, back in the eighties."

"Oh yeah?"

My friend continued chopping greens for the salad. I could smell the vinegar. It would be a nice supper.

I thought of telling her the whole story, the one I am telling you now, but then she would always think of it, every time she looked out across the darkening water, and I didn't want to curse her that way.

There were still patches of snow on the ground, and the lake had a flat, sullen look. The air was chilly. I wore a navy blue A-line skirt for my interview, black tights, and black oxford shoes with chunky heels that I'd thought looked responsible, vaguely academic—the right outfit for a *staff counselor* at a residential treatment center for troubled youth. Still, I felt self-conscious and wrongly dressed as I walked toward the building he'd called *the lodge* on the phone. Wide windows reflected the blotched April landscape, and it was impossible to see who was watching me from inside.

It was dark in the lodge. One big room with four or five long wooden tables, old couches, an empty fireplace, and a closed door leading to the "ICU" where confrontations took place. Next winter, one of the counselors, Sage, would break a kid's arm there, but I didn't know that yet. There was so much I didn't know that early spring day, walking into the lodge.

Three men were having lunch at one of the tables. One was tall and good-looking with a kind face and dark hair.

"I'm Garrett," he said, getting up.

"Sage," said the second man, older, also handsome, in a battered way.

The third man just looked at me steadily through wire-rimmed glasses. "I'm Elliot," he finally said. "And you are...?"

"Lorraine."

"Lorraine," Elliot repeated slowly, as if tasting my name.

All three men were wearing blue jeans and looked as if they hadn't shaved in a few days. They were different from one another, but they all had the same weary, sick-of-it-all look that seemed cool. I wished I hadn't worn the A-line skirt. Or the academic shoes.

"You here for a job?" Sage asked, giving me one of those appraising, up-and-down looks that were allowed back then, even among men like this who worked in social services, had facial hair, and smoked pot.

"Yeah. I'm looking for Doug Ritter." The guy I'd spoken to on the phone, the director.

"He's up in the office," said Garrett, jerking his head toward the stairs.

Just then, a tiny, pretty woman burst into the lodge. She was wearing a jean jacket over a hooded sweatshirt and big, clumpy hiking boots. Her hair was short and rumpled, as if she hadn't combed it all day. She looked furious.

"Which one of you is taking the hike out?" she demanded. "I got the van gassed up half an hour ago. This is getting old."

"Hey, calm down, Claire," Sage said.

She turned on him angrily, but Garrett said, "I'll take it, if nobody else will."

"It's Elliot's turn," Claire said.

Elliot had his back to her and didn't bother to turn around. "Yeah. But now I can't do it. We moved Group."

Like they were speaking a foreign language.

"Well, what am I supposed to do?"

Elliot shrugged, kept eating.

"Elliot! Look at me!" Claire demanded.

He put down his sandwich with exaggerated slowness, like a kid does, to annoy his mother.

"Relax, Claire," he said tiredly. "We can talk later."

She glared at him, and I wondered if Elliot and Claire were a couple. There was that shimmer between them, along with her outsized anger.

"Fine!" Claire turned toward the door. "Come on, Garrett." Then she left, not even glancing at me.

Garrett regarded Elliot for a moment with resigned disgust.

Elliot shrugged and continued eating his sandwich. He was wearing a wedding ring. Was Claire his wife? It was confusing. I felt like I was watching a play but had come in at the second act.

Sage, the battered-looking one, said, "It's her last day," as if that explained it. "Come on. I'll take you upstairs."

TWO

The first day on the job, I got twenty-seven blackfly bites. We took canoes across the lake, then, halfway over, it started to rain. Later, when the sun came out, some of the residents weeded the vegetable garden. This was part of the program at Sunrise: tending the garden and feeding the chickens was supposed to be therapeutic. It was way too hot. Although it was only May, it felt like July. I kept meeting staff and kids but couldn't keep all their names straight. Looked like there was no formal training—I was just supposed to learn on the job. Late in the afternoon, someone told me to "take the waterfront"—whatever that meant. Some of the kids were hanging out at the lakeshore, so I went over to sit on the bank beside a tall, dark-haired woman named Evelyn, who was older than the rest of the staff and wore large, dark sunglasses.

"I'm exhausted," I said, sinking down beside her.

"Get used to it," Evelyn said, then stood and stalked over to the lake, where two of the boys were shoving each other, knee-deep in the murky water.

"Cut it out," she said, and they stopped fighting at once. She came back to sit beside me.

"Your first day, right? It'll get easier."

"I hope so," I said.

I was beginning to wonder why I'd ever taken the job. While the other counselors seemed comfortable here, I was scared of the residents with their horrendous histories. They'd been in trouble with the law, kicked out of school, shunted from one foster home to another, caught stealing cars. Most were wards of the State, sent there by the courts. Sunrise was a last-ditch attempt to salvage them before they were sent to the Maine Youth Center, which was really a jail for kids.

At least I didn't have to live with them at the lodge. None of the counselors lived at Sunrise Academy, where the residents were housed in two dorms: one upstairs for the girls and another downstairs, at the back of the lodge, for the boys. There were day staff and night staff, so the kids were supervised around the clock. I was glad that I could go home at the end of the day to the small house I rented in Northeast Harbor and leave all this tumult behind.

The kids all seemed dangerous that first day, alien; they came from some other universe—not the universe I'd come from, which seemed tidy and calm in comparison. Their world was crazy and jumbled, full of poverty and drunken parents. These kids didn't act like people I knew, didn't talk like people I knew. They were from some other Maine.

A sudden ruckus broke out in the water, and the kids grinned and waved as a young woman climbed out of the blue Chevy Sunrise Academy van with a great big smile, her curly brown hair tied back in a pink bandana. She was stocky and wore khaki shorts and an old striped oxford shirt with the sleeves rolled up. She looked cheerful and ready for anything.

"Annie!" the kids yelled, "Come swimming!"

"Hey, guys!" she hollered back from the top of the bank, hands on her hips. "Hey there, Starr! Hey, Adam!"

A couple of the kids ran up the bank to greet her, throwing their arms around her. She didn't seem to mind getting wet.

"How's the water?" she asked.

"Fantastic!" they shouted, like regular kids. "Come on in!"

"Later! I gotta go talk to the chief!"

They all laughed. Clearly, she was a favorite.

Beside me, Evelyn was quiet. She glanced at Annie, then, as the hilarity heightened, stood on her long legs. "I'll be in the lodge. You and Annie can take over here."

"But she said she was going—" I started, then stopped myself.

I didn't want to get stuck there by myself. What if the kids attacked me? They seemed friendly now, but the other counselors had warned they could turn *on a dime*. They were like strange dogs you meet on a trail: could be friendly or might suddenly leap up and bite you. You could put your arms up and try to protect yourself, but they would get at you. These kids were like that. Wild dogs.

"You'll be fine," Evelyn said. The large dark sunglasses hid her eyes. "It's almost suppertime, anyway."

The kids were still romping around Annie, who suddenly pulled off her shirt and shorts, revealing a faded red bathing suit, and ran down the bank to the lake.

"Come on!" she called to the kids, "I'll race you!" Then, halfway to the water, she noticed me. "Hey there! You must be the new counselor. I'm Annie!"

"Hi," I said, awkward and shy, the way I always felt with big, breezy people.

"Want to go in?"

"Not right now."

I didn't have a bathing suit with me, and even if I did, I wasn't sure I'd want to take my clothes off—or most of them, anyway—in front of the kids. Some of the boys were like men already, with deep voices and hairy legs. I was afraid of how they'd look at me, what they'd whisper to one another.

They didn't bother Annie, though.

I watched her wade into the shallow water and wished I were like that—friendly and unencumbered. I'd always been shy and inward, always thinking too much. Maybe Sunrise would change all that.

"How do you like your job?" Jake asked.

"It's okay, I can't really tell yet."

We were on my porch in the slow summer twilight. Now and then, someone passed by, heading down to the harbor. Jake and I had known each other for almost a year, and lately, he had been coming over at dusk.

We sat close, side by side on the glider. We hadn't yet decided if we were going to be friends or lovers, but I was pretty sure we'd figure it out this summer.

Jake was the nicest man I'd ever known, besides my father. He was handsome and quiet and kind, and he made me feel safe, not jittery and excited. This was what I wanted now: someone nice who would love me, not like the bad boyfriend I'd had in Ohio—the one who scared and thrilled me, got drunk and slept with other women, turned up in the middle of the night, hammered on the door—*Let me in, Lorraine*—and I would. I could not resist him. He was no good, but wasn't that the attraction?

Jake wasn't like that. He was nice.

"Think you're going to be all right there?"

"Yeah," I said. But I wasn't sure. "I wish I could have a job like yours, where it's all outside of your head."

Jake's life as a carpenter was so simple. He built things out of wood: houses, mostly, additions. He made everything sound uncomplicated and good.

The air was soft, warm for spring. Hard to believe that just a few months ago, the road was covered with snow, the glider stored in the cellar.

"I better get going," Jake said after a while.

I kept thinking that some night he'd kiss me. Maybe he was shy, or maybe he just didn't want to. But still, this was pretty nice. Other times in my life, I'd rushed into the sex part, rushed right past this nice part of just being friends.

Jake got up. "So what time do you have to be there tomorrow?"

"Eight."

"Well, good luck," he said. He was waiting for me to stand, too. He had started hugging me good night. I waited for that brief contact. Maybe he did, too. In the moments before we embraced, I felt shy and lovely. Maybe I didn't need any final answers yet. Maybe I should just enjoy this fragile, expectant bliss.

He smelled good—like wood and some kind of soap—clean, like a forest. He held me like a friend and didn't press against me.

"Good night, Lorraine." He went down the porch steps and off down the road. It was getting dark, and soon, he was out of sight.

THREE

One morning, after I'd been on the job a few weeks, everything was in an uproar when I arrived. Garrett and Sage and the boys were outside the lodge with a pile of duffel bags, sleeping bags, rolled-up tarps. The van doors were open, the boys milling around.

I brushed through them, went into the lodge.

"What's going on?" I asked Evelyn, who was lounging against the wall by Elliot's office. I'd learned by then that he was also the staff psychologist at Sunrise.

Evelyn shrugged, elegant in her dark sweater. "They're taking a camping trip up to Baxter. Don't worry, you won't have to go; it's just boys this time."

"So what are the girls going to do?"

"They're staying here. You'll like it. It's a lot quieter."

She was right—it was better. As soon as they'd loaded the van and driven away, the lodge seemed more relaxed and spacious. Layla, the schoolteacher, led six of the girls up to the schoolhouse cabin for a "centering exercise." Layla was pale and plump, with soft brown hair streaming down her back. She wore Danish clogs, long flowing skirts, and a loving, opaque expression. I never knew what to say to her.

With the boys gone and most of the girls at the schoolhouse, I wasn't sure what I was supposed to do.

I wandered into the staff office and read some of the kids' files, which were kept in a locked cabinet. Most of the reports were written in crabbed, spiky handwriting, as if scribbled hurriedly in the midst of a crisis, and the stories were terrible. Father in prison. Incest. Foster family. Suspected abuse. Cigarette burns all over her torso. Alcohol. Guns. She had gotten in trouble; she had stolen something. Her mother had stolen something. A window got broken; somebody slashed his arm and had to get seventeen stitches. Their father had shot a dog. The police had been called. Taken into custody. Referral.

I was deep in their sad, sordid stories when I felt someone enter the room.

Elliot was standing in the doorway.

"Am I interrupting something?"

I looked up. "No, I was just—"

He cut me off with a brushing gesture; he didn't care what I was doing. He had that expression he always had—detached, considering, slightly amused.

"Want to do a girl group with me? Evelyn usually does, but she had to leave. One of her kids is sick."

Evelyn and her husband had seven or eight kids between them from previous marriages. Nobody here was just regular—but didn't that make it more interesting?

Elliot was looking at me. He wasn't tall like Garrett or handsome in a battered way, like Sage, who had served in Vietnam. Still, there was something about him—some power. The kids paid attention to him. You felt like he really saw you, really listened to you, like he was figuring you out.

We walked up the hill together, followed by a cluster of girls. One of them, Erin, was a Level Four, the top tier, which came with certain privileges and responsibilities. She had decided she didn't like me and wouldn't talk to me. When she had to say something as simple as *Please pass the salt*, she would direct someone else to ask me.

I wasn't sure what I would have to do in Group. Confront them? Tell them my secrets? Sometimes, I felt more like one of the residents than staff. At twenty-three, I wasn't much older than they were, and I'd had very little training. The philosophy at Sunrise Academy seemed to be that you learned on the job, and I still felt tentative and uncertain.

At the cabin, small windows looked out at the lake. We sat in metal folding chairs in a circle. I wound up opposite Erin, who still wouldn't look at me.

"First we'll do some warm-up exercises," Elliot said. "Say your name, where you're from, and something about yourself."

I felt as if I were about to be called on in class and didn't know the right answer. Luckily, the girls were used to Group and spoke right away. They were from towns I had never been to: Fort Kent, Millinocket, Lewiston–Auburn, Monson, Rangeley. Each one said the name of her town in a scornful way, then said something else: *I like cats*, or *I like to draw*, or *I want to be an actress*. Elliot said he was married and had a two-year-old daughter named Josie. When my turn came, I said I'd grown up in Baltimore and lived in Northeast Harbor on Mount Desert Island.

"Married?" Elliot asked. I shook my head no, surprised by the question. What did that have to do with anything? Unless he was interested in me…but wasn't *he* married? I looked at him curiously. He was already on to the next exercise: Say something nice about someone else in the room.

I began to relax. Group wasn't some complicated soup of self-revelation; I wouldn't have to discuss things I didn't like thinking about. My mother, for example. My relationship with my father. The man in Ohio. We were just going to say nice things so we'd all feel good. Fine with me.

When it was Elliot's turn, he looked directly at me. I noticed his eyes were blue-green, almost translucent.

"I find you very attractive," he said.

Some of the girls nudged one another and giggled. Erin scowled.

"Thank you," I said and blushed. Was he supposed to say things like that?

"Now you," said Frankie, a large, blowsy girl with orange hair, who had been assigned to me as my *special kid.* "You go!" Although she was large and as fully developed as a woman, she sounded like she was six years old. "Your turn!"

"I don't know," I said. "Well, I like Frankie's smile."

Frankie beamed. "Thank you, Lorraine!" she said in her loud, childish voice. "See?" she grinned at the other girls. "See?"

"Yeah, we get it," Erin said, sourly. "You're a ton of fun, Frankie."

A couple of the girls snickered.

"All right," Elliot said. "Let's talk about how things are going at the lodge," and the girls launched into a discussion of life at Sunrise Academy. They mostly complained about chores, said which staff they liked, which ones they hated. Gradually, Elliot led the conversation to more personal topics. I could see he had a gift for this. Somehow, he got these guarded girls to talk about how they felt.

Frankie said sometimes she was afraid of the other kids. She'd only just come to Sunrise. "Where I was before, people were really mean," she said. "So sometimes I get scared."

Erin surprised me by reaching over and patting Frankie's arm, saying kindly, "I used to feel like that. Don't worry, you'll get used to it. Just do what the staff says, and you can get up the levels pretty quick. Just don't get sidetracked."

"That was really decent," Elliot said to Erin, and she smiled but then, when she noticed me looking, ducked her head and scowled again.

When we were walking back to the lodge, Elliot asked what I'd thought of Group.

"It was interesting," I said. "Even though I wasn't sure what I was supposed to do."

"You did fine," he said. "You've got to establish credibility with these kids. They don't know you yet; they don't trust you. They don't know if you're here to stay or just passing through. They've been burned before—by their foster families, by staff that's come and gone too fast, by their parents. They expect abandonment. These kids have never known real honesty or how to get in touch with their feelings. You'll do fine here once you loosen up."

I wasn't sure what he meant by that—how *loose*, exactly, I was going to have to get, how *real* I'd have to become. It reminded me of conversations I'd avoided at college, when everyone was expected to tell big truths about themselves. To *put it all out there*—which always sounded like some man unzipping his fly and exposing the whole red wrinkly jumble that lay within, like the man in the cookie aisle at the Giant Food Store who'd pulled his penis out of his pants and waggled it at me, his face impassive. There were things I'd rather keep private.

But then I thought of Annie hugging the kids by the lake, getting all wet and not caring. It would be a relief to be like that—just do anything I felt like doing, say whatever came into my head, instead of always worrying what other people thought. Maybe I could learn to be open and honest and trusting. Maybe that's what Elliot meant.

"I was embarrassed, when you said that thing," I said, trying out being real. I meant when he said he found me attractive. I wanted him to explain—or maybe just say it again.

Elliot glanced at me. "Say what you mean, Lorraine," he told me quietly, but there was a shout from the lodge, and we both hurried in.

It sounded like an emergency, but it was only the usual mid-afternoon eruption. Kenny, one of the weekend staff, had arrived and was arm wrestling Annie, while the residents crowded around, shouting encouragement.

"How come you're on her side?" Kenny complained comically.

He was short and thick-set, with curly, reddish-brown hair. Dressed in jeans and a short-sleeved shirt, he was small and compact but looked powerful. He was older than the other counselors, maybe early fifties. "Hey Lorraine!" he called. "Welcome to Sunrise! My sincere condolences on your new position." Then, with a grotesque grimace, he bent Annie's arm down to the table. The kids cheered, and Kenny leapt to his feet.

"The champion!" he hollered. "Write it up!" he ordered Annie, who laughed as she received consoling hugs from the girls.

Elliot and I stood a little apart, watching the counselors' antics. The lodge felt large and empty with the boys away, and I was very aware of Elliot standing beside me.

"Come with me. I want to talk to you," he said quietly and led me upstairs.

We went down the narrow hall past the girls' rooms, with their single beds and wooden bureaus, and the noise from downstairs faded away.

It was late in the afternoon, and the upstairs office was closed. Doug, the director at Sunrise, had left for the day. Elliot took me to a large room at the end of the hallway, with a low, slanted ceiling and bookshelves lining the walls. I'd been here once before, that first day when I came for my interview.

The library, Doug had told me, although there weren't many books on the shelves. *Most of the kids aren't big readers*, Doug had explained.

Now Elliot led me across the room to a high-backed bench, like a church pew, facing broad windows that looked out over the lake.

"You see that island?"

I could see a small island, tufted with trees, midway out in the water, and nodded yes. I felt tremulous, sitting beside him. It was warm, and the library was secret and dim.

"I take groups there," Elliot said. "We take four or five kids and spend the night. It can get a little intense sometimes, but they like it. They consider it a privilege, to be asked to go."

I could feel him turn to look at me. He was sitting very close. I liked it and didn't like it. It made me nervous. He seemed to be regarding me carefully, waiting for me to say something; I wasn't sure what. Then, he turned back to look out the window, as if he were disappointed.

"Sometimes it's just boys," Elliot continued in that same quiet voice. "But sometimes I take girls, and, because we're spending the night, I have to take a female staff member. Claire used to go. Evelyn's been going lately. She's very good, but she has a family, and it's hard for her to get a night off."

Again, he paused, and I wondered if I was supposed to say: *Well, I could do that.* But could I? Spend the night on that little island with a bunch of surly teenage girls in a tent? Erin, pretty little Contessa, and that big girl, Kim, with the cold, blue-gray eyes?

"Maybe you'll go sometime," Elliot suggested, pleasantly, "when Evelyn can't get away."

I didn't answer. I wanted to ask what the deal was with Evelyn. A few days ago, I'd seen them hugging in Elliot's office. People hugged all the time at Sunrise, but their embrace seemed more intimate. Evelyn was *old*, I thought, and she was married. And Elliot was married. What went on on that island, anyway? I didn't want to seem stupid, or young, and I liked the way it felt, sitting close to him on that high-backed bench that was like a pew in a church or a booth at the Thai restaurant in downtown Ellsworth, I thought dreamily.

He didn't say anything else for a while, and neither did I. We just sat there in silence, and I began to feel a deep sense of intimacy, as if we were already lovers and this was where I belonged, upstairs in the darkening lodge, with this man beside me.

I felt as if I could turn and he would turn at exactly the same moment, and we would kiss, and it would all be completely natural. As if I could say anything, and he would immediately understand.

We sat there in silence as the room got darker and darker, and then, suddenly, we both started speaking at once.

"No, you go," he told me.

"I was just thinking," I said. "It feels like we're on a long car ride together." As if we were sitting in a tall, old-fashioned automobile with a wide windshield, passing through a summery, green, leafy tunnel of trees somewhere in the South.

He didn't say anything.

"You know," I said, "in the summer."

But the quiet spell was broken, and now I felt foolish.

"I'd be driving," I said.

Still nothing. He probably thought I was ridiculous.

But then he surprised me by saying quietly, "I want to drive," and he got up and moved around to my left, and we continued our make-believe journey. The air seemed to buzz around us. Through the window, we could see the lake and the island; everything seemed far away, through the dim scrim of screen. I was certain he'd kiss me, but, because he didn't even take my hand, I felt as if I were the one falling in love with him. He knew everything, and he had chosen me.

Years later, I would remember that quiet hour we spent in the library. I knew Elliot was seducing me but told myself I was only imagining the electric tension between us. He was my boss, after all, married, with a *child*.

But I liked sitting close and feeling the excitement, the possibilities, the intensity of his gaze.

FOUR

It was Starr's seventeenth birthday. Her special staff, Cassie, took her into the conference room with Doug for a phone call with her family.

I was cleaning up after lunch, getting ready to take the kids swimming at the waterfront. I liked sitting there on the grassy bank, watching the children at play. Sometimes, I dove in myself. The water was delicious. It was midsummer. I'd been at Sunrise for two months.

Suddenly, there was a shout from the conference room, and everything stopped—residents and staff frozen in various positions all over the lodge: Contessa and Darcy and Trixie in their swimsuits. Matt on the couch. Layla, the teacher, writing up her report in the logbook. She, too, was still. Everyone was silent and waiting.

Another anguished, wordless cry from behind the closed door. I could hear Doug's low-voiced murmur, then Starr's harsh voice: "No! No I won't!"

Starr yanked the door open, pushed past me, ran toward the exit, Doug rushing after her.

"Catch her!" he shouted.

Layla was out of the office like a shot, but I was still frozen. *Catch her?* I thought stupidly. Didn't somebody have to stay with the rest of the kids?

Layla bolted after Doug, galumphing along in her big, floppy skirt and large clogs, hair flying out behind her, like some peasant woman out of an old Dutch painting, clomping up the driveway after the runaway girl, who was lighter and quicker and had a head start.

Elliot came slowly out of his office, where he'd been holed up most of the day. He never seemed to be in a hurry. Always in control.

"Starr split?" he asked, casually. I was still standing there with my towel.

"You taking the kids out?" Elliot asked, coming over to stand beside me.

"We were going down to the waterfront," I said, edging away. I'd avoided being alone with him since that afternoon in the library.

"I knew she'd take off. Big mistake, letting her call her family."

He went back into his office and shut the door, and now I wanted to follow him there, to feel the tension between us, to pretend to talk about work while a second, unspoken conversation rippled beneath the surface, but I was supposed to be looking after the kids. Taking them to the waterfront. Tiring them out so that they'd sleep through the night and no more would run away.

While this wasn't a locked facility, there were consequences if they ran. They lost their privileges and their shoes and were put back on Reorientation. And, if they kept running, they would wind up at the Maine Youth Center.

And where could they go when they ran away down the country roads of Maine? Hitch rides back to their lousy houses and dysfunctional parents, their scabby yards, broken porches? Or would they try to go "outta state" as they sometimes threatened? They didn't know anything about the world beyond Maine's borders. Didn't know Canada or Massachusetts, even. They thought they knew. But they knew nothing.

Years later, my own daughter would run away. She would be gone a long time. Sometimes, I would think, for good. That's how it feels when they run away—your daughter, or somebody else's daughter—that they have gone forever, when they go.

Elliot came out of his office again. Saw me still standing there, uncertain, and took charge.

"Come on! Let's get down to the waterfront!" Elliot called the kids. Then, to me, "I'll come down later."

As we walked out, we saw Starr coming back down the drive. Doug had his arm around her, and Layla was lumping along in her clogs on the other side. Starr was crying, and her face was puffy, not sharp and pretty like she usually looked. More like a little girl.

I herded the other kids away, across the lawn, so Starr wouldn't have to speak to them. They were laughing and shoving, released from the tension of the lodge. They looked back over their shoulders at Starr, some curious and sympathetic, others scornful.

"It was stupid to run during the day," Erin said. "You have to go at night, or else they'll just catch you and bring you right back."

"What's going to happen?" I asked Evelyn later. We were sitting together on a blanket. It was really hot. I wanted to go in the water. It was full of teenage boys. A new one named Kurt had just arrived. He was big and handsome, with thick, floppy hair and blank chocolate eyes, like a dog.

Evelyn shrugged and stared at the water. I was intrigued by her connection to Elliot, her sophistication. With her large, dark sunglasses and wide hat, she had a sort of tall glamor; she could be on a regular beach somewhere in California.

"I don't know," Evelyn said, in her bored voice. "They might get Starr admitted to BMHI—Bangor Mental Health Institute—if she keeps trying to run."

"Wow. Really?"

Evelyn studied me quietly through her dark glasses. "Does that surprise you?"

"Well, I mean, does she really belong in a *mental hospital*?" I asked.

"What do you think?" Evelyn had spent so much time around Elliot; she was beginning to sound like him. She, too, answered every question with another question.

"I don't know," I said. "Maybe, I guess."

Evelyn looked at me for another minute, then back at the water, like she'd seen all she needed to see.

"You think these kids aren't crazy? You think Starr isn't? Where do you think crazy people come from?" she asked me. "Where do you think criminals come from? We're incubating them, right here. Look around. Do you think we're helping these kids—that we're changing them at camp? You think what we do here has any effect on their lives?"

"If you feel like that, why do you work here?" I asked.

Evelyn shrugged. "It's a job," she said. "I need the money and the health insurance. Plus the hours are fairly flexible. That helps, you know, with my family. And I like the people here."

She meant Elliot—whatever it was between them.

There was a coldness to Evelyn that I didn't get. I wanted to believe that the staff at Sunrise was dedicated and idealistic. Annie was and Garrett and Doug. Or I thought they were.

"But don't you think we can make a difference?" I persisted, knowing I sounded too earnest.

Evelyn didn't answer, just continued to stare out at the lake through her big dark glasses.

The boys were beginning to roughhouse.

"Uh-oh," she said. "I better break that up."

Kurt, the new boy, had Shawn in a headlock. Shawn was big and could easily throw him off. For some reason he was tolerating it. Both boys were yelling and splashing, maybe just having fun, but things could accelerate fast.

Evelyn walked unhurriedly toward the water, and, standing on the shore, without even getting her feet wet, she said something in a low, steady voice, and Kurt let go and backed off. Then he looked up at the bank and saw me watching, and scowled.

"What are you looking at?" he demanded, as if I'd been the one to correct him. It wasn't fair.

When the boys were out of the water and some of the girls had arrived in their two-piece suits, I went in for a swim. The water was cool and lovely. I floated on my back in the quiet lake, looking up at the clouds. The water lapped over my ears, so I couldn't hear anything, and I wanted to stay right there, just like that, for always. But then, suddenly, there was a surge in the water around me, and I got splashed hard in the face.

"Cut it out!" I said sharply, shaking water out of my eyes.

It was Kurt, the new boy.

"Cut it out!" I repeated. "No splashing!"

"No splashing!" he mimicked, and shoved some more water my way. "You don't like splashing?" He shoved again, flooding me with water.

My face was drenched. I was mad now and wanted to splash him back but restrained myself and spoke evenly, trying to sound like Evelyn: "Stop it, Kurt. No splashing. Get out of the water."

"Oh yeah?" the boy said, nastily. I glanced toward the shore.

The lake was shallow, and though we were only waist-deep, we were a long way out, and the others were far away. I could see Kenny there, on the bank, talking to some of the girls. Nobody had noticed our confrontation. They probably thought we were just having fun. No one would help me.

Kurt was bigger than I was and muscular. He stood too close, staring at me with his chocolate eyes. He looked menacing, slightly deranged, like a big, strange, dangerous dog.

"Come on, Kurt," I said. *Use his name*, I thought, trying to remember the odd bits of haphazard training I'd picked up in my weeks at Sunrise. "Let's go back in," I told him, starting to wade through the water, which seemed heavy, gelatinous, endless. "Let's go back to the lodge."

Kurt stood in the water, irresolute, as I slogged by. I was afraid he might hit me, but then he turned abruptly and headed for shore, thrashing noisily through the water. I followed him, feeling shaky and hoping my fear wouldn't show.

Kurt reached the bank before I did. By now, Kenny and the girls had wandered off, and only a couple of boys were lying on the bank: Adam, the tall, good-looking boy from Southern Maine, was talking to Shawn, the big bully. They glanced up as I clambered out of the water and whispered to one another, then both of them laughed. My one-piece bathing suit was not that revealing, but it was wet and clung to me, and I felt almost naked. Both boys, in their long swim trunks, seemed much more covered than I.

Kurt had gained the shore and was climbing the bank. I would talk to him back at the lodge once I got some clothes on. Garrett would help me or Sage. I wondered if we'd have to have some big session in the ICU—or, as we counselors called it, the rubber room. Probably. They'd want him to learn right away that he couldn't act like that here at Sunrise. It wasn't tolerated. The thought of that small, windowless room, the smell of it, was particularly uninviting on this warm summer day.

I trudged up the bank past Adam and Shawn, who lounged on their towels, watching me. I tried to pretend they weren't there, but Kurt was aware of them. Maybe he wanted to impress them with his rebelliousness, or maybe he was just dumb and dangerous. It was possible that I reminded him of someone—some mother or teacher or sister who had enraged him in his shadowy past. In any event, he suddenly bent down, picked up a good-sized rock, and, before I could figure out what he was doing—thinking only that the rock looked like a potato—Kurt hurled it at me. It missed but only by inches. I felt the air stir as it whizzed by my arm. In a minute, he had another one.

I was frozen in place, didn't even duck as he threw it, just stood there dully, stunned by his brutishness and then by the rock itself, which hit me in the side of the head. There was a shout from the boys. I was shocked by the blow, aware of the force of it more than the pain: a hard and permanent feeling. I stumbled, barefoot, backward, on the damp grass.

Then there was someone beside me. It was Adam, gripping my upper arms, steadying me with his young, sure hands and shouting at Kurt.

"You asshole! Stop throwing rocks!"

And Shawn, who was big but quick, rushed over and tackled Kurt, pulling his arms behind him, holding him tight while Kurt twisted and flailed, trying to get free.

Garrett ran out of the lodge. Sage appeared. Kurt was yelling. His face was bright red. I saw all this without knowing what I was seeing. I was dizzy and weak and sagged against Adam, who held me away from his body.

Because I'm wet, I thought dully. *I'm so wet.*

"You're going to get quite a lump," Annette, the nurse, said, holding an ice bag to my temple. "You're lucky that's all it is. Could have been your eye." She wanted me to go to the emergency room; I said no.

"I'm okay," I kept saying, embarrassed I'd gotten hit. I could hear Kurt's shouts from the rubber room. Garrett and Sage were in there with him. Adam and Shawn were the heroes, and I the stooge who couldn't control the new kid.

"You okay, Lorraine?" Frankie asked, looking into the office. "I brought you something." She held out a little paper cup full of blueberries. "I picked them in the field."

Frankie looked excited by all the drama, as if there was something glamorous about the incident, and it had rubbed off on her. It was her special staff, after all, who had been attacked.

I took the paper cup from her and managed to smile. I still felt dizzy, but I didn't want Annette to know that. I wanted the nurse to think I was all right.

"I better go home," I said.

Annette was bustling around in the meds cabinet. "Not for a little while. I don't want you driving yet. I want to observe you," she said. "Make sure you're all right, before you go driving anywhere. Or maybe…is there someone who could come get you?"

"I'll be okay to drive," I said.

"Are they good?" Frankie asked, watching me. She wanted me to eat the blueberries right away.

I took one or two, put them in my mouth. "They're delicious," I told Frankie. "Thank you." Then standing up, I said to Annette, "No, really—I want to go home."

I was careful not to stagger, to walk very straight, as I left the office. I was still in my bathing suit. It was no longer wet, so I'd just pulled my clothes over it. Slowly, without saying anything to anyone, I went out of the lodge and into the dizzying brightness of the afternoon.

"Aren't you going to write that up?" someone yelled.

I just raised one hand and kept going. I could write it up tomorrow, if at all. Now I was going home.

Just try to stop me, I thought.

"I don't think you should work there anymore," Jake told me that night. "It's too dangerous."

We were on my little porch on the old, cushioned glider. He was on the bad side of my head and looked at the lump, which was larger now, purplish gray.

"It looks worse than it is," I told him. I liked the way he looked at my injury, as if it hurt him to see me hurt. Something had changed between us. He was sitting closer to me, and he seemed less hidden.

Gently, he reached out and turned my face toward his, careful not to touch the sore place. He was so tender, and when he suddenly kissed me, I was entirely happy.

"Don't go back there," he said, after a while.

"Can't we just keep kissing?" I asked.

I didn't want to talk about any of it. Just wanted to sit on this nice cushioned glider, all clean and relaxed from my bath. Not talk about anything, just lean against Jake, kiss him once in a while. Safe in my little house on the sweet, quiet road where I lived. The Maine night all around us, a few lightning bugs coming out, the sound of a faraway car.

FIVE

That night, there was a big fight in the girls' dorm between Kim and Starr. Nobody seemed to know how it started, but sometime after midnight, Starr ran again, and this time, she got away.

Doug met me at the door when I arrived the next morning.

"Elliot thinks Starr might have headed north, though why she'd do that," he said, shrugging. "There's nothing up there for her. Her stepdad is terrible. We know he's abusive, but nobody wants to press charges. Her mother's too scared. Starr's better off here, but Elliot thinks she'll go there. We want you to drive up to Van Buren, so you can pick her up."

Van Buren? Where *was* that, anyway? Somewhere way up in The County.

"Okay," I said.

"Take a couple of Level Fours. I don't know. Erin, I guess," Doug said. "She can calm Starr down. And Adam."

"Okay," I said, again, even though I was doubtful. Erin was still scornful of me. She didn't bother insulting me out loud, just glared at me in my bathing suit, my cutoffs, my raggedy thrift-store dresses. She looked at me like I was dopey and weird and outlandish, though I was no more outlandish than the other staff—Layla in her long homemade skirts and clodhopper shoes; Sage, with his beat-up face;

and the night guy, Lou, who looked like a scarecrow. But Erin was used to them and scorned me, the new staff who had no status at Sunrise. She didn't openly disobey me; she just moved extra slowly if I was around, to show who was really the boss.

"Call in every hour or so," Doug said. "We'll let you know if we hear anything."

It sounded like a dumb plan, but Doug was in charge. He told me to take the Sunrise car—a small yellow Subaru station wagon, not the big Chevy van—and he gave me some cash.

"For gas, if you need it. And you can buy some lunch, if y'all get hungry."

So then it was like an excursion, a lot easier than staying at the hot summer lodge with a bunch of surly teenagers: nobody wanting to go to classes, some dogged outing in yellow canoes meandering sullenly across the shimmering lake. It wouldn't be so bad, driving up into Northern Maine on a summer morning with two Level Fours.

As for finding Starr, I was doubtful. She was small, but she was also strong and wiry and street-smart. I had no confidence in my ability to *bring her in*. Even so, Erin and Adam and I left the lodge like heroes. Sallying forth to capture the wild escapee. Off in our yellow Subaru. *Northward ho.*

On the way up 181, we didn't say much. Adam sat beside me in the passenger seat, handsome and genial. He was so polite. He came from a good background, as he liked to make clear. What was less clear was what he was doing at Sunrise. Unlike most of our kids, his file wasn't very thick; he hadn't always been in trouble. There was no long police record or any history of abuse, though his father was in prison, reason unknown. His parents were divorced, and Adam had lived with his mother, who had remarried. He never mentioned his stepfather.

Adam dressed better than the other kids. He wore expensive sweaters, had his own good leather hiking boots and North Face jacket. He'd been at Sunrise for six months, skipping his way up the levels. He was seventeen.

"By the time I'm eighteen, I'll be out of here," he'd told me, smiling with his nice white teeth. He was charming.

Oh yeah, Elliot said one time. *He's charming, all right. We haven't even scratched the surface there—and we're not going to. He won't let us. He's just gliding through, biding his time until he gets out of here.*

Today, Adam was easy and cheerful beside me in the Subaru with the windows open and the hot July breeze blowing in. Erin was scrunched up in the backseat wearing her sunglasses, dark hair hiding her face. She didn't have her seat belt fastened, but I didn't mention it, and, because I didn't, Erin put it on, then slouched back and stared out the window as the landscape slid by.

Adam and Erin talked to one another, not to me. At Sunrise, they were king and queen of the prom, the only Level Fours in residency. They got picked to lead everything, do everything, whereas I, the new staff, got all the shit jobs—like this one, I thought sourly, driving north on this fruitless errand.

"Do we know if she's even there?" Erin asked from the back.

I shrugged, looking up at the rearview mirror to answer her. Erin was hunched forward, talking to Adam who, she assumed, had a better grasp of the facts than I.

"I mean, why would she go *there*? She hates her parents. She was all upset after she talked to them."

"Yeah, maybe," Adam said, gazing out at the countryside. He didn't care. He had his elbow propped up on the door: a young man out on a drive. He might have been driving the car himself, one hand slung lazily on the wheel. "But where else would she go?"

"You ever do it with her?" Erin asked, as if I were not even there.

Adam laughed uneasily, glancing over at me.

"No," he said. "You think I'm stupid?"

Erin shrugged. "Everybody else did."

"Shut up, Erin," Adam said, crossly.

I didn't say anything. I wanted them to like me, these two popular kids, as if I were still a kid myself. I wanted them to know I was cool, too, but I had the same lumpy, mulish feeling I got in junior high.

"Want the radio on?" I asked them.

Adam shrugged, "Can we get the Z up here?"

"Yeah!" Erin said, brightening in the backseat. "Turn on the Z."

Adam leaned over and fiddled with the radio. This one wasn't as good as the one in the van, and we only got static.

"It's AM, doofus," Erin said from the back.

"Oh, right. Can't you get BLM up here? I want to hear Darrell Martinie, the Cosmic Muffin." He fiddled some more, and when nothing came through, he switched over to AM. He slid the tuner up and down the dial, but all he could find was some old country song on WDEA, and he flipped it off.

Meanwhile, the miles were passing. We were somewhere north of Bangor when I glanced at my watch. We'd been gone for almost three hours.

"I better call in," I said. "Want to look for a phone?"

"How about that gas station?" Erin asked, so I pulled over. Erin was a little nicer now, away from the lodge. She seemed like a regular kid, but I'd read her chart. A lot of foster homes and some bad abuse. Still, *She'll turn out all right*, Elliot had said. *Oh, yeah, she's a survivor.*

Today, maybe because I wasn't trying to be friendly, Erin didn't seem to mind me as much. I got out of the car, pocketing the key so the two of them wouldn't drive off without me, and Erin actually sounded amiable when she asked, "Can I use the bathroom, Lorraine?"

"Sure, if they have one. Let me know if it's not too gross, okay?" I called after her.

It was one of those funky old country gas stations you would still come across back then: old-fashioned gas pumps, a small store with a battered porch painted a scuffed blue-gray. The screen door slapped shut as Erin went in to find the bathroom. Adam got out of the car, stretched his long legs, looked around. He was wearing tinted aviator sunglasses, like a rich boy visiting from Massachusetts.

I didn't know this part of the state; I had never been to Greenville, Presque Isle, or Caribou. I didn't know Augusta, Bethel—any of those places. When I had gone exploring, I'd kept to the coast, driving to Camden's pretty harbor, downeast to Lubec and Campobello. This felt strange to me, this inner Maine: the dusty countryside, the flattened land, wide sky, and distant line of tees. I wondered how far we'd get today before we gave up and turned back. But now that we'd reached a truce, it was starting to feel like an adventure again.

Maybe Starr would be there, after all, walking toward her parents' house as we drove up. Maybe we'd be the ones to find her, not the police. We'd be driving along the road, and suddenly, Erin would shout from the backseat: *Look! There's Starr!* and I would pull right over and Adam would jump out and tackle Starr and bundle her into the car, and maybe she'd be mad at first—well, sure—but then we would disarm her with jokes and banter, so she wouldn't open the car door and fling herself out. She wouldn't roll in the dust of the road and get all banged up; instead, she'd sit, resigned and docile, in the backseat, with Adam beside her, and Erin up front with me, and the radio station would come in—not Sinatra, not hokey AM country, rather, something we'd all like, some old Beatles song, maybe—and we would sing along with the radio, all four of us, all eating ice-cream cones that I'd purchased, all the way home. *Butter pecan*, I thought. *Pistachio*. Good on a hot summer day.

Against my ear, the faraway phone rang and rang.

"Sunrise Academy."

It was Elliot.

"Hi, it's Lorraine."

"Oh, hi." He was all business. "Where are you?"

"Somewhere north of Bangor." Leaning back from the pay phone, I looked up and down the road. "Not sure where. We passed Howland and Mattawamkeag," I said, liking the sounds of the names.

"Okay," Elliot said. "Stay there."

"Stay *here*?"

"We haven't heard anything yet. No sense going further north if she won't be there. Van Buren's a long way up. You look on a map?"

I hadn't but didn't want to admit it.

"Yes. I've looked on a map," I said in this big, patient way. It was meant to be playful banter, but it came out rude. There was silence.

"Here's Doug," Elliot said. "He'll tell you what to do," and he was gone, without saying good-bye.

What an asshole.

Doug was friendly; he always was.

"Where are you?" he asked in his unhurried way.

"A couple of hours north of Bangor."

"That's good," he said vaguely, as if he were thinking about something else. "Well, stay put for now."

"Here?"

"Where are you again?"

"A gas station somewhere. The side of the road."

"Yeah—okay. Stay there. Check back in an hour or so. Can you do that?"

"Sure. But don't you want me to keep going north?"

"Uh, not yet. She might not be headed there. No sense your— wait a minute"—there was a scuffle, and someone shouted in the background—"You still there?"

"Yep."

"Well…" Doug sounded distracted. "Stay there for now, okay? We think someone might have spotted her, just not up that way. I'll know more in an hour. Want to call back then?"

"Okay."

"That's terrific," he said. "You're terrific, Lorraine. You're doing a great job."

Doug was such a nice guy. Much nicer than Elliot.

I said good-bye and hung up the phone. Erin and Adam had wandered up and were standing nearby. They didn't look at me or at one another. Erin had her hands in the back pockets of her jeans. She had a way of hiding behind her glasses, with her hair in her face, so you couldn't see her expression.

"Well!" I said brightly. They both looked bored already by whatever I might have to say. Later, it would be my own child looking at me like that, but now it was these two.

"Doug wants us to stay here," I told them.

"Here?" Erin asked, indignantly.

"Yeah. I'm supposed to call back in an hour."

"Where's Starr?" Erin demanded.

"They don't know."

Adam shook his head, admiringly. "Wow, she might actually get away with it," he said. "Good for her."

Then he must have realized how that sounded.

"I mean, it would be kind of cool, wouldn't it? If she got really far? Like, I don't know, California?"

I looked at my watch again. It was twelve-thirty.

"Why don't we get some lunch?" I asked. "You guys hungry?"

Of course they were hungry. They were always hungry. They were teenagers.

"What do they have in there?"

Erin shrugged. "I don't know," she muttered. She followed us into the dim little store where, surprisingly, they seemed to have everything in the world.

We got hot dogs and sodas and a big bag of Humpty Dumpty barbecue potato chips, and I paid with the money Doug had given me back at the lodge. I had plenty; it was 1979. The hot dogs were only a dollar apiece, the sodas thirty-five cents. We carried our food to an old, stained picnic table under a tree.

"At least there aren't any chickens running around, like at Sunrise," Erin said, and Adam laughed.

It felt like a picnic, with the hot sun and the cool shade and the hot dogs and the salty chips, which tasted so good. And the two kids, because they were on this outing that felt like an adventure, forgave me for being staff, and new staff at that, and we just sat there and ate together like three regular people. It wasn't so long ago that I'd been the surly teenager in the backseat, not talking to some dumb adult, and on some level, they must have known that. And I knew enough not to push it, to let them talk without horning in.

I stared off at the trees, only half listening to their conversation. The hot dog tasted wonderful; I hadn't had one in ages. I thought I might just eat hot dogs from now on, all the time. Drink cold Cokes; eat these salty and delicious chips. Be like this. It was summertime; we were somewhere in Maine. At that moment, I loved my job, I loved Maine, loved these kids, even Erin with her dark, hidden little face and her terrible history, and tall, handsome, affable Adam, with whatever secrets he wasn't yet ready to share.

I was dating a man who loved me. A man who probably, before the summer was over, might ask me to marry him. My life would move on, away from Sunrise—that would all disappear—and I wasn't going to let some wily staff psychologist distract me from the radiant future that spread out before me. This is the beginning, I thought, as I sat there sipping the sweet, fizzy Coke. I would look back on this summer as the beginning. When I started my one true life.

They were still talking. Something about some movie they'd both seen or some song Erin liked. I was hardly paying any attention to them as their voices rolled on.

Then the food was all gone, even the chips, and the empty Humpty Dumpty bag skittered a few inches across the picnic table in a small breeze.

"I better call in again," I said.

I stood up, stretched, and went over to the pay phone mounted on the side of the little store. Peeling paint; a tracked-down dirt yard; short, scrubby grass. A few people had gone in and out since we'd been sitting there: some Mainers in blue jeans; a tourist couple who'd driven up in a red convertible, top down and windblown; an old man with a boy.

Doug answered the phone. "Sunrise Academy."

"It's Lorraine."

"Oh, right! Well, you might as well come back. She's not up there." Doug sounded tired.

"You okay?"

"Yeah," Doug said. "It's just—I feel bad about Starr. It's our job, you know, to keep these kids here, keep them safe."

I hadn't thought that Starr might be in danger, but of course she was. It was only a few years ago that I was hitchhiking all around the country, thinking nothing of it. And, in a few more years, it would be my daughter out there, somewhere. And then I would know. I would know how to be afraid.

On the way back, none of us said much. The kids were relaxed, the windows open. Erin rode up front, Adam in back. She and

Adam talked a little, Most of the time, they sat back and looked at the passing landscape, like any kid would do in a car, thinking whatever it was they thought. I wished we could drive just like this, across the countryside, in summertime Maine, forever.

When we got back, though, the lodge was tense and twitchy. I could feel it the minute we walked in.

"Uh-oh," Erin said, and she actually smiled at me. I tried not to look as pleased as I felt and gave her a warm smile back.

"Thanks, Lorraine," Adam said, loping off to his room to avoid the ruckus.

The main floor of the lodge was noisy, with kids hanging out on the couches, and in the smoking area, a Plexiglas cage full of smoke.

Two staff, Cassie and Layla, were standing in the middle of the room. The door to the ICU was closed; somebody must be in there. They'd brought in Lou, the night staff, and he was trying to calm things down. I saw Sage and Elliot in Elliot's tiny, windowless office, face-to-face like two angry dogs.

"What's with them?" I asked Evelyn, as I came into the staff office.

Evelyn was writing in the staff logbook in her slanty, decisive black script.

"What?" she asked, without looking up. "Why don't you take some of the kids down to the waterfront?" she said, still writing.

"Well, I just got back."

"And?" Evelyn did look up, now. "Look, Lorraine, the kids are about to erupt. Take them down to the waterfront. That'll cool them off." Seeing my face, she added, coldly, "It's our job, Lorraine," and turned back to the log.

I felt quick tears prick my eyes, and I hated the feeling. Hated Evelyn. Wanted to say something back. *I'm tired*, I wanted to tell her. *I got hit in the head with a rock yesterday.* The caffeine from the Coke had worn off. I just wanted to go read a book or something.

Couldn't we have story time now? Evelyn was right, of course. I'd signed on for this. And hadn't I been thinking, just a few hours ago, how much I loved my job?

I turned and walked out of the staff room, past Elliot's office where the men were still locked in confrontation. Sage glanced over as I went by.

"Everything go okay up there?" he asked me.

"Yeah," I said. "I'm just going to take some of the kids down to the waterfront."

"Good idea," he said. "I'll join you there in a minute."

But it was Elliot who came down the bank to where I sat on an old army blanket, watching the kids sun themselves and play in the shallow water. He sat down beside me. Even though it was very hot, he was wearing long pants. He always did, I noticed. I'd seen his bare arms but never his legs, all this time, and it was really hot that summer.

"I'm exhausted," he said, staring out at the water. "I've been fighting all day with Kim."

"Yeah, she's tough," I said. That big girl with the strawberry blonde hair, the flat blue-gray eyes. "What did they find out about Starr?"

Elliot sighed. "Oh, you don't know, do you? She's really gone. Nobody's seen her. Everything's a dead end."

"Won't they keep trying to find her?"

"Well, sure. We sent out her picture, description, and so on. But she could be anywhere by now. It really pisses me off," Elliot said, suddenly. "It really stinks. Why wasn't somebody watching her? Night staff was *asleep*."

I tried to look shocked, but everybody knew the night staff slept. I'd slept myself, when I had to fill in on the overnights. You just did. You got tired. But there were always two on duty, and one stayed awake. You took turns.

"Anyway, I'm exhausted," he said. "Sometimes this place just gets to me, you know?"

I could tell he was looking at me. I could feel his shirtsleeve brush the bare skin of my arm. It was so hot out.

"Want to go swimming?" I asked.

"Good idea," he said, getting up. "I'll go see if I can find some shorts."

He went off toward the lodge, and he didn't come back, even though I sat there on the bank, watching the kids for a long time.

Later, it seemed like much later, I saw Elliot ride off up the driveway on his motorcycle. He was wearing a white helmet and didn't look back even once.

SIX

The next morning was my day off. Jake and I went out to climb the Jordan Cliff Trail early, before it got too hot. It was seven a.m. when we pulled into the parking lot at Jordan Pond. The previous summer, the old restaurant had burned down. In a few years, it would be replaced with a big new building—as garish and out of place as a Howard Johnson, with bright shingles and turquoise trim—but for now, the area was quaint and quiet; no one was around. We hid the car keys under the back left tire and headed into the woods. On the other side of a wooden bridge, the trail led up stone steps, then down, then up again. It was leafy and cool in the woods. It was almost chilly.

We crossed a carriage road to the rocky path. From there, climbing swiftly, we looked down at the long, smooth oval of Jordan Pond, with the Bubbles at one end and Pemetic Mountain on the other side. From up there, the parking lot looked small and innocent, the green lawn sloping down to the water.

It got hot as the sun rose higher, and we were both sweaty by the time we paused on a narrow ledge to drink water. Then came the tricky part, where we had to pull ourselves up by an iron rail, the smell of iron cold and familiar, medicinal, then the always-unexpected downward dip, and we crossed a small ravine on a notched log, holding onto the crude wooden railing.

There was the steep place where we hoisted ourselves onto a large boulder, then barged through tough little bushes to the open slope. Then on until we reached the top and leaned against the tall rocks, surveying the land before us: the other mountains—Sargent, Cedar Swamp, Parkman, and the others beyond—the span of sea to the left and the outer islands.

It was a clear day, bright and hot, and it would get hotter. We were sweaty, but we felt wonderful; we could see the shadowy, green-blue shimmer of Sargent Mountain Pond between the trees and headed down through a cool little valley full of flies to the pond itself.

We left our shirts and backpack by the log and waded into the water.

Seeing Jake there, at the pond, in his bathing shorts, I had a feeling that felt familiar: a kind of wondering regret at the finality of life. This was the body I had gotten to know, the body I would marry. The body I would lie beside, the one I'd bury. I couldn't quite believe that life could be so definite and so abrupt. I always used to think the future was some big, vast, limitless landscape, spread out before me, going on forever, changing, then going on. Now, here, in his waist, in the slope of his shoulders, the mole on his back, it had ended, and I was struck by the way love could define life and make it finite. My own arms were brown with the sun, and, when I looked at my feet through the shallow water, my bare toes looked white and unfamiliar.

Jake dove in and swam strongly across the pond. I continued to stand knee-deep in the water, afraid to go in. It wasn't that it was too cold. There was something about getting wet that suddenly seemed like a weird and alien concept. I thought I might stand there all day, thinking about what scary things might be under that smooth surface. What twisty reeds, what snaky vines, what dangers and slippery fish. But, sooner or later, I would have to get wet. So, holding my breath and terrified, I, too, dove in.

It was delicious. The water was as perfect as silk. I swam forward briskly, then, halfway across, I turned in the water, as if I were turning in bed, to float on my back, looking up at the beautiful sky.

Jake was already across the pond and called something. I couldn't hear what he said, only the faraway sound of his voice. The water lapped around my face, and I held my arms out, letting the water rock me gently.

Jake called again, and a little flicker of annoyance darted through me, and suddenly I wished I were alone. But would I have felt so peaceful, so free, lying there in the water if I were all by myself? If he were not there on the other side of the pond, waiting for me? Ready to dive back into the water to save me if something did rise from the depths, something snaky and dangerous? With him there, I was burdened but safe.

I rolled over again in the water and then swam toward Jake, pulled myself up onto the warm, rough rock, and lay down beside him.

Sometime that night, maybe around three a.m., a big storm began with thunder and lightning. Battering winds hurled through the branches of the trees, and the rain poured down. It sounded wonderful and mixed with my dreams, until I woke and lay still, enjoying the sound of the storm. All the windows were open, and I let some of the rain splash into my hot, tight little house before I got up and went through the dim rooms to pull down the sashes and shut out the storm.

I didn't go back to sleep. I lay there listening to the rain until it stopped and the slow dawn rose beyond the backyard trees.

"Did you hear the storm last night?" Jake asked me on the phone.

"Yes. Wasn't it lovely?"

"You're lovely," Jake said. "I wish you were here."

"I will be," I said. I was in the staff office, and I could hear how my voice sounded on the phone with him—different than the voice I usually used in this place.

"Bye," I said in that secret voice, and hung up.

When I turned, Elliot was standing in the doorway.

"Sounds like a boy," he remarked.

"It was," I said, waltzing past him. "My boyfriend."

"I didn't know you had a boyfriend. Tell me more. What does he do?"

"He's a carpenter."

"Ah!" Elliot said. "How long have you known him?"

I didn't have to answer. Somehow, it felt dangerous, giving Elliot this information.

"What are you—my father?" I teased, putting him off.

"How long?" he persisted, and his face was serious.

"About a year." I tried to act confident even though my voice sounded reluctant, defiant, like one of the kids.

"A year? You in love with this guy?"

"I guess so."

"You *guess so?*" Elliot said.

"I've always been a bit uncertain about these matters." I wanted to keep it light. He could so easily trip you up with your own words. Talking with Elliot was like walking on wobbly rocks through a fast-moving stream.

"You still are," he said. "And you lack spontaneity. You have to be smart and spontaneous to work here. You're smart, but you're very uptight."

Why did it matter so much what he thought? Somehow, it did.

"I didn't mean that as a put-down," Elliot said.

This was the kind of stuff he did with the kids. I admired it, but now it felt as if he was prodding and poking at me, trying to goad me. And the worst part was that now I wanted to tell him everything—all my uncertainty about getting married to Jake, sweet though he was. Elliot knew things. He had some wisdom, or acted as if he did. But he was so unpredictable. One minute, he seemed kind, and the next, he was critical and harsh. I didn't trust him, so I only said, weakly, "It sure sounded like one."

"I would never do that to someone I care about."

Just then, Kim came barreling in.

"Elliot! I need to talk to you. Right now," she said in her loud way. She looked over at me. "Do you mind?" She pushed past Elliot.

Kim had been writing poems since I'd led a girls' poetry lesson one rainy July afternoon in the schoolhouse cabin. The girls seemed to enjoy the class, especially Kim. Since then, she'd been writing piles of poems, decorating the pages with hearts and flowers and hanging them on the walls of her room. Kim's poems tended to be about love and sunshine and kitties—girly things—which seemed odd, because she herself was loud and rough.

At first, I'd been afraid of Kim. She was as tall as me, taller maybe, with big hands and broad shoulders, and when she got mad, she would shove the other kids or punch them. She'd even swung at the staff a few times and had to be restrained.

But there was another side, too. Kim was beautiful, with milky white skin, strange, pale eyes, and reddish-blonde hair, and since the poetry class, she'd been friendly, inviting me shyly upstairs to her room to hear her latest poems, asking for my opinion about her new jeans.

"Do you think I look fat?"

"You look lovely."

As she pushed past into Elliot's office, her eyes were flat and cold. I could hear Kim's loud voice behind the closed door, complaining about one of the staff members. Everybody had been on edge since Starr took off.

I wouldn't be surprised if another one runs any day now, Sage said. We were all on guard for the next explosion.

But when Kim came out of Elliot's office, she seemed calmer, and, as the afternoon wore on, the lodge was quiet. A couple of older boys lounged in the smoking area, while I stood at the window, looking out. Evelyn had taken some of the girls to the waterfront and was sitting on one of the army blankets, fully dressed, as usual, in long pants and a long-sleeved shirt. I had never seen her go into the water, never even seen her in a bathing suit. Maybe because she was so old—in her forties, maybe forty-five.

I saw someone get out of the water and walk toward Evelyn, a boy I hadn't seen at Sunrise before: pale-skinned and out of shape, his dark hair slicked back by the water. As he drew closer, I realized it was Elliot. From the window I could observe them unseen.

Evelyn looked up as he approached her. She didn't seem to notice his white skin or the way his stomach pooched out over the elastic waist of his swim trunks. She picked up a white towel and handed it to him in a familiar way, like a wife would do, and he used it to rub his head and face. When his face was dry, he looked down at Evelyn; she was still looking up at him. It was a naked look and full of something so intense that I had to turn away from the window. I was so full of hopeless and jealous rage.

SEVEN

The next morning, I found out there'd been another big fight. Frankie, my special kid, came rushing out of the lodge to tell me. Her hair was wild, and her face was puffy. There were red marks on her upper arms, and she pulled down her pants to show me a big bruise on the white skin of her hip. The night before, Frankie had been beaten up by Kim and Tina, a big, mean girl who hung out with the boys.

At first, I wasn't sure I believed her story. Frankie said they had come into her room in the middle of the night, that she woke up to find Tina standing over her.

"She didn't say anything, Lorraine!" Frankie wailed, and I couldn't tell if she was excited and proud or terrified. Tina had held the door shut while Kim punched her.

"They broke my glasses!" she told me. "I can't even find them!"

Frankie looked weird and vulnerable without her glasses. One blue eye wandered.

I gave her a hug. "You okay now?" I asked, then went into the lodge and asked Kenny what had happened.

He just jerked his head at the logbook. "It's all in there."

Doug called Big Group, and we all trooped up to the school-house cabin. Elliot had come in early. Cassie and Lou, the night staff, gave their report, even though they'd been up all night and must have been exhausted. Since Starr had run away, they weren't allowed to sleep on the job anymore. They said they'd heard nothing. The girls could be very quiet; they were stealthier than the boys, whose fights were out in the open, full of shouts and punches. The girls slid into one another's rooms in secret, bolted the door shut, came at their prey in the dark.

"They hit her numerous times," Cassie said, with the stilted verbiage of a police report. "Finally, she managed to get away. She came down to tell us what happened."

"And then what?" Elliot asked, his voice cold. He was being theatrical; he already knew the answer.

"I took her back upstairs," Cassie said, looking down at her lap. "I didn't believe her." She looked over at Frankie, who was sitting beside me. There were tears in Cassie's eyes.

"I'm sorry, Frankie," she said. "I should have listened to you."

"Go on," Elliot said, sternly. I could see he was enjoying this, though later he'd say how terrible the place was, how it made him sick.

"I checked around," Cassie continued. "Tina and Kim were both in bed. They appeared to be asleep, and everything was quiet up there. I waited until Frankie got settled, and then I came down."

"And then?"

"A little later, Trixie and Contessa came down and said they were scared; Kim was hitting Frankie. I brought Frankie downstairs. Kim followed us down. She punched Frankie some more before I could pull her off."

Cassie was crying now. Some of the kids were, too; even Annie's merry face looked grave. I was almost crying myself, I knew Frankie's story. She'd been beaten and abused all her life. She should have been safe here at Sunrise.

Suddenly, Elliot started yelling. "This stinks, Kim! Why would you do that? And you, Tina, you're a bully. You got that?"

If Elliot was trying to break through their teenage veneer, it wasn't working. They stared back at him stoically, their faces expressionless. His own face was red now. He'd gotten up from his chair and was standing in front of them, yelling, but they remained impassive.

Then Layla, Kim's special staff, started yelling, too, and crying. "I'm so disappointed," she said to Kim. "I believed in you!"

I was surprised by this. Why would Layla believe in Kim? I never had. For all her talk about poetry, all those pages decorated with hearts and flowers, there was something cruel about Kim, her always flat, cold eyes.

Everybody took turns yelling at Kim and Tina. It was an emotional free-for-all, though it seemed a bit forced. This was the "tough love" part of the program at Sunrise. I wanted to join in, but I was too self-conscious. It felt fake to be yelling and yowling at those two girls. Yes, what they did was horrible, and they ought to be punished. But was this really the right way to go about it?

It reminded me of something—another day, long ago—another person yelling. Yelling at me. My own mother. Had that helped in any way? It had changed me, certainly, marked me; the question was, had it made me a better person?

There was something else that kept me from joining in— something I was only vaguely aware of, but it comes back to me now as I remember that scene in the schoolhouse cabin. I was afraid if I really let go of what I was holding inside, I would never stop yelling. I might say something I didn't want to say—about how angry I was at Elliot and how I desired him, how confused I felt about Jake—should I actually marry him?—how terrified I was of my life. Was this all there was? Everything, all my fears about the job, about myself, it would all come out in a big, messy, vomitty heap. I'd be like one of the residents: uncontrollable, raging.

So I kept quiet and sat there, miserable with embarrassment, Frankie leaning against me with her soft damp weight.

Frankie looked very young without her glasses, wobbly and sweet, like a giant toddler. She was no longer crying, just staring, fascinated by the drama. She was still whimpering a little, but proud, too, because this was all about her. Maybe it was healing for Frankie to be defended like this, after years of abuse. But what did I know? I wasn't trained in this. Only Elliot was, and now he was yelling again. His face was red, and he was standing so close I could see a little vein sticking out on his temple and a bubble of spit at the corner of his mouth. Tina and Kim sat unmoved, waiting it out, so all the mayhem seemed stagy and insincere. Lots of people were crying—the residents, staff—but I didn't know how much was real or what they were actually feeling inside.

Elliot turned, suddenly, to me. "Don't you have something to say, Lorraine? Frankie's your special kid," he reminded me, as if I had failed her.

What was I supposed to say? Did I really have to add my own wild roar to the rampage? Yelling wasn't working. These girls had been yelled at before, all their lives. They knew all about yelling. All of these kids had been raised in chaos: noisy and drunken parents, houses full of shouts and slaps, broken furniture, smashed glass. They were inured to it. They knew how to deflect it. It had strengthened them, made them clever. They attacked in the dark and in silence, their stealth more sinister than all of this futile clatter.

Somehow, I kept my composure. I could feel a calm certainty gathering inside. There was a faint sneer on Kim's pale face as she waited to hear what I'd say. She stared at me as the room fell silent, and I stared back. I felt as if I were staring into the face of my mother, the mother who had bullied me, raged at me, loved me—all of those years. The mother I'd fled. If I could face this one angry girl, if I could find the right words to say, my lifetime of fears would fall away, and I would finally be free.

I held the silence and Kim's gaze, gathering strength, for a full minute. Everyone else in the room had faded away. Everything else—the residents and the staff, Elliot in his theatrical, tyrannical pose—none of that mattered, only Kim, Tina, and Frankie, this soft, damaged child assigned as my "special." None of the rest of it mattered: the fear and the awkwardness, the shyness and inhibition. All of it faded away, and I felt very clear.

Elliot, impatient with this break in the drama, said sharply, "Lorraine!" but I held up one hand to silence him and waited a full minute more.

"Kim," I said, finally. "You told me just yesterday that you're a poet. Well, I don't believe it. A real poet has to have feelings and empathy for others. All your little poems about love and friendship—I don't believe them. How can you write those words about love and peace, when you don't feel compassion for someone right down the hall? I don't believe your poems, Kim. They're not real. They're just pretty words."

That stung.

Kim looked furious. She stared at me with her strange, pale, alien eyes, and I knew I had touched her at last. We sat staring at one another in silence, as if I had cleared a little pathway between us with my words.

The ranting resumed and roared on, and by the end of the session, practically everybody was crying, even the staff. Some of the boys looked stricken, though a few, like Shawn and Adam, seemed kind of bored. It had gone on too long, and it was way too hot in the cabin.

Despite the sickening knot in my stomach from all the yelling, I felt victorious; I knew that my arrow had struck home. Still, it was a sad, sick victory. What would come of it? Had I really made a lasting impression on Kim or just pissed her off? What we did here at Sunrise—did it repair these kids or only humiliate them and damage them further? None of us really knew what we were doing, except Elliot, maybe, or Annie.

"I've got some housekeeping business to go over," Doug said. Nobody was listening anymore. We were all tired and wrung out and hoarse from too much yelling. Sage and Jed and Garrett would take a group out on a hike. I would have waterfront later. Extra staff would stay on at night to watch Kim and Tina, posted in the tight, narrow hallway outside the girls' rooms. Cassie, the night staff, was going home, slumpy and sad and ashamed.

Frankie, still sniffling, seemed bewildered. Suddenly, instead of the geeky one, she'd become a star. The other girls took turns giving her hugs and offered to lend her things: a ring, a stuffed animal. Darcy gave her a piece of Juicy Fruit gum. Frankie stared at me, astounded by her sudden popularity.

Kim looked back over her shoulder as she was led away by the staff. She mouthed something I couldn't make out. It seemed like a witch's curse.

As everyone shuffled down to the lodge, Elliot came up beside me. "That was perfect—you did good. You broke through something in there, didn't you?"

He was right. I was part of things now.

Elliot looked sad and weary.

"How are you doing?" I asked in my new, therapeutic tone. It was the way other staff talked, even to one another, and had always seemed pretentious and far beyond me. Now, I'd earned the right to speak that way too.

"I just want to get out of here," Elliot said, as we went into the lodge.

"Come on," I said and led him upstairs to the cool dim library and the tall-backed bench that had felt, that other time, like a car somewhere in the South. This time, I sat on the left; I was the one who was driving.

We sat very close, and I was no longer afraid of him. Because of what we had been through, I felt like his equal. I could feel the attraction between us, and this time, it didn't bother me.

My heart was beating fast, but it slowed as we sat there in silence.

Elliot reached out and took my hand, and we sat like that for a long time in the quiet room, holding hands and not speaking. It was very quiet.

Suddenly, Annette the nurse and Frankie burst in and started rooting around behind the old wooden wardrobe that stood on one side of the room.

"We'll find them," Annette said, briskly.

"I can't see without them," Frankie said.

They were looking for Frankie's glasses, which had gotten lost in the scuffle the night before. They didn't seem to notice us sitting there.

"I feel like I'm watching a movie," Elliot said.

"Maybe you are," I answered.

I loved how we sounded, as if we really were in a movie, like people used to sound at college: profound but at the same time ironic.

The nurse and Frankie were on their hands and knees with their behinds sticking up as they searched in the narrow space in back of the wardrobe. Every once in a while, one of them would sit back on her heels, push the hair out of her face, then dive in again.

"I'll find them later," Elliot called. They didn't hear.

"I'll find the glasses later," he repeated.

They still didn't respond.

Now Annette had opened both doors of the wardrobe and was searching in there, pulling out paperback books with their covers torn off, old sweaters, and balled-up notebook paper.

I started to laugh.

"We *are* in a movie," I said.

Elliot spoke again; this time, his voice was impatient. "Stop it!"

At last, they heard him. Annette looked over then jerked her head for Frankie to come, and they left.

We were alone. The silence felt different now, dangerous.

Elliot turned to me with a look so intense that I had to look away. I could feel his gaze, feel him staring at me.

"So, what do you think?" he said quietly.

"What do you mean?" I asked.

"You know what I mean," he said. Then he kissed me once, on the cheek, and started to get up from the bench.

"Don't go," I said, and he sat back down, put his arms around me.

Now he was stroking my back, putting his hand up into my hair, pulling me toward him.

"This feels good," he said, his voice hoarse.

"It feels terrific," I heard myself whisper. I felt sexy, unleashed. This was territory I knew—the land of seduction—where I felt strong and beautiful and desired.

I turned toward Elliot, put my face against his, my breath hot. As I pressed against him, I got a sudden flash of his white body coming up the bank from the lake: a dwindled, smallish man with wet, thinning hair. Picturing him like that didn't make me desire him less; instead, it made me feel more powerful. He was married, and I wasn't—not yet. I was the free one. I was younger, taller, wilder. I was the one with adventure and life, the one driving this old-fashioned, straight-backed bench of a car through a make-believe countryside. He was only along for the ride. I was the one who got to choose whether I wanted him or not. I was in charge.

But then we were kissing, and I stopped thinking.

We kissed for a long time in silence, deep in our hidden place opposite the abandoned wardrobe with its doors open wide and the rubble of lost kids spilling out into the room. Faraway, we could hear the noise from the waterfront. An innocent sound of children laughing.

Then, there was another noise, a different one, closer.

I pulled away from him, peered around the tall back of the bench, and saw Annie in the doorway. She must have been there for some time, must have heard us.

The minute I spotted her, Annie turned and walked quickly away down the hall, without looking back.

"It was Annie!" I whispered to Elliot. "Do you think she saw us?"

Elliot didn't seem to hear; he was staring into my face. He looked naked.

"It would be awfully easy to have an affair with you." He reached out, and his hand was nothing like Jake's. It was smaller, more like a woman's. He ran the back of his hand down the bare skin of my arm in a way that, because of the delicacy of his touch, felt almost sinister, and it made me shiver. He smiled then and got up. And, because he was the one who got up first, I felt as if he had won something—whatever this contest was.

I didn't want him to leave. I wanted him to stay there, in that dim, sacred room with its jumble of forgotten possessions. I wanted to take my clothes off and show him my body. I wanted to see in his face the look men get when they look at a body that's new to them.

I wanted to take his strange, delicate hand and put it on my breast, to take his other hand and push it between my legs. I wanted to make love to him on that dusty wooden floor, in the dim, cool air of the library, with the faraway shouts from the waterfront drifting up from below.

But he was already standing, and he gave me a rueful smile.

"Help me look for Frankie's glasses?" he asked.

We moved through the rooms as though in a dream, always aware of one another. Once, he came up behind me, massaged my shoulders, and pushed against me, then walked away.

The glasses were in the back of a drawer, buried deep under socks and underwear, in Contessa's bureau. I held them up triumphantly.

"Look what I found!"

"They were all in on this. You see that, don't you?" Elliot asked me. "They all conspired against her."

Like a pack of dogs.

When we came downstairs, the lodge seemed abandoned. I hurried outside, wondering if we'd been missed. Maybe Annie hadn't noticed us, sitting there in the library shadows. Maybe she hadn't heard us: the unmistakable murmurings, the sounds of love. I tried not to think about it as I sat by the water with Evelyn, so stern and old and elegant on her striped towel.

But later that evening, after Elliot had gone home and the kids were helping Alice, the cook, wash up the supper dishes, Annie drew me into the conference room with a serious look.

"Can we talk, Lorraine?" she asked.

She had seen us, after all, and now I was in trouble.

"First, I want to tell you what we've decided to do about Kim and Tina. We're sending them to Bangor Mental Health for a couple of weeks. We need to get them out of here, and we want them observed. They may be beyond the scope of what we can deal with here."

"Will they come back?" I asked.

Annie sighed. "I don't know. I hope we can bring them back. I hate to give up on anybody."

She paused for a moment, looking out the conference-room window at the darkening water of the lake.

"And there's something else. I'm not going to ask what was going on up there in the library," she told me. "It's none of my business, and I'm not here to judge you. It only becomes my business if whatever it is distracts you from doing your job."

Her face was kind, and she smiled her crinkly smile. She was really nice. Annie was the kind of person I wanted to be but wasn't.

"Believe me, Lorraine, I know how intimate this place can feel—how it can pull people together. Especially when there's a situation like this morning, so raw and emotional. We all get very...well, *vulnerable*."

I nodded but didn't say anything. I felt too ashamed.

"I do think I should remind you, though, that Elliot's married. Have you met June yet?"

June was Elliot's wife. I had seen her photograph on his desk and a photograph of the three of them: Elliot, June, and their little girl, Josie.

"She's great," Annie said. She looked out the window of the conference room. She seemed to be considering the island that lay on the lake out there. "I know Elliot can be quite...persuasive."

I looked at her. *What?*

"You're not the first staff here he's taken a shine to," she said, with a smile, as if of course I knew that already, and it was our little joke. We were in this together, two grown women who knew all about these silly, silly men.

"You know about Evelyn, I assume?"

I stared at her dumbly. I thought nobody suspected their affair except me.

"Oh, come on, Lorraine," Annie said. "This is Sunrise, after all. It's like a small town. It's hard to get away with anything here. Everybody finds out eventually. No one would think any less of you—well, some of them might, but I get it. We're under a lot of stress. It's a stressful job. I just wonder if that's how you want to be known here, Lorraine. You're pretty good with the kids, getting better each day. Like what you said today in Big Group. That was pretty amazing. I just think you can do better than to get involved with a married man who is, really, after everyone. Everyone he hasn't already had."

I looked sharply at Annie. Did she mean that Elliot had been after her, too? Had Annie maybe even messed around with him? Was that how she knew so much? Annie was so healthy and jolly in her big, clompy brown hiking boots and many-pocketed shorts. She wouldn't have fallen for him. He probably wouldn't go for her, either, I thought. Annie wasn't his type.

While she meant all of this kindly, I resented her butting in. She hadn't been the one kissing him. She didn't know how it felt. Still, I wanted Annie to approve of me, because she was so good, so kind and right-thinking: the way I wanted to be. Or, at least, the way I wanted to be now, sitting here with Annie.

"You're right," I said finally. "We got carried away. It's just… you know, like you said—you get so emotional here."

"Oh, I know. And I'd like to say you'll get used to it, only you never do. In fact," she said, standing up now, to show our conversation was over, "when you do get used to it, when you find yourself getting hardened to it, *that's* when you should worry. Because you've got to *care* about these kids. This is tough stuff, Lorraine—what these kids have endured, what we're trying to do here—it's not easy. You should be proud to be part of it. It doesn't always work out, but if we save one kid, we can make a big difference in the world."

"Do you think they *can* change—most of them, I mean?" I asked her, thinking of Kim's cold eyes and Tina's belligerent glare.

"I have to believe it, Lorraine. Or else why would I do this?" Annie said. "I think every child comes into the world a good person. Stuff happens to them. They get wounded and hurt, but inside, they're still good—still pure. We just have to help them find their way through the brambles, help them recognize the best part of themselves, and bring it out."

She truly believed what she was saying. This was Annie's gift—this belief in the strength and beauty and resilience of the human spirit. And like any gift, it was also her weakness. It would be her undoing, but I didn't know that then.

EIGHT

I didn't have to go in until noon the next day, so I had a lazy breakfast on the porch glider, the morning road dim through the screened-in porch, then set out to climb Eliot Mountain, not missing the irony of the name.

It was almost nine. Downtown, the sidewalks, so empty in winter, were bustling with people going in and out of the post office, down to the Colonel's Deli for doughnuts, stopping to chat in front of the Mount Desert Apothecary and the Pine Tree Market.

I parked in the gravel parking lot by the Asticou Inn and left my keys under the front seat. Some people wouldn't do that anymore, not after what happened last summer. Before that, everyone had felt so safe and protected here in our little village. Nobody locked their car, locked their house. But it had shaken the town up—what happened to that girl in the Azalea Garden. She'd been hitchhiking, someone said. People had seen her around town: a young girl with a dog. The dog had a red bandana around its neck. Later, there was a crude, inelegant drawing of her face in the newspaper. She could have been anyone. Nobody knew who she was.

The gardeners found her. She was in the back of the garden, beyond the azaleas in that grassy part, lying partway under one of the bushes. She was dead when they found her and *partially clothed,* it said in the paper, with a tire iron lying close by. They never did find the dog. *It must have run off,* someone said, *but you'd think...*

I overheard people discussing it at the gas station when I was putting air in my bike tires; they talked about it in the post office. Nothing like that had happened in the village in years, maybe ever.

A few weeks later, the girl's family came forward. They hadn't even known she was missing. Her family lived in Massachusetts or someplace. Maybe New Hampshire. She hadn't been home in a while. Maybe they didn't even know that she'd had a dog or that she'd been traveling in Maine or anything. But you didn't get the impression, from what you read in the newspaper, that she'd had any big problems with her family. They seemed like nice people; they'd just lost track, the way you can, if your kid's in her twenties and away at college or has a job somewhere. That was long before cell phones. I hardly ever called my parents, and I was only twenty-three at the time; the girl who got killed was twenty-seven. Or that's what it said in the paper.

I went across the road and up the steep, uneven stone steps toward Thuya Garden, a public garden once part of a private estate. I'd slept badly the night before, and my thoughts were muddy. The walk would make me feel better. Behind me, the harbor was full of its summertime fleet. I stopped at the little pavilion that, years later, my own daughter would name the House of the Swans because of the graceful curve in the wooden railing.

I could hear the little stream just up the path and the cars going by below on the road. The morning air was cool. The mail boat was coming into the harbor from the Cranberry Isles, gray and white against the green water. Beyond the pier lay a clutter of trees and houses that was the village of Northeast Harbor, where I lived.

This was what was real, I thought, sitting there. This and Jake. Nothing could touch me here. No clever, seductive psychologist, no burly girl with pale eyes—nothing. As long as I could summon this perfect place, remember this moment, I'd always be safe.

I got up and continued over the stream and across that one big, open rock to the broad path of sandy pink gravel, carefully raked and groomed. No other visitors had come yet that morning, and the marks of the rake were still distinct on the path. In some places, circles, other places, straight lines, as if the path had been combed.

The little museum was already open, and one of the lady volunteers was sitting in the cool shadows by the unlit fireplace. Maybe she was reading a book, maybe knitting. Maybe she could smell the faint, cool odor of ashes in the unlit hearth. Years later, I would know the woman who worked there. She would be a friend, or a friend of a friend, and she would be my age and then, eventually, the woman in there would be younger. That's how things are in a little town—or anywhere you live for a long time.

The garden was quiet and magical. Nobody there but one gardener at the other end of the flowerbed. There was dew on the grass, and my sneakers got wet as I crossed the lawn. I passed the small frog pond with grassy banks and went to the wishing well. I had brought two bright pennies: one for my wish and one to leave behind for the person who came next.

After I made my secret wish, I went to the back gate with the wooden sign: THROUGH THIS GATE TO ELIOT MOUNTAIN TRAILS. I opened the door to what lay beyond: Narnia. A narrow path with trees on either side, a leafy cool.

As I disappeared into the forest, the gate swung shut behind me, and the garden was gone.

Things were quiet at the lodge when I went in that afternoon. It was so much better now that Kim and Tina were gone. I took some of the girls out to the vegetable garden, and they seemed to like the weeding and quiet conversation. I thought they'd enjoy Thuya Garden and wondered if I could take them someday. Give each girl a penny to make a wish at the well.

Later, we went down to the waterfront so they could swim off the dirt from the garden. Kurt, the dog boy, wasn't around. I still didn't trust him and had kept my distance after that incident with the rock. Kurt had been confined to ICU during free time, although lately Garrett had been taking him running.

The girls came out of the water and sat nearby. They were finally getting used to me and had decided they liked me.

"You were so mean at first, Lorraine," Contessa said in her baby voice.

I'd been scared. The kids had seemed like wild animals, feral and unpredictable. Now, just a few months later, they were almost like family. I knew Darcy couldn't stand creamed spinach, Frankie was scared of the water, and Trixie still slept with a stuffed rabbit. Just regular kids. Things seemed so peaceful, but later that afternoon, in the conference room, Sage shook his head.

"We're barely in control," he said. "Just barely."

As if to prove his point, there was a sudden yell, and we all jumped up and ran out. Some of the residents were running up the drive toward the schoolhouse cabin, and Sage and Garrett took off after them.

"Answer the phone! Keep an eye on things!" Sage hollered back over his shoulder.

The lodge was nearly empty. Kurt regarded me sourly from the open doorway of the ICU. He scowled at me but didn't try to come out. He knew if he exploded again, he'd be sent to the Maine Youth Center. And none of the kids wanted that. *It's like a jail,* they said, and the counselors agreed. *This is summer camp compared to what you'll get down there.*

Out in the driveway, I could hear yelling and cheering, and then everyone was coming back to the lodge in a big parade. The kids were laughing, and some of the staff had their arms around the residents.

"What happened up there?" I asked Annie.

She shrugged. "No big deal. Some roughhousing got out of hand, and a bunch of the kids piled on top of Trixie. Nothing major."

As I looked around the circle of increasingly familiar faces—Contessa's little heart-shaped face, Frankie and Trixie, big Matt and handsome Adam, Manny and little Roy—I felt a wave of love for all of them. Maybe it was just because my vacation was coming up, and I was feeling nostalgic, but I felt as if I belonged there.

Looking back now, I realize it was then that my life seemed to turn inside out. Until then, the main part of my life, the real world, was outside of Sunrise. My dates with Jake, my hikes in the forest, the neighborhood where I lived, my little house. Sunrise was just a job, the place I worked: immediate and intense when I was there, fading into the background when I was home in Northeast Harbor.

Now, everything was reversed. It was as if Jake was the foreigner now, the staff and kids at the lodge my real family. The rooms at the lodge were the rooms where my dreams took place. The muddy bank by the lake, the yellow canoes, the blueberry fields, the dim library upstairs at the lodge. That was my true home now. I remembered how it was when I first started working there, driving up to Sunrise in the early spring: gravel and salt on the road left by the plow trucks, clumps of leftover snow dark with exhaust, a bruised-looking sky the color of a hard-boiled egg.

Now, everything was different. It was August, and the air had the crystalline promise of early fall, though it still got warm by midday.

In the morning, on those days when I didn't work, I sat in the old glider on my screened-in porch, writing in my journal, sipping coffee that I set on a glass-topped table beside me. But the whole time—all the time I spent alone or with Jake—I was waiting. Waiting until I could go back to work. Waiting for Sunrise. I looked out at the pale blue sky of the summer morning. Earlier, when I'd gotten up, I could still see the last streaks of dawn in the east, that pink drift of cloud signaling early morning.

A little neighborhood boy named Brian trundled past on his bicycle, raising one hand in greeting, then pedaling off to the Neighborhood House. They were having an outing today, he'd told me importantly when I'd seen him the night before. They were going to the *outer islands*. His mother might pack lunch for him. He was wearing a backpack. Someday, I would be packing lunch for my own child, and she'd have a backpack. The whole world felt safe and lovely. I stood on the porch of my house and thought: What'll it be today? Which mountain shall I choose? They all had their own personalities; they all seemed like friends to me now.

I remembered the sad, wet days last fall when I was still getting acquainted with the Island. I would drive to some point in Acadia National Park and pull out my map of the trails and study it closely. *Turn left at the crossroads*, I'd say to myself. *Cross two carriage trails. Keep going up.* The trails had seemed mysterious then and uncertain. They were muddy and strange, and I never knew how long it'd take to hike them or what I would find at the top. Would it be like Mansell: just trees and a signpost? *Nice view*, I'd heard one lady mutter bitterly as she approached the summit. *Nice view—if you like looking at a bunch of fucking trees.*

I'd dawdled behind them so I wouldn't have to share the rocks. Then, when they had grumbled their way down toward Bernard, I scrambled up, only to find they were right. The earlier overlook had been more dramatic: a view of Southwest Harbor and Little

Cranberry Island, where Brian was going on a picnic today with his summer camp.

"You're avoiding me, I think," Elliot said one afternoon in late August, coming into the staff room.

"I think you're projecting," I said, using one of his favorite phrases.

"Is something the matter?" he asked.

"I don't know," I said. "You tell me. I thought we were friends." He'd been cold to me after that time we'd kissed in the library.

"It's hard to be friends with conditions. You're pretty uptight."

"You're married," I countered. "And I heard June's going to have another baby. Doesn't that mean anything to you?"

He sighed. "You're all tied up in knots. My family is one thing. What goes on here is another."

I remembered what Annie had said about him: *You're not the first staff here he's taken a shine to.*

"I think you're sneaky," I said and left the office before he could say anything else.

It was kind of like high school, yet I had to admit that I liked the tension between us. I felt daring and sure of myself, now that I'd decided for myself that it wouldn't go any further. I didn't owe Elliot anything; plus, it was kind of fun to play this game knowing I had Jake waiting at home.

Annie and I were taking a group to Aqualand. Someone knew the owner and had gotten free tickets. The kids on Levels Three and Four could go. They were all excited. At the last minute, Annie decided to let Kurt come, too.

"You've done good work, Kurt," said Annie, giving him a sideways hug.

He reared away, like a nervous horse.

Annie hung on. "Aww, don't be so shy," she told him. Annie wasn't afraid of anyone.

But when we got back from the water park, Elliot was furious that we'd taken Kurt. He pounded the wall with rage, shouted at Annie, then stormed into his office, slamming the door.

"What's with him?" Annie asked. She didn't seem to feel, as I did, completely undone by his fury. She seemed to think it was his problem, not hers.

"Talk about overreacting," she said. "Well, something must be going on with him. Want to help get supper?"

"Are you afraid of the kids?" Annie asked me. It was my three-month job review. We were in the conference room. She looked at me kindly.

"I used to be," I said. "Not so much now. I feel more at home here these days."

"Are you getting too comfortable?" Annie asked. "Do you need to stretch? Like, are you ready to take a camping trip out?"

"I don't want to do that," I said. "I don't think I would like it."

Annie looked at her notes. She had comments from other counselors, but I couldn't see what they said. Annie looked them over carefully, glanced up at me, out the window, then back.

There was something about the way she looked at me—not judging, exactly; more considering. Kind of like the way Evelyn looked at me but without the hard edge. As if Annie were thinking not about what I did wrong. What I might do better, like she really cared—not just about the kids, about everybody. She was good, I thought. A good person.

Tina and Kim seemed subdued when they came back from BMHI. The staff had been warned not to make a big fuss at the girls' reappearance, and we'd promised we were going to "try."

Frankie was still afraid of Kim and clung to me. "Don't let her near me, Lorraine," she pleaded.

Layla took Kim up to her room, and they were there a long time. Later, Layla came gently down the stairs in her long, flowing skirt, as if she had just put her child to bed. She practically had her finger up to her lips: *Shhhhhh, baby is sleeping.* She walked over to the staff office and looked in, serious and serene.

"How's she doing?" Elliot asked.

Layla nodded gravely several times in a knowing way. "I think okay. I'm off now, Elliot. Can you keep an eye on her?"

"Sure," Elliot said. "And Lorraine's going to be here till ten."

"Oh, right." Layla turned, so she was facing me. "I think she's fine," she said in that quiet, motherly voice. "She just needs to resettle. She knows this is her last chance at Sunrise."

"How soon do you think I should check on her?"

Layla looked at her watch. Her wrist was white and plump. She was wearing a peasant blouse with embroidery and puffy sleeves. She looked restful, pretty. Her long brown hair was parted in the middle and fell over her shoulders in smooth, shiny waves. Her blue eyes were gentle. I tried to like Layla, but she kind of got on my nerves.

"Yeah, I think in an hour or so?" she said. "You could go up there and just kind of look in?"

"Okay," I said, made awkward by her quiet calm. I could feel Elliot watching us, amused, taking it all in.

"Well, I'm gone for the weekend," Layla said. "But you can get me. I mean, if there's anything…" Her voice trailed off.

By three o'clock that afternoon, it was warm and humid. Lately, we'd had mostly sunny weather, but today, it was cloudy and strange, the air heavy, waiting for rain. Some of the kids were at the waterfront, just lying around on their blankets; nobody felt like swimming.

The kids didn't welcome quiet time, as I had when I was a child. I was always reading. I remembered the wonderful, private bliss of it, stretching out on my bed with a book. Reading filled all the empty spaces between the events in my life. It was an event in itself, the wonderful comfort of story.

The residents didn't seem to share that feeling. At home, they would probably be watching TV, and they seemed aimless and sad when not actively engaged in some task or outing. They hung around, smoking cigarettes in the smoking area, if they were Level Four, or sat despondently on the couch, staring out at the flat, gray lake. What did they think about? Was it all just ramble and fluff?

I wished I were reading now; the lodge was so quiet. Elliot was writing a report in his office, getting ready to leave. Doug had already left, and Garrett and Jed were still out. It would be pleasant to be deep in a book, glancing up now and then: the fond mother, the slightly bored babysitter.

Suddenly, Trixie came clattering down the stairs.

"Elliot!" she shouted. "Something's wrong with Kim. She looks weird."

Elliot rushed for the stairs, and I hurried after him. Everyone in the lodge looked up, alert as animals.

Kim was lying on her bed, holding the pink stuffed bear that Layla had given her. Her face was damp and dead white. Packets of birth control pills were strewn about on the floor. Trixie and Adam crowded in to see.

"Get Annette," Elliot said to Adam, taking Kim's wrist.

"I'm going to throw up," Kim said weakly.

"Good," Elliot said. "Lorraine, get a basin."

But I didn't get it in time, and Kim vomited all over the floor. Her windows were shut tight, and the smell in the close air was putrid. I had to hold my breath or I might have thrown up, too.

"Jesus Christ," Elliot said. He usually didn't swear around the kids. He looked furious.

"What the hell did you do?" he asked Kim, impatiently. "Try to OD on birth control pills?"

"I thought I was pregnant," she said.

"How could you not know?" Elliot demanded of Layla when she got back to Sunrise, and we were in the conference room. She was crying, her face all blotchy. She looked like one of the kids. Like Kim, I thought. That same puffy, soft skin.

"Didn't you talk to her? Didn't she tell you?"

"I knew she'd seen him up there," Layla sobbed. "Of course, they would have *seen* each other."

It turned out that Kim was having sex with Shawn at BMHI. She thought she might be pregnant and, with stupid kid logic, had taken a lot of birth control pills to abort the baby. In case there was one.

"I can't believe you let her have all those pills!" Elliot said. He was furious. I had never seen him so mad. I felt a little sorry for Layla. How could she have known, after all?

"She's your special kid," Elliot said. "You're supposed to look out for her."

"All right!" Layla said, crying harder, eyes streaming. She wagged her head back and forth, as if bewildered. "I didn't know. All right! Don't you think I feel bad enough already?"

Elliot sighed and got ahold of himself, pressing his lips together in a tight line.

"Can I at least say good-bye to her?"

"Where's she going?" I asked.

"Maine Youth Center," Elliot said. He didn't look at me. He still had that stern expression. I had a feeling that somewhere, deep inside, there was a capering delight in the action. He'd been getting bored, I thought. This was what he lived for.

That evening, after supper, when the long pink light of the sunset filled the sky, Kim left Sunrise Academy, carrying a red suitcase and a white vinyl pocketbook with long fringe.

Cheryl, her caseworker, had come to drive her to Portland. She was a tall young woman with glasses and short brown hair. She had met with Elliot and Layla and me, got the full report, and taken notes. She didn't seem sad about what had happened, just nodded and listened, then said, briskly, "Well, where is she now?"

I wanted to ask Cheryl how she could stand watching kids run through all their options and wind up at the Maine Youth Center, but I kept quiet. I didn't want any attention focused on me. I just wanted to get through the day.

Driving home, I went over the events of the afternoon. It wasn't my fault, I assured myself. But I kept remembering how I had been sitting there, thinking I'd rather be reading a book, while upstairs, Kim was eating those birth control pills and changing her life forever.

NINE

One afternoon, a week or so later, Elliot invited some of the kids to his house.

"Want to come along?" he asked me, raising his eyebrows. It felt like a dare, so of course I said yes.

We took a select group of residents who'd been "good," because this was considered a treat—not a *big long hike up some fucking mountain*, but almost like a trip to the mall or something. It seemed frivolous, not therapeutic, but Elliot said it was fine. He was a psychologist—almost; he practically had his PhD. You could call him *Doctor* now, and he'd laugh, but I knew he liked it.

"Turn on the radio, Doc!" Manny called.

This was one of the kids' perks: riding somewhere in the van, listening to music, feeling as if they were free. Residents weren't allowed radios at the lodge for some reason. Secret messages? Forbidden ideas? Somebody going to prison or getting out? I never found out.

When I leaned over to turn on the radio, Elliot, pausing the car at the end of the driveway, put his hand over mine.

"No," he said softly. "We're not going to have the radio. We're going to have quiet."

"Aww—come on, Elliot!"

He smiled, unswayed by their pleas.

"Not today," he said, and the kids subsided.

We turned right, toward the fish hatchery.

"Hey—it's the other way," somebody shouted.

"We're going this way," Elliot said, in that same quiet voice.

"I don't know this route," I said, as the trees spun by on either side.

"No?" he asked, conversationally, turning his head slightly in my direction while keeping his eyes on the road. There was something sexy about the way he did this. The connection between us felt stronger here, on this country road. And, because it was summertime and the windows of the van were open, with the warm, sultry air drifting in, and I was wearing a cotton dress, and Elliot a casual, short-sleeved shirt, I felt as if we were on a date together or as if we were married and these were our children in our van on a summer day.

"We should get them ice cream," I murmured.

Elliot smiled. "Already thought of that. I called ahead and asked June to pick up some ice cream and cones. It'll be at the house when we get there."

June. That brought me back to earth. I had forgotten, for a moment, his actual wife. Elliot had a whole life outside of Sunrise: a wife and a child and another one on the way.

"He's *married*, Lorraine," my sister would have told me. "*Married.*" Even if he was flirting with me, even if I found him attractive, it was *Not Right.*

"We almost there?" Contessa called from the back.

"Nope," Elliot answered. "It's a really long way. Could be hours."

"He's kidding," Contessa said to the others. "Isn't he? You're kidding, right?"

"Me? Kidding?" Elliot said with his little smile.

That was the problem with Elliot. You could never tell whether he was kidding or not.

June and Elliot's house was smaller than I expected and shabbier, with a small, scabby-looking front yard, a rickety fence, and asbestos siding. The house sat right on the road, the backyard trailing off into some woods, with a little creek that ran alongside.

"That'll be nice," I said, trying to think of something good to say about Elliot's disappointing house.

"What's that?"

"The creek," I said. "I mean, when your kids get older, they can play in it."

"God," Elliot said. "I sure hope we won't still be living in *Maine*." He said the state's name like it was poison or something you'd leave on your plate and cover with your napkin: a bit of bad gristle, maybe, or indigestible fat.

"You don't like it here?" I asked, astonished. I thought everyone felt the way I did—that Maine was a chosen place, special and magical, and we were lucky to live here, even with all the poverty and the lousy weather. There was so much more than the lostness of Maine. There was the kindness, too. The dear nosiness of the small town where I lived. The way everybody knew everything and accepted one another despite it. The way we could rally around one another. Finally, for the first time in my life, I felt I was home. Even in summer, with all the tourists and rich summer people from Philadelphia, I still felt Maine was mine in some essential way. That I belonged there.

"You really don't like living in Maine?" I asked again.

"God, no! You think I want this?" Elliot held his hand out to encompass everything: the old blue Chevy van we were riding in, his own shabby yard, and the house where his wife was waiting.

"This is just temporary, Lorraine, until I get my dissertation done, save up some money, and get a real job somewhere."

I didn't answer. The kids were already scrambling out of the van. Elliot opened his door. "You coming?"

He hadn't promised me anything—that he loved Maine as I did, that he cared about the kids, that he wanted to make Sunrise succeed—but somehow I'd assumed that was all true. Now, I saw it was only a job for him, just a stepping stone to the real world. We didn't really matter to him. But everybody was getting out of the van, so I got out, too.

Elliot's wife, June, stood in the open door. She was small and quiet and friendly and very pregnant.

"Lorraine!" she said, taking my hand. "It's so nice to finally meet you. And this is Josie."

A little two-year-old girl with curly hair was hanging on to June's leg, pushing her face into her mother's dress. June's belly was round and definite under her denim jumper, and her bare legs were pale and narrow. Her light blue Keds looked like something my grandmother would wear. I could tell she was nice.

The kids crowded around her. Some of them had met her before at a Christmas event at Sunrise.

"Well, hello, Tessa," June said. "And Erin! You look so pretty! Did you get your hair cut?"

She seemed to know all of them.

"Want to help me get the snack ready, Lorraine?"

Together, June and I went into the tiny kitchen. It was not the kind of kitchen I'd have imagined for Elliot, which would be much cooler, with Mexican pottery, kerosene lamps, and interesting plants or something. This was just an ordinary kitchen. Almost like a student-apartment kitchen—everything makeshift and secondhand, with little touches that were not even ironic but pure kitsch. The potholders had little blue ducks that matched the dish towel and table runner and the duck stencil that ran around the top of the wall. I knew that June, or maybe Elliot, had painted those ducks.

I tried to imagine Elliot, on some lost Saturday morning, standing on a battered metal step stool, painstakingly spraying the light blue paint through a cardboard stencil from the Craft Barn on Route 1A. Because he wasn't that tall, he'd have had to be almost on tiptoe, reaching upward in an awkward and undignified way. I imagined him getting annoyed, and that made him seem petty to me; then I imagined him being tolerant of the whole thing and even excited about the prospect of the ducks decorating his kitchen, and that was somehow even worse.

I imagined Elliot sitting at that kitchen table eating whatever he ate for breakfast—Cheerios, I thought, glumly disappointed by his ordinariness, maybe waffles on Sunday morning—and reading the paper. Did Elliot even read the paper? Did he wear a plaid bathrobe and go around the house unshaven and in a bad mood? Humbly agreeing to whatever June told him to do because she was pregnant and his wife and maybe, under her sweet veneer, a little bossy? I tried to imagine all that, and it wasn't easy, because for months I had regarded Elliot as a sort of wise, sexy sage—someone with knowledge and keen insight. If I had imagined his home in Brooksville, I would have thought of it as, well, *hipper* than this. Not that it would be fancy or even big but at least interesting. An older house, not a split-level ranch with mildewed siding. It would have candles, exposed brick walls, arty furniture, not a brown plaid couch in the living room and a leatherette La-Z-Boy recliner facing the television set on one of those wheeled stands.

I wondered what their bedroom was like. If they still made love, even now that June was pregnant. June's big breasts sloped out largely under the blue denim tent of her jumper, and her belly was a hard, oval thing. I imagined Elliot putting his hand on June's belly, the same hand that had closed over mine when I tried to turn on the radio in the van.

And then I was thinking about Elliot's hands and the hairs on the backs of his hands and of kissing him in the library on that dim, dreamy afternoon as I stood in the duck-bedecked kitchen with his wife, who now, as she took a carton of ice cream out of the freezer, turned to look at me as if she understood my desire for Elliot, since, after all, she desired him, too. She had married him, had a child with him, and would have another. June's smile was gentle and understanding. She said only, "Could you bring the cones and the scooper? We'll go outside. There's a picnic table out there. It won't be as messy."

A few years later, long after I'd left Sunrise, I heard June and Elliot had moved out to California. Several years after that, when I'd almost forgotten him, I met someone who knew him. My daughter and I were visiting my friend Cynthia in Santa Monica. Cynthia was also divorced; we were both raising our children alone. Though we lived miles apart, we'd become very close.

It was spring, and we were at a ball field. Cynthia's son was playing baseball, and we'd gone to watch. His team was up. Cynthia, bleached into somebody else by her years in the California sun, sat beside me on a pink blanket, where we sipped Diet Cokes, watching the game together. Our daughters were on the swing set, pretending not to love it. They considered themselves too old for playgrounds and wanted to scorn them, so they talked continuously, as if they were doing something else entirely, as they swung higher and higher into the warm blue Santa Monica sky.

A blonde woman with gold jewelry lounged nearby. She, too, had a Diet Coke. Long legs in tight white jeans and a gold bracelet watch. She looked expensive, cared for, married. Cynthia and I were both struggling financially. Our children were wearing castoffs and hand-me-downs. I was surprised at the way my life had turned out. We talked about our daughters, our jobs, the books we were reading, and our shadowy, unimaginable futures. We didn't discuss our ex-husbands or our terrible loneliness. We had shared all that already, in early-morning phone calls, Maine to California, when the children were still asleep. *I don't know if I can do this*, one of us would say, and the other would offer encouragement. We were like two exhausted marathoners running in tandem on opposite sides of the country: *You can do it, don't give up, you will survive.*

The next week, home in Maine, I would rise at five a.m. and go to my desk to write in my journal. Pull on my boots and coat for a hurried, predawn walk around the frigid town. It would be six o'clock and just beginning to get light. I'd walk by the ocean beyond the Swim Club, then to the end of the pier at Gilpatrick Cove to toss my prayers onto the water. Four fishing boats far out on the pale horizon, the sun coming up. It would be very cold. I'd walk home, get my daughter up, help her find her mittens, give her breakfast, get her out the door. By 7:45, I would be in my car on my way to work, up 198 and over the bridge to Ellsworth.

By the time I passed the Green Moth Cabins, my old car would start to get warm, the cold hard blocks of my feet begin to thaw out. There would be dirty snow along both sides of the road, snow on the fields. I'd pass that curve in the road where a fence runs along one side. Sometimes, I'd see horses standing there in the field. A little further along, I'd come to the Cheese House, then the Hilltop House on my left. I'd be so tired.

The day in the newspaper office lay ahead, with whatever had piled up in my absence. The haste and waste of life, the hurried moments. The phone calls, messages, urgencies, stories that must be written. And I would think: *I can't do this. This is impossible. This is too much.* Having been away for a week, I'd be able to see that. *It's too much, I can't do it.* But I would. Until, of course, I couldn't anymore.

And then, sitting on the pink blanket, on vacation in California, observing the golden jewelry of the other mother, I thought: I have nothing in common with this careless, wealthy woman. She knows nothing of my life in Maine, the tough, chapped nut of it. The cold, relentless clutch of the winter air and the steel sky. But then the woman, who'd overheard us talking about Maine, turned her perfect face our way.

"Did you say *Ellsworth*?" she asked. "Ellsworth, *Maine*?"

It turned out that her former brother-in-law had worked in Ellsworth. A therapist, she said. I asked her, idly, what his name was, in case I might have heard of him. The woman said, "His name's Elliot Greene. I *hate* him."

"Really? Elliot Greene?" I said, sitting up. "I used to know him."

"You're kidding, right?"

"No, really," I said. "I used to work with him. At Sunrise Academy."

"Poor you," the woman said. "He's such a prick."

After our visit to Elliot's house, on the drive back to Sunrise, the residents were subdued. Erin only halfheartedly asked if we could put the radio on, but nobody chorused, *Aww, come on!* or muttered, *Fucking staff*, when he shook his head. Instead, they slumped back, quiet and full of ice cream, staring out at the landscape of Maine as it slid by. Nobody spoke much. Not even the usual bickering that occurred in the van—*Move over! You're taking up too much room! Did you cut one? Eww!*

In the front seat, I was very aware of the man beside me. He had shown me the life he shared with June, outside of Sunrise. A real life he could disappear into when he wasn't working, where he probably never even thought about me or the kids at Sunrise. I imagined him absorbed into the quiet rooms of the house, brushing his teeth in their shared bathroom, June waiting for him in their bed. Sitting with her in the living room in the evening, watching some stupid show like *Laverne & Shirley* or *Bosom Buddies* or *Three's Company* on TV and finding it clever: the two of them side by side on the couch, their buttery fingers fumbling in a shared bowl of after-supper popcorn. His life seemed small to me, ordinary, and strictly off limits. But somehow that only made me want him more.

TEN

The next day, there was a big camping trip going out. It was all boys this time; Jed and Garrett were taking them to the Allagash for two weeks. Doug and I took seven kids out for a day hike up St. Sauveur. The trail was easy and crackly this time of year, after the long, dry summer. When we got to the top, the kids stood around, dissatisfied with the plain rock space surrounded by trees. *Is this it?* they complained, as they grudgingly continued toward Valley Peak. On the way, I pointed across the Sound to the village of Northeast Harbor.

"See that clump of trees in the middle? That's where my house is," I said.

They were oddly excited, seeing me in this new way. *Do you have a husband?* they asked, though they already knew I didn't. *Do you have a baby? Got a dog?* They sounded younger than they were when they asked these questions.

When we emerged from the forest near the top of Valley Peak, the trail looked dusty and western in the open sun. The kids were getting tired; they didn't say much. They were not familiar with Doug, who didn't often go on these hikes. They knew he was head staff and were awkwardly respectful around him. I liked Doug; there was never any hidden agenda with him, and he was always kind and respectful. Doug was tall and lanky with pale skin and orangey hair, but he turned out to be very fit and hiked easily, loping along the ridge without having to stop for breath, while the kids, many of whom were smokers, panted and wheezed and complained at the slightest incline.

They had started complaining now; they wanted to stop and eat lunch. I said we were almost there and led them out into the view at Valley Peak, where they threw themselves down on a large, flat rock, drank their water, and ate their sandwiches, cookies, and apples. Some of the kids stared out at the beautiful water and the islands beyond, and some just lay on the rock letting the sun shine down on them. There was no breeze. In a few weeks, it would be cold again, but today, it was lovely and warm, and everyone was well fed.

When we got back to Sunrise, Elliot was waiting for us at the lodge.

"Where have you been?" he demanded. "I got called down on my day off because they couldn't reach you. Really not cool."

"What's going on?" Doug asked in his mild way.

"Three kids ran away from the camping trip. Justin, Kurt, and Roy. They located Justin and Kurt, but Roy's still missing. Somebody's got to drive up to Mars Hill, and it sure as hell isn't going to be me."

I'd never seen him so angry, and I wondered if it was because I'd been hiking with Doug. Was he jealous?

"I'll go pick 'em up," Doug said quietly. "I'm on it, Elliot. You go on home."

"And, Lorraine?" Doug said, turning to me, "Thanks for a great hike today. Felt good to get out of the lodge, be with the kids in the woods."

Then, without another word, he got back in the van and headed off to Mars Hill.

The next days at Sunrise were horrible. Everyone was on edge—with the runaways. With the change of seasons, the changes in staff. With everything. We had softball games and relays and hikes to exhaust the residents so they would sleep soundly and not run away in the night. Everybody was taking vacations at once, which meant we were understaffed; the days were irrational and hectic, and we were all mad at each other. Only Annie seemed amiable and unflappable in the midst of the chaos.

Some days, I felt as if I were just running back and forth across the lodge all day long, up to the schoolhouse cabin, down to the waterfront, into town for frozen pizzas because Alice was on vacation, then back to the lodge again, down to the garden. Breaking up fights. Looking for kids who might be missing. The whole place seemed to be teetering on the edge of a major crisis.

Some of the older staff, who had been there for years, seemed to take a perverse pleasure in the disintegration of Sunrise.

"I knew it would get like this," Sage said to Garrett one afternoon in the conference room. They liked to hang out back there, feet up on the conference table, case folders spread out before them, pretending they were writing reports. Elliot stood in his office door looking out at the lodge, the clusters of residents, the staff running hither and thither. In the past, he and I used to talk, but since our trip to his house, I'd decided to avoid him. No matter how much I wanted him, nothing good could come of our flirtation. He was married—and, besides, I had Jake. He was my future, not Elliot. And Elliot picked up on it. He was cooler toward me now, almost disdainful; there was no longer any playful banter between us. He acted as if I didn't even exist. Like he was bored with me and with everyone.

"I need a vacation," he said.

"I'm taking one," I told him, triumphantly. Jake and I were taking the Blue Nose to Nova Scotia.

"Oh really?" he said. Another time he would have asked, *With lover boy?* laughing, but now he just sounded resigned, as if I'd disappointed him by being so ordinary. Monogamous. Boring.

Late in the afternoon, on the last day before my vacation, I was in the staff office, getting ready to leave. Elliot came in and stood in the doorway, watching me pack—the sweater I usually left at Sunrise, some books, my striped beach towel, a pair of jeans.

"So, you're really going on vacation. I'm going to miss you," he said.

"Yeah, you'll have to find a new girlfriend." To show him I was joking, I smiled. He didn't smile back.

"I don't want one," he said. "I want you."

I turned away, blushing hotly, and got very busy putting my things in a canvas bag, zipping up the top. He came closer, and I felt as if we were the only ones in the building. The noise of the lodge receded as Elliot stood very close and put his hands on my shoulders.

"Are you really going to marry this guy Jake?" he asked me, urgently.

"I think so, yeah."

I thought he would say something snide; instead, he stood there silently, his face very close to mine. I was expecting one of his sardonic smiles. He just looked sad.

"Come into the conference room for a minute," he said.

"Why?"

"Because I can't kiss you here."

In spite of myself, his words thrilled me, and at that moment, all I wanted was to press against him, to feel his mouth on mine, his hands on my body. I didn't care about his daughter or his pregnant wife—didn't she know about birth control? I didn't care what Annie would think or the kids watching us through the Plexiglas window of the staff office, the boys in the smoking room in their clouds of smoke, the girls on the Naugahyde couch. I didn't care about Jake or anything else beyond Sunrise. I didn't want to be comfortable or safe. I wanted to be thrilled. So I turned and walked into the conference room, with Elliot right behind me.

The room was dim, nearly dark in the autumn dusk. Elliot closed the door and leaned against it. I turned, and we faced one another.

"Come here," he said.

I moved closer and pushed up against him. And then, because we were doing this in secret, because anyone could come in at any moment, I felt like the sexy, wild girl that I used to be, the one I had left in Ohio. This was more exciting than kissing Jake. This was more thrilling, risky.

He kissed the side of my mouth, but not yet my mouth. I wanted his lips on mine and turned my face toward him. His lips were soft, but his mouth was smaller than Jake's, and his teeth seemed closer together. He kissed me as if he had all the time in the world. He was an expert kisser, but so was I.

"You've done this before, I think," Elliot murmured, when I finally pulled away. He sounded like a character in a movie—or he was trying to sound like one.

I didn't care. My lips felt bruised; my face felt flushed and beautiful.

I moved in to kiss him some more.

"Wait," Elliot said, putting his hand on my chest. "I want to know what the rules are. You always have rules."

"Oh, shut up," I said.

I loved it, this reckless feeling, as if I were tossing my hat on the bed. *Come on*, I thought. *Come and get me.*

"Oh really?"

He moved in closer, slid his hand down until it covered my breast. His other hand moved to my waist, touching me lightly, as if he were measuring my body: the scope and texture of it, how it might taste.

I loved how his hands felt. Different than Jake's and more certain. I felt as if he could do anything—touch the palm of my hand, the side of my neck—and I'd come. I moved closer, but he held me away as his hands moved over my body. He wanted me simply to stand there. *This is what it would be like*, he was telling me with his hands. *How I'd make you feel:* precious, delicious, alive.

I made a small sound.

"I knew it," he said, very quietly. Then, he took his hands away, kissed me once more on the lips, very gently this time. "We'd better stop now," he said. "Or I won't be able to."

I stumbled back, awkward in my desire. Bumped into the conference table with an odd little laugh.

"But what if I don't want to stop?" I asked him.

"That's what you have to decide. You know I'm married. I don't plan on not being married."

"I know," I said, my voice hoarse.

"We have to be clear about this," Elliot said.

We stood there in silence, looking at one another in the room that was almost dark now, then he turned and opened the door.

"You all right?" he asked, looking back.

I didn't answer, just walked past him quickly, grabbed my bag from the chair, and, without saying good-bye to anyone, I walked right out of the lodge, got in my car, and drove home.

ELEVEN

I'd only been gone a week. It seemed like much longer. Jake had taken the time off, too, and after our trip to Canada, we'd moved in together. It was a bright blue fall with sunny days and crisp nights, when we'd read contentedly by the woodstove. *This,* I kept telling myself. *This is what's real.* I looked at Jake's dear face and thought how much better a man he was than Elliot, who was sneaky and opportunistic. What had I been thinking? This was what I wanted. Who I wanted to be all the time. Back at Sunrise, I resolved to be different. I'd pitch in more, come up with ideas. Be more like Annie.

"Can I make a fire?" I asked Kenny one cold October afternoon.

The lodge had a huge stone fireplace, dark and empty in the shadowy far wall, the stones black and greasy-looking from long-ago fires. In the hearth, there were ashes and bits of charcoal that nobody had bothered to clean out. There weren't any fireplace tools—no poker or tongs. Too dangerous. Too easily used as weapons. There was a big pile of wood outside, most of it old and mossy, but some looked all right. I pictured the kids sitting around the fireplace after supper, the way my family did, when I was a kid. Maybe we would tell stories. Something like that.

"Yeah, sure," said Kenny. "Get some of the boys to bring in the wood."

We had moved into colder weather. The days were shorter; we no longer lay around by the waterfront. There was frost in the morning, and everyone needed new clothes.

Twice a year, spring and fall, my mother would bring down big boxes of clothes from the attic. In spring, my sister and I saw once again the creased, flattened folds of our summer dresses; in fall, she would bring down the woolens, smelling of mothballs and must. All of the boxes were marked with their contents, and we would go through them, trying on clothes we'd forgotten, dreaming of warm summer days in mid-March, when there might still be snow on the lawn, with the first green grass sticking through.

Some of the clothes would be too small, and those were discarded. Some were too babyish now. *I'm not wearing that*, my sister would say, and so the sashed dress and the print blouse with the Peter Pan collar went into the pile.

When we had picked through the clothes, our mother would box up the rejects for *the poor*. I never knew exactly who *the poor* were. They did not have individual faces. They were just a vast, needy sea of nameless people, happy to receive our castoffs. They would be thrilled with our outgrown dresses—the one with the red rick-rack trim, the one with the smocking. The plaid wool kilt with the giant safety pin and two leather straps that didn't really unbuckle but that still seemed foreign and proud and vaguely Celtic, eliciting dreamy images of foggy moors and bagpipes, Loch Ness and lost horizons.

When we were done with the weeding out, our mother would take us on our biannual shopping trip to Best & Company to replenish our wardrobes. In spring, there were new dresses and party shoes. In fall, wool or corduroy jumpers, new saddle shoes or brown oxfords, and sometimes a winter jacket. We got new clothes. *The poor* got our old ones. That was how it worked, in the world where my sister and I grew up.

At Sunrise, most of the kids were *on the State*, which meant that Maine was responsible for their care and feeding. They were given an annual clothing allowance, meted out by their caseworkers. The Sunrise staff could put in a request for new clothes if their special kids' wardrobes were getting thin. Most of the kids were still growing, and sometimes their clothing was outgrown. Usually, it just disappeared; it was never clear how. Someone stole it. They had an overnight at a staff's house and claimed they had left it there. In any event, it was gone.

Their rooms were a mess, their clothes stuffed haphazardly into shallow drawers. They'd never been taught, as I had, to keep their socks in a certain drawer, pile up their panties, fold their shirts into thirds with the arms tucked back, and then folded again, in a neat, narrow-chested parade. The girls got their periods and bled all over their new jeans and their tiny, terry-cloth shorts. They were ashamed, and didn't know to soak the bloody clothes *right away!* in cold water to get the blood out. Instead, they hid the stained clothing, which would reappear, weeks, even months later—behind the tall wardrobe in the upstairs library or in a dusty corner under the bed, scrunched up and stiff, crusty with brown, dried blood.

The boys' clothes weren't as messy but smelled worse.

A few of the residents were oddly fastidious. Darcy, for example, always looked as if she had washed and pressed her clothes that very morning. She would have a fit if she got a smudge on her white shirt and all summer refused to sit down on the dirt patch by the lake that served as a beach. Instead, she stood, looming over us all, on her pale, narrow legs, unwilling, even on the hottest day, to get her hair wet in the muddy water.

My new special kid, Nita, was like that, too. Tiny, dark-haired, and pretty, Nita kept her things nice and always looked put together.

And, when it was time to take her shopping, I was impressed at how she could navigate the wide, garish, brightly lit aisles of Ames, the discount department store at the Maine Coast Mall. I myself felt lost there, accustomed as I was to the sleeker, carpeted hush of Lord & Taylor, Woodward & Lothrop, and Saks.

That fall, Nita had been awarded a voucher for fifty dollars. She needed underpants, bras, some slacks, her caseworker had written on the order; socks, warm clothing for winter.

"And I want a bathing suit," Nita told me, "in case I get to go swimming at the Holiday Inn. And new shoes."

She needed hiking boots but wanted stilettos. I was dismayed by the fact that the voucher specified Ames, a store I thought of as a place to buy household supplies, inexpensive stationery goods, and Christmas tree lights, not clothing. But Nita, delighted by the outing—even if it was with her clueless special staff—leapt out of the car and strode through the wide glass doors, grabbing a shopping cart and moving purposefully and fearlessly into the vast array of merchandise in the crowded store. It was a Saturday, and the aisles were full of people, but Nita expertly wielded the cart through the maze of women's clothing and junior wear, cocking her head to one side as she considered a sequin-strewn sweatshirt, a pair of cheap black jeans, a sateen bra on a tiny plastic hanger, fake suede boots, and—*I guess I've got to get them*—a package with six pairs of thick white crew socks. *Yuck.*

Nita was easy to be with, dear and neat as a cat. She liked to sit close by me in Group, smiling at me in scoffing clubbiness at the other kids' remarks. She would give me a glance: *Oh, honestly! Can you believe it?* I felt tender toward her, and maternal. I would feel this way toward my own little girl when I had a daughter some-day—this same tenderness and longing, a complicated mixture of despair and hope and terror. It was a new feeling, and I considered it apprehensively, as if there were something dangerous about it. And, of course, there was.

I wanted to be the one to discover unknown depths in Nita. Wasn't there something about her that was decent, deep? Some hidden talent, some artistic or intellectual bent? Some proclivity or aptitude that no one else had discerned?

Maybe it was this, I thought now, following her through Ames, watching as Nita expertly tossed piles of bright clothing into the shopping cart. Maybe this was her talent: the ability to navigate the cluttered aisles of a cheap department store in Downeast Maine. A gift for discount shopping. A profound understanding of a world illuminated by television commercials and acute desire. I didn't have this particular talent, that was for sure.

And so I trudged behind, slow and cow-like, as Nita pranced ahead.

"I'm done!" she announced, suddenly.

"Aren't you going to try those things on? You don't know how they'll look," I protested. My own mother had always insisted we try things on, then stood in the door of the dressing room, arms akimbo. *Don't be silly, girls! They can't see.*

"I already know how they'll look. I know what fits me," Nita said but didn't resist when I urged her gently toward the dressing rooms. This was an adventure for her, I realized, an adventure for both of us. I was tasting what I would taste again, years later, shepherding my own little girl toward the dressing rooms in various stores and cities. Her brave, impossible little body, her flamboyant impatience with her mother's taste. *I want the leopard-skin one. I want the one with the glitter.* Where had she come from, this daughter? Same place as Nita, I guessed. Some distant shore.

Years later, I would hear that Nita was working as a high-priced hooker in downtown Portland, but that might not have been true.

Nita called me one time, a few years after we'd both left Sunrise.

You know who this is?

No.

It's Anita!

I hardly recognized her voice. It sounded so hoarse now, so old. It's cigarettes, I thought. That's what happened. *A whiskey voice*, my mother would have called it.

Anita?

Nita Pelletier! You know!

She wanted to come and visit. *Might be up that way*, she said.

I looked around at my house, which was full of sunlight. I was still married then, and we had a child. I imagined Nita coming into our house with her hoarse voice, her furtive look, peering down at Susannah.

That would be nice, I said, guardedly.

Nita never did come, of course, and I never heard from her again.

We'd all pledged to remain in touch back then, when first one, then another, left Sunrise Academy. We'd felt glued together by what had happened. But then, the way things go, the feeling had faded away.

Nita stood before me now in a white bathing suit I never would have picked for myself. A one-piece, with a single silver-toned buckle that twinkled in the fluorescent glare. But somehow, on Nita, it looked exquisite, showcasing her tiny, perfect, voluptuous young body.

I felt uneasy, old, and used up. I was twenty-three.

"What do you think?" Nita asked, turning this way and that. She already knew what *she* thought. So, too, the black jeans, the pink shirt, the black sweater. Everything was transformed when Nita put it on.

"You're not going to make me try on the bras too, are you?"

"No, of course not."

"Let's see how much it costs," I told her, once again the mother, coming into the tiny, drab dressing room with some lady coughing next door. The cold, merciless lights overhead were for Nita, like everything else, somehow flattering.

She had thrown all the clothes she didn't want on the floor, and they lay inside out on the beige speckled linoleum.

"Pick those up," I told her, gently, adding up the prices of Nita's selections. It wasn't very much, altogether. My mother and I could have spent five times that much on a single dress for some special occasion.

Nita looked at me. I wasn't sure she could add. She simply stood there, waiting, in her regular clothes, holding the white bathing suit in her hand.

"I want this, at least," she said, used to disappointment.

"I think we can get it all," I said.

I didn't say it was too much, although of course it was. Nita's would-be purchases added up to nearly one hundred dollars. The State had apportioned half that amount. I would pay the rest. It wasn't like I was rich or anything, but I was richer than Nita. I was making, at the time, about $12,000 a year. I was vaguely beginning to understand, after years of comfort and luck and security, there were pillars behind me. Safe oceans. Financially, at least, I was secure. This little girl stood alone.

"We can do it," I told Nita, when we got to the register.

Nita didn't understand or try to follow all the intricacies of the transaction. I paid in two batches, so I could turn in the correct receipt to Nita's caseworker. The second receipt, the one showing the items I paid for, would be my secret.

It was cold—early December, often the coldest month of the year on the coast of Maine. That biting, gray-fanged wind. The clashing waves. When I drove up to Sunrise Academy in the early morning, the sea was dense and choppy on either side of the bridge leading off the Island. The fields of Trenton were brown now, and beyond them lay dusky trees and sullen cows. Further on, the Cheese House was closed for the winter. They'd covered the giant mouse on the roof with a bright blue tarp, or maybe they'd taken him down.

Some of the residents needed new jackets. All of the kids needed boots. Someone had donated a lot of outerwear and a big batch of moon boots in various sizes to Sunrise for winter outings. They were really warm.

"But I'm not wearing fucking snow pants," Erin announced.

"Language," said Garrett.

The lodge smelled of wool and smoke.

I looked around at the kids trying on their donated clothes, smiling, grousing, but safe and warm enough to complain. Sometimes it is hard to see how lucky you are—until your luck runs out.

TWELVE

We were having a Christmas party at Sunrise.

"You bringing Jake?" Annie asked.

I shrugged. I hadn't decided yet, but I didn't think so. Too awkward.

Elliot had never met Jake, and I wasn't sure I wanted him to; I was afraid of Elliot's judgment. Things had cooled between us over the fall, and he hadn't tried to kiss me since that time in the conference room. I wondered if he was waiting for me to make the next move. I could feel the buzz between us, liked the quivery nervousness I felt around him, and liked him watching me as I moved about the lodge. In my dreams, sometimes, we were kissing.

When I woke beside Jake's kind, warm body, I lay there, feeling guilty and scared.

The day of the party arrived, and the lodge was decorated with a tall Christmas tree, some kind of red ribbon bunting, lots of little white lights. There was a big fire in the fireplace, and Matt, who was Level Four now, watched over it, proud of his responsibility.

Adam was standing nearby. He might be able to finish the program and go home in a few months. *I can't wait*, he'd told me. His mother and stepfather were coming up for the party. Afterwards, they'd take him back to Cumberland for a week, on a trial visit.

"By next Christmas, this will all be forgotten," he said. "It'll be like it never even happened. I'll be back at school, back with my friends. Getting ready to graduate."

Adam's parents arrived nervously early. His mother, who was thin and stylish with blonde hair and gold earrings, brought cupcakes decorated with little Santas. She carried them on a big tray. Her husband, Adam's stepfather, followed her, big and gruff in a good wool coat. He seemed nice, but the staff didn't trust him.

Adam's real father wouldn't be coming. He was still in prison. I had seen his photograph, which Adam kept in his room. *I hate him*, Adam said. *For what he did to my mom.*

Elliot said Adam wasn't ready to talk about what his dad had done. *When he does, there's gonna be an eruption.*

But, right now, it was all cupcakes and candy kisses. Strings of tiny white Christmas lights looped along the black windows. *Gets dark so early*, somebody said, *this time of year.*

"Doesn't it look pretty?" Frankie asked, running up to me, all excited.

Nita, who was standing nearby, turned away, with a little *puh!* of contempt. Nita hated sharing me with Frankie. *How come they gave you two special kids?* she'd ask, her back stiff. She wouldn't look at me when she asked that.

"What are you giving me, Lorraine?" Frankie asked, oblivious. "You got a present for me?"

I did: a makeup kit with perfume and all kinds of lipstick and eyeshadow—not actually allowed at Sunrise, but I knew Frankie would love it.

For Nita, I'd bought a white furry hat with matching mittens. She'd either love them or hate them; I didn't know which but was afraid it would be the latter. Of course I wanted Nita to love them and felt as nervous about my gift as I would when, years later, I bought my own daughter a fuzzy blue sweater.

"Thanks, Mom," she would say, casually ironic, and I would read into that whatever I could.

Adam's mother stood awkwardly by her cupcakes, as if guarding them. She was clearly scared of the kids. Adam was doing an act for her: the young delinquent, standing across the room with the other boys, after giving her one quick kiss.

"Want to see my room?" he'd asked her, finally, at Annie's urging.

Now, the residents were giving their special staff presents. Nita gave me a Christmas tree ornament she'd bought in a kiosk at the Maine Coast Mall. It was red and shiny, with *Anita* in glittery script.

"Annie helped me," she said. "She got me the glitter and helped me write my name."

I could tell Nita was proud of what she had made and pleased when I exclaimed over the gift, though she looked aside, with a bored expression.

I kept that ornament and still had it years later, long after Sunrise Academy had closed down. I put it on the tree every Christmas, told my daughter about it. *This was a gift from a girl I knew at Sunrise Academy. She was my special kid.*

What do you mean by special kid? Susannah would ask.

Later, of course, my daughter would find out firsthand, when she herself was somebody's special kid, in some other place not unlike Sunrise. But that was still years away.

Frankie rushed up from across the room and threw her big fleshy arms around me. Nita stepped back at the onslaught, dainty and disdainful.

"Look at my new pants!" Frankie hollered.

She had on new, light blue corduroy pants. "My caseworker Lynda gave them to me," she said, all excited. "They're kinda big, though." She put her hands in her pockets to demonstrate how much extra room there was. "I think they're for a guy. See how I'm missing something?" She pulled at the loose fabric at the crotch. "Something's supposed to go here?" she cackled.

"Oh, honestly, Frankie," Nita said, disgusted, and turned away.

Frankie whirled around to her. "See the big boxes, Nita?" She did not understand that Nita didn't like her, thought she and Nita were meant to be special sisters or something, because they had the same special staff.

"Look, Ma!" she shouted. Her blue eyes were shining, her face big and eager. Her reddish-blonde hair was wild all over her head. "Look what they brought us!"

The male staff had carried in big boxes of clothing donated by one of the local churches, collected from their parishioners, I supposed, *for the needy*. The stuff they had donated was not fancy or expensive, only old, worn, and outgrown. There were two boxes each for the boys and girls. Evelyn was in charge of distributing the boys' clothing, and Annie planted herself with the girls'. As the kids lined up eagerly, a veil of unreality fluttered over me, as if my own clothes might be in those boxes—my own outgrown skirts and sweaters, donated by my mother, years before, *to the poor*.

Annie began handing out the girls' clothes.

"I'm the worst one to be doing this," she proclaimed, laughing. "As you all know full well, I have absolutely *no* fashion sense. Here, Darcy," she said, handing over a green sweater. "This'll match your eyes."

Across the room, Adam was sitting with his mother on the big couch near the fire. Manny tried on a plaid flannel shirt over his regular clothes. He turned this way and that, and Elliot gave him a thumbs-up.

"Nice, Manny," he said. "Lookin' good!"

Manny gave a small, unwilling smile that he tried to hide.

"Nita! These'll fit you!" Annie called. "I can't think of anyone else who's small enough to wriggle into them!" She indicated her own broad, friendly hips. "I certainly couldn't, but you're so tiny! Nita, come here!"

Nita took the clothes and retreated to the other side of the room, where I was standing.

Frankie had waltzed off, eager to show everyone her new makeup kit.

"Look at this!" she squealed, waving it indiscriminately at Doug and Garrett. They glanced at the gift, feigning interest.

"Really nice, Frankie," Garrett said, kindly.

Frankie was getting too excited. Later, there would be tears and a tantrum. We would blame the sugar. The kids were all eating way too much of it. Cookies already, before dinner, which would be a feast. *I'm making something special*, Alice had told us. There would be a big chocolate cake for dessert.

"Think she's going to blow?" Elliot asked, sidling over to me. A chilly wind came off the lake, and I could feel it sneaking in through the cracks and chinks in the log walls.

Nita came up carrying her hand-me-down clothes with a sour expression.

"I'm not wearing these!" she said indignantly, as if it were all my fault. "Flared pants! I don't wear flared pants!" She was furious. "And look—they've got a stain!"

She waved the pants at me. They were pink jeans. That was the first thing. Who wore pink jeans? Not Nita. And not with a *stain*.

Over the holidays, Jake and I got officially engaged, and then, suddenly, it was the end of the year. It was almost 1981. Reagan was going to be president. Everything seemed dull and settled. The country, Republican. There was no war or no war anyone knew about until later. There was no draft, and there weren't any protests. Stuff that went on in the sixties and seventies, that was all over. This was a different decade. Drearier, more grown-up, resigned.

In my new journal, I made a list of everything I wanted to do that year: knit a sweater, do well at my job, get married. Then I mapped out the next few years. I'd have a baby in 1982, I thought, and another one a few years later, maybe '84 or '85. I'd work until I had the babies and then stay home for a few years.

I didn't think about what this would feel like, just that I would do it. When I was married, I'd be a different sort of person—a married person, a person who stayed home with the kids, not someone who made out with her boss in the conference room. I'd read *Redbook* and learn to cook complicated casseroles with various healthy grains. I'd make all our bread. Kneading and kneading while, outside, soft snow fell on the rumpled brown dirt of the yard. I'd have a garden. I'd grow vegetables, clean the house, make the children's clothes, and do art projects with them. I'd make friends with other mothers, and we'd exchange wifely lore. That was the sort of thing you could still do in Maine in the eighties, when lots of young mothers stayed home. I'd be one of them, and I'd be content.

Contentment seemed like a pancake, circular and perfect, that I must eat.

THIRTEEN

By mid-January, the Christmas lights had been taken down at Sunrise. The browned tree was gone, the flared, stained clothes thrown away. There was a new man on staff named Randall, a big old bald guy with a patchy beard, a youngish wife, and five children. He arrived each evening in his overalls to work the night shift.

"I don't mind," he shrugged, when I asked him if it was hard to work nights. "It's a job." He was just glad *this gig*, as he called it, came with health insurance.

His wife's name was Sandra. She had plump, pale skin; a large bosom; and all those children. *Did she really sleep with this old man?* I couldn't imagine being married to a man like that, with bad teeth and those shabby ribbed undershirts under big denim overalls. He had a scabby place on the back of his thick, red neck. But his eyes were kind and understanding, and the way he looked at me reminded me of Elliot, like he knew things about me.

One evening, Sandra brought Randall to work but didn't come into the lodge. Her headlights shone in through the windows as she dropped him off.

"Truck's out," Randall said. "Sandy brought me down."

Later that evening, I noticed a glow in the trees near the parking lot.

"There's somebody out there," I told Kenny.

He looked out. "Yep, sure looks like it," he said. He didn't seem very surprised. "That your car, Randall?" Kenny asked sternly.

"Yep."

"Kids in it?"

"Yep."

"That's no good," Kenny said. "You know that."

"Couldn't leave them home," Randall replied. He didn't seem fazed by any of it—Kenny's rebuke, his pale wife and children outside in the frigid night.

"Lemme talk to you," Kenny said, leading him into the conference room and closing the door behind them.

I watched the lodge floor. Cassie, a tall girl from rural Maine—out west, up north, someplace else—was on night shift along with Randall. I could leave at ten. Just one more hour to go. Tomorrow, if it wasn't too bitterly cold, we'd take the kids hiking.

You gotta watch them, Kenny said, *this time of year. Winter's hard for them; they get ideas.*

Now Kenny came out of the back office with his arm around Randall.

"We got it worked out," Kenny said, as Randall headed for the door.

"What's going on?" I asked.

"They only got the one car working," Kenny explained. "They live way out near Milo, good sixty miles from here."

"He drives sixty miles to get here?" I asked, astonished.

Kenny shrugged. "It's a job," he said. "Couldn't leave the kids home alone—they're still pretty young—so they're all out there in the car, all six of them."

"Out there? In the parking lot?"

I looked at the black night window.

"Yep. The kids're doing their homework by flashlight," Kenny said. "They were planning to spend the night out there, sleep in the car."

"They were going to stay out there all night? It's so cold."

Kenny shrugged again. "Guess they're used to it. He told them to start up the car and run the heater every half hour or so. It's probably not that cold, with all of them in there. Though it must not smell very pretty."

"I said to send them on home. We can drive him up in the morning. Take a van ride up north, you and Jed. You're going hiking anyway, aren't you? You can hike up there."

"Is there anywhere up there to hike?"

"You'll find something. Now write me up," Kenny told me and dictated a few lines for the logbook. Called his wife: "Come get me," started to pull on his jacket.

I wanted to say something to him. I didn't know what. Something about how nice he was, how he noticed things, when anyone was in trouble or needed help. He never made a big deal about it, just always knew what to do. But then Randall came back in. He didn't even glance at Kenny. They'd worked it all out and didn't need to say anything more.

Some of the staff played cribbage on quiet winter nights when the kids were doing their homework or hanging out in the smoking area. Annie and I were equally matched; Annie would win one game, then I'd win the next. It wasn't like playing with Randall, who was really good and always skunked me, in spite of his overalls and that weird scabby thing on his neck.

"Do you like him?" I asked Annie, even though I knew she wouldn't say anything bad about anyone. She and I were playing cribbage at one of the long tables where the residents ate their meals. It was late in the evening; the lodge was quiet; the girls were asleep upstairs, the boys in their rooms down below. I liked her more now; imagined us staying friends after I quit working there. Because I knew in my heart this was just temporary; it wasn't going to be my career or anything. I had an inkling that maybe I'd become a writer someday. I liked writing, but one thing was sure: I knew I wasn't staying here.

"What's your story, Lorraine?"

"What do you mean?" I pretended to be studying my hand, but really I was scouring my mind, scanning each room for incriminating evidence that Annie might find. Was she asking me about Elliot again? Had she seen us kissing that time in the conference room? What if she'd glanced in the window and seen us, or somebody else had seen us and told her about it?

"Don't look so scared," Annie said. "I mean, how did you grow up? I know you're from Maryland. What's your family like? Do you have siblings? What was your life like when you were a kid?"

I relaxed a little. I had practiced answers to questions like this. I knew what to say.

"Oh, just normal," I said, breezily, pretending to be offhanded. "You know. There were two of us, my sister and me. My dad had a job with the government." That's what I always said. We weren't supposed to say what he really did. Not that we knew. He was gone a lot, when we were little. Later, of course, just gone.

"And your mom? Did she work?"

I stiffened. I didn't like to talk about her.

"Oh, she had a job for a while. But then she was mostly home."

I pictured her in the living room. The room quiet and dark. Sitting there alone on the couch when I came home from school. You never knew how you would find her. Whether it was a good day or something else.

"That must have been nice," Annie said, like she knew there was more to my story. It wasn't the avid curiosity I was always on guard against. People wanting to know my family secrets. Teachers asking why I was late, where I got that bruise. There was kindness in Annie's face, which was, somehow, worse. I could probably tell her everything, but I had carried my secrets for so long, held close in my arms that familiar, unwieldy bundle, that I didn't know how to unpack it. I glanced up at Annie. Could she be the one I could tell? Maybe some day.

At the end of February, Sage and Annie and Garrett took some kids up north on a camping trip. I was surprised Annie wanted to go, but she seemed elated.

After they left, the lodge felt empty. Jed and I took the residents walking on Ocean Drive where the road was plowed out or swimming at the Holiday Inn in the heated indoor pool. On winter nights, with half the kids on the camping trip, the lodge was quiet and cozy. Elliot wasn't around in the evenings, so it seemed more relaxed. We made a fire in the fireplace, or Doug brought over his VCR and we watched some G-rated movie, and Alice made popcorn. Outside, it was always cold.

"I'm glad I didn't have to go up north," I admitted to Cassie. "I can't imagine camping out in this weather."

"Yeah, me neither, but Annie loves it. She was so excited to go. She's got a wicked crush on Garrett."

"Really?" I couldn't imagine having a crush on him, though he was very handsome. There was just something about him. Good looking, yes, but not sexy, and he didn't seem to fit with Annie. She was so—well, rumpled. So large and jolly. They didn't match one another.

I was surprised by how much I missed Annie now that I'd gotten used to her; she'd become a friend. Everyone there seemed like a friend, in a way, even Margo, who worked in the upstairs office, even the kids.

When the campers got back, Annie and Garrett were different. He had his arm around her waist as they walked in, each lugging camping equipment, their big winter boots flapping open. She was wearing his flannel shirt.

"Oh goody!" Cassie whispered. "She got him!"

They were in love. All the staff members knew right away and were proprietary about the couple, as if they'd invented their union. They teased Annie, asked when they were going to get married.

There was a poignant twist to their romance, because Garrett was about to leave Sunrise to hike the entire Appalachian Mountain Trail, starting in Georgia. He was leaving in just a few weeks.

Annie was so emotional now, teary and happy. She started telling me personal things. How much she loved him. How she wished she hadn't been so shy for so long—*Annie?* I thought, *shy?*—that she'd gone after him sooner. She admitted she was jealous of his old girlfriend Donna, who used to work at Sunrise.

"She's so pretty and little," Annie said. "She always made me feel like a big oaf."

Annie was so nice, and her love was touching. She seemed to have none of the doubts that plagued me. Those terrible doubts. Should I really get married? Wouldn't Jake eventually, sweet as he was, just get on my nerves? Wouldn't I rather be on my own? It was so much simpler just to be by myself, not to have to worry about someone else, all their little ways. Then I'd think how sweet it could be, the two of us. Sweet and normal like everyone else.

But I wasn't like everyone else. I was spinier, different.

In the woods, however, I felt wonderful.

On a cold day in early March, I walked up the steep crumbly driveway across from the Asticou Inn and entered the woods at the Map House. The path was still full of snow, trodden down, mostly by me, on other, earlier forays. Years later, I would take Susannah there and regale her with scary stories, and my daughter would look back fearfully over her shoulder at the path which I strode now, alone.

The path continued toward Jordan Pond, passing the branching turns to Cedar Swamp and Sargent Mountains, pausing on the rickety bridge across Hadlock Brook, where water ran sparkling over the rocks. If I turned right there, I could follow its crooked course all the way down to the sea, passing those sandy banks that seem to belong out west somewhere. A random crow cried overhead; far off, I could hear the gulls. Beyond the bridge, the path rose again to a long straight passage past that tree with the one bent leg, like a knee to sit on.

Overhead, beyond the tall trees, the sky was a far-off blue. The path unfurled before me. I could walk all day.

In mid-March, we had a good-bye party for Garrett. He would fly south to Georgia, where an old college friend would drive him to the trailhead to begin his three-month trek. Garrett had taped a big map on the wall in the schoolhouse cabin, so the kids could follow his progress.

Annie was seated beside him, and he took her hand in his. They seemed so certain of one another. I never felt sure of anything. I loved Jake, of course, but did I love him enough? Sometimes, when I looked at him, I saw the most wonderful man in the world, while other times, he seemed meager.

"Annie's going to come down and meet me on the trail," Garrett said, still holding her hand.

Her face had the crinkled, dazed look of love.

"If I can get the time off," she said, glancing over at Doug.

"I'll see what we can do," Doug said, smiling. "I bet we can work something out."

The kids were excited, restless. There could be a fight tonight; they were all wound up. There was tension in the air—Garrett's leaving, the chocolate ice cream, all this visible love. Something was bound to happen.

FOURTEEN

On Saturday afternoon, I took Frankie to J. J. Newberry's in downtown Ellsworth. Frankie had gotten some money from her caseworker, and she needed new clothes. I led her to the upstairs section that, years later, would be an indoor flea market. Back then, in the early eighties, it was full of inexpensive, serviceable clothing: pastel cotton house dresses in XXXL with snaps down the front; large white underpants; big, pleated-looking bras. Black socks, dark green work pants, pale blue ladies' Keds.

Frankie picked out a flowered dress made of some kind of filmy, synthetic fabric. "For Easter Sunday," she said, though Easter was still weeks away. Frankie got new shoes, new underwear, and nylon stockings. Back at the lodge, she got all dressed up for supper and right away ripped one of her stockings, but she was happy all night.

"I got new clothes," Frankie kept telling everybody. "Lorraine took me shopping."

One afternoon, Annie came to my house. I'd made orange bread the night before, and we had it with coffee. Annie brought a bouquet of spring flowers in a green paper cone from the florist.

No one had ever brought me flowers before, except Jake, and I was touched by the gesture.

"This is so nice!" I said. I sounded just like my mother.

"A friend of mine got me doing this," Annie said. "She would always bring fresh-cut flowers. They're pure pleasure. You don't have to do anything with them except put them in water and enjoy them. Then you can throw them away. They're not a responsibility, like giving somebody a plant they have to take care of, or a book they have to read."

I showed her around my house—how everything was miniature: the living room, the tiny upstairs with the slanty walls and the old-fashioned rose-strewn wallpaper. I showed her the ironing board that folded out from the kitchen wall. Annie exclaimed over everything.

"It's so cute!" she kept saying. "You've got everything!"

We went for a walk around the town. I felt proud—as if I'd created it.

Everything I said made Annie laugh, so I started elaborating on things—the little old lady named Augusta who walked her dog very fast down the sidewalk, the brothers who lived in that house at the end of the block.

"They're both really fat," I told Annie. "And they look exactly alike. We call them Tweedledum and Tweedledee. They wear matching outfits."

"Stop," Annie said, bending over with laughter. "Oh stop it," she gasped.

Frankie came down to spend the night at my house. I made her a pallet on the living room floor out of all the big pillows I'd sewn. Frankie loved the house, too. She liked Jake and called him Whitey.

"Why do you call him that?" I asked her.

"I don't know. 'Cause he's got kind eyes," Frankie said.

I planned to make French toast for breakfast. "Or would you rather have waffles?" I asked.

"Oh, waffles, please!" she replied.

Frankie was very polite at the house. No yelling, no carrying on. She took lots of time in the bathroom—a really long shower—and hung up her towel just so, though at Sunrise, she threw her damp towel on the floor, like the other girls. Here, she was quieter, different. I'd been afraid she'd be bored in my quiet house, but she seemed content.

The next morning, I had to take care of some bills and write a few letters. "Do you want to watch television?" I asked Frankie.

"No," she said, folding her hands in her lap. "I'll just sit here."

I was a little worried about leaving her in the living room when I went back upstairs to my desk. It was ominously quiet downstairs. I resisted going back down to check.

When I did go down, Frankie was still sitting there in the chair, exactly where I had left her. She was playing with a little wind-up R2-D2 toy Jake had given me.

When I came into the room, Frankie quickly put the toy down.

"That's okay," I said, "you can play with that, if you want to."

I wondered what Frankie would be like if she'd grown up in a house like this, with two regular parents making a waffle breakfast on Sunday. The kind of home I was going to give my children when I had them, or so I thought then.

I felt bad when it was time to drive Frankie back to Sunrise, as if I were taking her back to jail, though Frankie didn't seem to mind. She wanted to show everybody the sweater I had given her, one I didn't wear anymore.

We got a new staff person on weekends. Her name was Elizabeth. She was from Virginia, she told us, and she and her husband had moved up to Maine to live. He was in boatbuilding, she said, vaguely. Elizabeth couldn't hike; she had something wrong with her knee. *But I used to*, she said. In fact, she and her husband had done the entire Appalachian Trail together a few years ago, when she was thirty. They went by horseback the whole way, she said.

"Wow," I said. "That must be a long trek, with horses."

She agreed.

Elizabeth was sharply pretty, with black hair pulled back in a ponytail and a small, narrow body. She always wore tight black pants and a bright-colored sweater. Her diamond ring glittered brightly. She had gold earrings and a little gold chain at her neck with a tiny gold cross, which she fingered in Group. Pulled it out of her turtleneck and then slipped it back under again.

"What do you think of Elizabeth?" Annie asked me one afternoon when we were fixing supper.

Alice was off that week, so day staff had to make all the meals. Today, we were making chicken with ginger and honey.

"It's really good," Annie told me. "Wait till you taste it. You like it when things are kind of burnt and crispy?"

"I love that," I said.

"Then you're going to love this," Annie said. "So what do you think of Elizabeth?" she asked again.

"She's okay," I shrugged. I was careful what I said about other staff, especially with Annie, who always took the high road and rarely said anything bad about anyone.

"Yeah, I guess," Annie said. "Did you hear about her accidents? Cassie told me about them."

It turned out that Elizabeth had been in two really bad car accidents.

"First, she fell asleep at the wheel," Annie said. "That was maybe eight years ago—something like that. Back when she was in college, in Delaware—is that where she's from? Anyway, she was in this terrible accident and broke her leg—the bone just splintered. It came out through the skin, and her foot was broken in seventeen places. She was in the hospital, in traction, for seven months."

"She told you that?" I asked.

"She told Cassie. Anyway, she was in traction all that time and then home in bed for another seven months, and her husband—only he wasn't her husband then—was in divinity school at the time. He came every day to sit with her, drove all the way, every single day, to the hospital, then to her house."

Jake would do that for me, I thought.

"Then, the day she was driving back to the hospital to get the last of her stitches out—they'd put a rod in or something—a drunk driver smashed into her car, and she went through the windshield, and the force of it shredded her eyelids. Her scalp was practically torn off. She had to have total facial reconstruction."

I was staring at Annie while she was talking. Annie's face was animated the way people get when they tell a terrible story.

"Completely reconstructed," Annie repeated, and I tried to picture the doctors putting Elizabeth's face back together, all the odds and ends. Flesh from the thigh or something.

I pictured Elizabeth's face now. Come to think of it, hadn't I maybe noticed some little scars?

"Wow," I said.

"Yeah, I know. She still has nightmares about it," Annie finished, triumphantly. "Even now—eight, maybe nine years later."

Kenny had come into the kitchen and stood there listening with a tight, disapproving look.

"What?" Annie asked him.

"You believe that?" he asked. "Smells like bullshit to me."

That hadn't occurred to either of us, but after that, we started wondering if other things Elizabeth told us were true. That whole thing about the Appalachian Trail, especially when it turned out they didn't allow horses on the trail. And there were other things, too. Things about her husband's job, which first she said was in boatbuilding, and then sales, and then, when one of us said, innocently, *I thought you said boatbuilding*, she said *Well, he sells supplies to boatbuilders, so it's sort of both*. How could she keep it all straight in her head?

It turned out she couldn't.

Her stories started to fray at the edges, and it became a game for the rest of us, trying to trip her up. The funny thing about Elizabeth, though, was that she didn't lie about things on the job. If she told you she had taken one of the kids upstairs, then she really had. It was just her own life she invented.

I kept thinking we might be wrong about her; maybe all those things were true. I stared at Elizabeth's face, when I thought she wouldn't notice—when she was writing in the staff logbook or looking out at the lake. I would search her face, studying it carefully, looking for tiny scars.

Two ladies came from the Rape Crisis Center to talk to the girls. We had an all-girl Group session in the conference room and talked about self-esteem. One of the women told the story of her own rape. She looked around the table as she told her story, her hands in her lap and her eyes full of tears. The other woman, who was a little older, kept looking over supportively and touching her arm. The girls were unmoved.

"What do I want to hear about that for?" Darcy demanded when Group was over. "That supposed to help us?" she scoffed.

She threw out the index card she'd been given. Each girl was supposed to write three things she liked about herself, three things she was proud of, and three things she wanted to improve. The exercise felt familiar and futile. They'd done this before in other groups with other counselors. So far, it hadn't really taken. Or maybe it had. Maybe this *was* self-esteem, rejecting the words of the rape victim. Maybe that's why Darcy could throw out the index card and scorn the two women who had come to Sunrise Academy.

One night, Trixie had to be rushed to the hospital. She kept writhing and screaming, clutching herself. *I can't stand it!* she kept screaming. *Make it stop!* They kept her overnight for observation and then released her the next day. They couldn't find anything wrong.

Cassie, the night staff, freaked out when she found bloody clothes upstairs in Tina's room. It turned out it was just someone's period, but the clothes had been stolen, and everybody was mad. Cassie thought it was an aborted fetus and couldn't stop crying. She had been trying to get pregnant for years. She was a born-again Christian and kept miscarrying and thought it was because of her sins. Annie gave her a few days off, but she never came back after that.

A week or so later, when I came in to work, Justin was being restrained by two male staff in the middle of the floor. Frankie was yelling at the top of her lungs, and all the rest of the kids were racing back and forth across the lodge.

Elizabeth had suddenly quit. Her husband had cancer, she said. Nobody believed that, either. Annie had left to meet up with Garrett on the Appalachian Trail. She'd be gone for a month. There wasn't enough staff, and it was bedlam.

I decided I wasn't going to work there much longer. I wanted my own quiet life.

I took some of the girls in Levels Two through Four to see *Raiders of the Lost Ark* at the Maine Coast Mall Cinema. I bought them popcorn and soda with my own money to make it seem festive. Everybody was in a good mood. But the next morning, I found out that when the girls had returned to the lodge, four of them had tattooed themselves with straight pins and India ink that they'd saved from the calligraphy class with a visiting artist.

One day in mid-April, I took the Asticou Trail to Seal Harbor again. It had snowed two days before, and now, it was warm and mild. The path was muddy at first, just past the Map House, and then it got better. Old leaves from last fall littered the trail, and there were only a few patches of snow on the ground. The woods were noisy with birds.

When I was almost to Jordan Pond, I turned down the path that led to a small quarry where someone had built a little stone hut with a wooden roof. Inside, three rocks were arranged like two chairs and a little stone table. Sun shone in through the chinks in the roof, and the whole place was sunny and quiet.

I imagined I would return often to the little hut, that Jake and I might even spend the night there sometime, sit in those stone chairs, eat at that granite table. It was years before I would go there again. I brought Susannah when she was six or seven; the stone hut was all toppled over by then, and there was trash on the ground and beer cans lying around. It seemed, then, a desolate place.

Annie had been gone for a few weeks, hiking the Appalachian Trail with Garrett. She'd flown down to meet him somewhere in

Virginia. Nobody had heard from them in a while, which was kind of weird. They'd been sending a postcard every few days, so we could track their progress. It probably just meant they were between mail drop-offs, and we'd be sure to hear from them soon.

FIFTEEN

Because Annie and Garrett were away, Sage asked me if I'd go on the next camping trip. It would be a big one: Sage, Jed, me, and nine of the residents. We'd be gone for three days. I didn't want to go but didn't know how to get out of it. Annie would have jumped at the chance. *You bet—I'm in!* she would've said. *Sounds terrific! When do we leave?*

"You're going to love it," Sage assured me. "The kids are a lot easier when you're out of here. It's not like a day hike, where they complain and bitch and can't wait to get back to the lodge. When they're out there, they get into it. Baxter's pretty great this time of year, but make sure you bring bug dope. The blackflies can get pretty bad."

We were going to climb Katahdin at Baxter State Park, up near Millinocket. The forecast was good, fairly warm for this time of year, so Sage thought we'd be able to get up to the top.

It was a mixed group. A couple of the tougher kids were going: Kurt had tried to brain me with a rock last summer, and Shawn was burly and unpredictable, but I liked Trixie and Darcy and Contessa, and Frankie was going. We had at least two Level Fours: Erin and Adam. He would be discharged from the program at Sunrise in a few weeks, so he was practically a counselor himself. We could count on him.

"You're coming? Great!" Adam said. "You're going to love it up there."

"I don't know," I said. "I'm not much of a camper."

"Don't worry," Adam told me. "I'll make sure you're all right."

Adam was in a great mood. He was leaving Sunrise at the end of June. *If I don't fuck it up*, he said.

We pitched our tents beside a stream in a pretty camping spot with an outdoor grill. Jed was in his element, efficient and capable, cooking our supper over the fire while the kids set up their tents. Because there were only four girls on the trip, they were sharing one large tent, and I had a smaller one to myself. Trixie and Erin helped me get set up.

"It's good to have your head near the door so it's easier to crawl out," Erin advised me.

I remembered the weird stuffy funk of a closed-in tent from childhood camping trips and the warm, animal exhalations of the air mattress. It would be good to be near the front, breathing the clean, chilly night air. When I crawled into my tent after supper, though, I realized it wouldn't work. The way the ground sloped, I'd be better off with my head at the far end, so I repositioned my sleeping bag before wriggling into its soft, swishy folds.

The men were camped out with the boys on the other side of the fire, but I could hear the girls whispering in their tent, and their voices, drifting in and out, sounded sweetly familiar. I was surprised by how cozy I felt. Maybe this camping trip wouldn't be so bad after all.

In the morning, I could hear the girls whispering again. Had they been at it all night?

I lay in my sleeping bag. The air outside would be chilly, but inside, it was nice and warm. And it didn't smell bad, after all; I felt safe and content. It was going to be a long hike today. Sage and Jed knew the way. There was that one scary part that everyone talked about—the Knife Edge— I was sure I could manage it. After all the times I'd climbed the Precipice Trail, I wasn't afraid of heights. Some of the kids, especially Roy, were nervous about it, and I wondered if that was what the girls were whispering about. I doubted it. They were teenage girls, after all. Probably discussing boys, I thought, or their hair.

The men were already up and moving around when I emerged from my tent. Jed was cooking pancakes, and I could smell bacon.

"Bout time, sleepyhead," he said.

Sage had taken some of the boys to check out the trail, and the girls had gone off to the toilets.

"We'll have breakfast and be on our way," Jed told me.

"You're all set to go already?" I asked.

"Sure. I've been up for hours."

The blackflies were pretty bad, but we had lots of bug repellent. The oily pine-tar smell of Old Woodsman would always remind me of Baxter.

The hike went well. It was warm enough so that, by the time we got to the top, we could laze around on the rocks, eating our sandwiches and reveling in our accomplishment before heading down. Parts of the trail had been challenging, but we'd all been able to do it. I could tell that the kids felt proud, sitting high on the top of the mountain with the wide span of Maine all around, and I felt a comfortable sense of belonging and knew they must feel it, too. I glanced over at Jed, and he raised his thermos cup in a silent toast. *You did it*, he mouthed, and I grinned. I had always wanted to climb Katahdin, and now, here I was with this odd little band of kids and counselors who had become my family.

On the way down, we were chatty and complimentary, telling the kids what we'd do when we got back to the campsite. We had chocolate and special treats. We would make s'mores. I was glad I'd remembered to bring the fixings, as Annie would have, if she were along. I wondered how she and Garrett were doing, somewhere on the Appalachian Trail and wondered, again, why we hadn't heard from them in a while.

The kids clumped together in bunches. Adam laughed at something Shawn said, then glanced back to see if I'd heard. Probably some sexual comment about one of the girls. They always had secrets, and I decided to ignore it.

We tried to make the evening special, but things seemed a bit off. Jed cooked steaks over the fire and buried potatoes in the coals, and we had the s'mores, but the kids were all subdued, kind of quiet. It had been a long hike; they were probably exhausted. I thought we could sit by the fire after our supper. Maybe tell ghost stories, the way, years later, I would tell my own daughter scary stories. The kids weren't interested, and, without much fuss, first the girls, then the boys, disappeared into their tents.

Jed, Sage, and I stayed up awhile, staring into the fire, tired and content. It had been a long day, but a good one. We didn't talk much; it was quiet, chilly. Away from the firelight's glow, the night was black, and the shadowy trees loomed up.

"I'm wiped out," I said. "Think I'll go to bed."

"You going to be okay in there alone?" Jed asked me.

"I could sleep anywhere tonight," I said. "I'm really tired. That's quite a hike."

"You did good," he said.

"Thanks, Jed. 'Night, Sage."

I went off to pee, brushed my teeth, and crawled into my little tent. It smelled musky and familiar. I made my way down to the far end of the tent and burrowed into my sleeping bag. The nylon fabric made a whooshing sound as I pulled it up to get warm. Then I lay back, savoring my exhaustion, happy with the sense of accomplishment. A few times, the kids had gotten surly, but mostly, they had been remarkably well-behaved. Sage was right; they were different out here. They seemed closer to one another than back at the lodge, more like siblings than strangers thrown together by chance.

I could hear the girls whispering companionably in their tent, and I smiled. They were still whispering as I fell asleep.

Sometime in the night, I woke, disoriented.

It was very dark. I could hear a commotion outside the tent. Somebody saying something—one of the girls—in a low, urgent tone. Then a boy's voice. "Do it!"

"*Shhhhh*. Don't wake her up!" someone said. "Not till we're ready."

I heard low, intense whispers outside my tent, very close; then, the *swoosh* of a sleeping bag, the sound of night footsteps. What were they doing? I knew they were up to something. I ought to go out there, I told myself. It was my job, I thought wearily, starting to ease myself up.

I was half sitting up in my sleeping bag when everything happened at once. There was a sudden yell. Jed shouted *No!* Then another loud shout, like the roar of a wounded animal. The door of my tent ripped open, and someone lunged in.

I felt rather than saw him. The night was so dark, he was only a shadowy shape—I couldn't see who it was.

I pulled my feet up toward my body as he plunged into the tent, thrusting something—hard!—in the place where my legs had been just moments before.

I tried to scream, but my voice came out a hoarse rasp. The dark figure, whoever it was, reared up and came at me again with some sort of weapon. This time, he was closer—he was inside the tent—and I cowered away, felt the clammy nylon fabric of the tent stretch out as I tried to escape him. He lurched forward a third time, but somebody—Sage?—threw his arms around him and dragged him out of the tent.

"*What the fuck are you doing?*" the intruder yelled.

I knew that voice. *Shawn.*

Someone wrestled him to the ground.

A scream from one of the girls. Then somebody shouted, "Oh shit! Get back in the tent!" There was a scuffling noise and somebody grunting.

I crawled forward, peered out of my tent.

In the last light from the dying fire, two shadowy figures were struggling. One was Shawn—I recognized his bulky shape—but the other, I couldn't tell. Was it Sage? Whoever it was, he was tall and getting control. He managed to pull Shawn down, then sat on him, holding his wrists, forcing him to let go of the knife. It dropped to the ground, glinting briefly.

"What the fuck, Adam?" I heard Shawn, his voice hoarse. "I thought you were in. You fucking traitor." It was Adam holding Shawn down as he struggled to rise.

"I'm not a total asshole, Shawn," Adam said. He said something else, but I wasn't sure if I heard him right. He was still on top of Shawn, breathing hard. Then, turning his head, he asked, "You all right, Lorraine?" I couldn't see his face in the dark.

"I'm okay," I said, surprised at how clear my voice sounded. It was not even shaking, though my heart was pounding too fast.

"Stay there," I commanded. "Where's Jed?"

I scrambled out of my tent to look for him. He was all right but wounded. When I shone my flashlight on him, I could see that his arm was bleeding.

"What did they do to you?" I asked, kneeling beside him, trying to see.

"I'm okay. It's not too bad," he said.

Sage had Kurt on the ground, both breathing hard.

"You okay, Lorraine?"

I nodded. My heart was still pounding. I felt a white-hot bolt of anger inside me. How dare these kids attack us after everything we'd done for them.

"Get something to tie up Jed's arm," said Sage. "I'll take care of this asshole."

"Let go, man!" Kurt twisted around under Sage. He was big and young, but Sage held him down. Kurt continued to struggle, until Sage did something—I couldn't see what, some kind of jerking motion. Then Kurt cried out and lay still.

I heard a scuffle behind me. Shawn was trying to throw Adam off.

In two strides, I was beside them. I took aim and kicked Shawn— hard—in the ribs. Adam looked up, startled. I did it again. And again. I didn't want to stop. Couldn't stop.

"How dare you!" I yelled. "You ungrateful little shit!"

I would have kicked him again if Adam hadn't grabbed my leg.

"That's enough, Lorraine," he said sharply. "He's done."

My heart was pounding so fast. I'd never felt this kind of fury before, had felt only the brunt of it, the force of another's anger. Now, the frenzy was mine, and I could feel its power—the energizing, intoxicating power of rage.

After we'd taken their knives and searched everyone for more weapons, we sat them around the fire, the girls in a huddle on one side, the boys, surly and silent, on the other. The story came out—or some version of it.

It was beginning to get light by the time we got the gist of the story. The attack had been Shawn's idea. Kurt went along with it because he admired Shawn. We still weren't sure about Adam. Only the smallest boys, Roy and Justin, were unaware. They burst into tears when Sage dragged them out of their tents.

"I didn't know what they were going to do," Roy said. "Honest!"

Sage was silent for some time. He looked disgusted.

"We're going to break camp and hike out right now," he said. "We'll deal with this when we get back to Sunrise."

"What about breakfast?" one of the girls asked. Sage ignored her.

"Yeah, what about it?" Erin said. "You can't expect us to hike on an empty stomach. That's child abuse!" she protested.

Any other time, I would have laughed, but at that moment, nothing was funny. My earlier anger had faded away, leaving only a dull, bleak feeling. Just the day before, the residents had seemed like ordinary teenagers. Climbing up the mountain along the dirt path, clambering over the boulders, complaining amiably. Now, they seemed like felons. Their faces, in the gray light of the early morning, looked tough and older. Seedy. They looked like people you'd see late at night in a bus station in some far-off city. People you'd be a little afraid of because of the location and the hour. These kids were criminals or criminals in training.

Evelyn was right. Some of them—most of them, maybe—would wind up in jail.

Where do you think criminals come from? Evelyn had asked me. *Don't be naive*, she'd said.

But I had been naive. Believing that I, young and untrained, working there for a year or two, doing this as a lark, really, before

I settled down in the real world—that I could make a difference in these kids' lives. I'd been naive to think that I was going to save anybody. I'd be lucky if I could save myself.

And that whispering I'd thought was about boys and hair, things I'd talked about when I was their age. They hadn't been gossiping, I realized now. They'd been plotting. The girls were in on it, too. Jed showed me a note he found in their tent. *You hold her down*, it said, *and I'll slash her face with the razor.*

"But we weren't really going to do it," Darcy said, her face earnest. "We were just pretending. It was, like, you know, a game."

I didn't believe any of them. Even Adam, who'd come to my rescue. Did he switch teams last minute so he could graduate from the program, as planned, in a few weeks? What was it he'd said to Shawn when he tackled him—something like *We weren't going to get away with it anyway.*

When I asked him about it later, Adam denied it. *I wouldn't have said that. I think you're mixed up.*

We packed up the camping stuff in the chilly dawn. The campfire burned out quickly; just some old embers were left. Jed got the girls to pour water over the charred logs, and they sizzled, briefly, then turned a dull black.

"Come on," Jed said, hoisting his backpack onto one shoulder. He had a bandage on his arm where he'd been cut. *Only scratches,* he said. *Nothing serious.*

Jed led the group down the trail. I was in the middle, and Sage brought up the rear, so he could keep an eye on any stragglers. *And keep close together,* he said.

Jed was usually smiling, but now his face was pale and grim. He said he was fine, but I'd seen the place on his shirt where the blood had soaked through. *Good thing I was having trouble sleeping,* he told me. *I heard them before they came in.*

We'd gotten bits and pieces of the plan: The girls were the sentries, in charge of holding me down after Shawn stabbed me. Their plans were romantic—I guess you could call it that—fantastical. No real motive other than the attack, the haphazard revenge of children against authority. But they were big children, large as adults. If I hadn't been sleeping with my head at the far end of the tent, I thought. If Jed hadn't been half awake.

I didn't know what would happen when we got back to Sunrise. I felt wooden and dazed as we walked single file, hardly speaking. It was a damp, chilly morning, and the trail seemed endless. Once in a while, one of the kids said something softly. I didn't try to understand. I didn't think they would strike out again; I was too dull to think anything. I just wanted to get back to the lodge, turn them over to somebody else, go home, and never come back.

When we'd packed up the van and driven a few miles down the road, Jed stopped at a pay phone to call Sunrise and tell them what happened.

"They'll want Doug and Elliot down there," he said to Sage, who nodded somberly. Sage was in back between two of the residents. He looked dangerous. This must have brought up old war stuff for him, things he didn't like to talk about from Vietnam. He was tense and silent. Other than a few angry words at the start of the trail, he'd said almost nothing. The kids seemed wary of him, and the ones seated closest held themselves away. Some of the girls were asleep or pretending to be. Jed drove, and most of the kids were quiet. A vanquished army, and now they were going to jail.

So what? I thought. I hated all of them, even Frankie, who kept trying to catch my eye.

"Come on, Lorraine," she said in her whiney, little-girl voice. "You know I would never hurt you. I didn't even know about it."

I didn't trust any of them. Something had gone out of me, some kind of light or something. My clothes smelled from the smoke and the hiking. My skin and my hair felt dirty. My mouth tasted terrible. I was tired of caring about them. I half hoped they all would be sent away.

"What'd they say when you called?" I asked Jed.

"They're going to send somebody to meet us partway, so we can split up the kids. It'll be Lou or Randall. They're calling in other staff, too. We're going to have Big Group when we get back. Do not pass Go."

I knew he was trying, in his Jed-like way, to cheer me up.

"There's something else going on, too," he said. "But Doug wouldn't tell me over the phone."

"Doug was there?"

"I know, on a Sunday. Weird, right? Something must be going on. I mean, besides this."

We met up with the yellow Subaru just north of Bangor. Randall the night staff was driving; his head looked huge in the small car. We split up the kids, put some in with Randall and Sage, who still wasn't speaking. Then, in the two vehicles, we drove back to Sunrise Academy.

It was still fairly early when we pulled into the drive. Chilly, and the fields were still wet with dew. The lake was gray, and the water looked dirty, which was odd, because the sky was pale blue.

Everyone got out of the van without speaking and walked toward the lodge.

Kenny met Jed and me by the van. I expected his mischievous smile—sure he'd find a way to joke about what we'd been through—but his face was serious, older, as he watched us haul the camping gear out of the van.

"You can leave that for now," he said.

"Might as well—" Jed began.

"No, let it go," Kenny said. His voice was a monotone.

We stopped, and the three of us stood there.

Then Kenny spoke without looking at us.

"They found the bodies," he said. "Annie and Garrett are dead."

SIXTEEN

It had happened at a campsite on the Appalachian Trail. Garrett was shot in the head. Annie was stabbed many times, maybe tortured.

"Doug's here," Kenny said. "We haven't told the kids yet. We were waiting till you guys got back."

He didn't say anything else, just turned and went back down the drive.

Jed and I stood in the middle of the camping gear, which was lying all over the ground. We just left it there and followed Kenny down to the lodge. It was all too much.

Most of the residents were still sleeping. It was Sunday; they might sleep for hours. The kids from the camping trip had been sent to their rooms, and the lodge had an empty feeling. Kenny went into the smoking area, sat smoking a cigarette there. I'd never seen him smoke before.

I wandered outside and walked down to the waterfront. It was still early morning, chilly, and I hugged myself. I was shivering, not sure if it was the temperature or the news.

There'd be more. There'd be lots of things.

Doug was up in his office, now, talking to Annie and Garrett's families. Everything was solemn and scary. There'd be Group. There would have to be after what happened on our camping trip and now Annie and Garrett. Elliot would be there and as much staff as they could summon up on a Sunday on such short notice, or maybe they'd wait till tomorrow.

I wished it were over—all of it—the news and the discussion and the expressions on the kids' faces. I didn't even like their faces anymore, after what had happened at Baxter. I wanted it to be over: the confusion, the startled comprehension, the crying and anger, the staff's measured explanations, and then Elliot, in his Elliot way, trying to work them through it. I didn't want any of it. Didn't want to be there with those lying children. Those children who might have killed me, though they'd said it was just a joke. *Just a prank, Ma*, Frankie had said. *Jeez.*

In a few hours, I'd be driving home to Jake. Home to my little house. Home to my approaching marriage, my sweet little life. I would take a long shower and wash it away: the tent, the smoke, the hiking, the kids—and I'd be okay.

I wanted this bad story not to be true. *Annie?* Could she really be dead? That bright light gone? I went back into the lodge and stood in the staff room. I felt filthy and heavy; I was exhausted. I'd barely slept the night before, and the emotion that had propelled me through the morning had faded away. I was only a lump. Dirty and messy, my ratty hair tied back in a haphazard ponytail. Mouth sour and sticky.

"I just want to go home," I said out loud. "I want to go home right now."

"But you can't, you know."

It was Elliot. He had come up behind me. He looked serious, even sad.

"How are you doing, Lorraine?" he asked, putting his hands on my shoulders and pressing his fingers into my sore muscles. "God, you're tense."

It felt good, and I didn't care that I was dirty and probably smelled. I let my head drop forward, willing myself to stop thinking—the whispery voices outside the tent, Jed's shout, the knife, the orange firelight caught on its blade. Let that disappear. Focus only on feeling Elliot's fingers on my tight, sore muscles.

"We're going to make a plan in a little while," he said. "Can you hold out that long?"

I didn't say anything, only nodded slightly.

"Come here," he said and, putting his hand on my upper arm, led me into the conference room.

I moved automatically, allowing myself to be led. It was the same room where we'd kissed last fall—before everything. Before Jake and I had decided to get married. Before Annie had started going out with Garrett. When everything was different and the kids seemed young and salvageable, as if a hike in Acadia could save them. It seemed like a million years ago, when kissing Elliot, letting him touch my breasts, seemed like the biggest deal in the world. Like it even mattered.

Now, everything was unreal. The window in the conference room looked out at the lake, which looked dead.

"Sit down, Lorraine," Elliot said, and he pressed me into a chair. "Let me do this for you."

Elliot began rubbing my shoulders again, kneading the muscles of my neck. It felt wonderful as he gradually worked his way up, rubbing my scalp, loosening the ponytail so my hair fell around my face. I let him rub my head, rub my shoulders, and my neck. It was not thrilling, like other times when he'd touched me. Still, it felt good to have the terrible tension squeezed out.

It seemed to go on for a long time. Elliot said nothing. I could hear him breathing. He was standing behind me, and the room was dim. I didn't move, not even when he slid his hands down to cover my breasts. It didn't matter. It felt good—a distraction from my churning thoughts.

He didn't say anything. If he had, it would have ruined everything. It would have been entirely different, if he had made some stupid remark about my breasts, about the texture of my skin. But he didn't. He just continued to touch me, and I made a sound like a sound someone else was making.

Elliot drew in a breath and stood still, his hands on my breasts. Then he walked slowly over and locked the door to the conference room.

I turned my head to look at him, and his face was serious.

"It's okay," he said. "You need this."

Everything in that moment seemed simple.

"And, you know what, Lorraine?" Elliot said. "I need it, too."

There was a couch along the far wall; we used that. I thought later I should have been ashamed. I was so dirty. Years later, when I remembered that scene, when I was more finicky, I thought: How could I have made love to that man when I'd been camping for days? I hadn't even brushed my teeth! But at the time, it didn't matter. Nothing mattered except getting my clothes off, seeing the look on his face—a look almost of reverence.

"Oh, God," he said. "You're so beautiful."

In another place, with another man, I might have scoffed at that remark; made some awkward joke. But that morning in the conference room, with all that had happened and all that would happen next, all I wanted was to stop thinking—to be entirely in my body. To get him inside me, feel him pressed against me, feel the rough fabric of the couch, and let go of everything—my thoughts, anger, sadness, my identity, even—and be entirely there.

I almost cried out when I came the first time, but Elliot said, "*Shhh. Shhh.*" He looked kind, smiling down at me. He took his time, moving more carefully and slowly than Jake. Drawing me on, holding back, until finally, closing his eyes, he stopped for a moment before pushing in deeper and making his own small sound.

He didn't make some stupid joke, like some men do, and he didn't collapse on top of me or pull right out and leave me there, wet, chilly, and lost. Elliot touched me gently, put his hand on my face, smoothed my hair. Looked at me with his beautiful eyes, with a look that meant he loved me, had always loved me. That he was sorry our lives had taken us in different directions—that he was married to June, that I would be marrying Jake. That he had a daughter. That my life was going in a different direction, with a different man.

We lay there, staring at one another, our bodies still joined.

"What's going to happen?" I asked.

"Nothing." Elliot shifted, so he was lying beside me. I felt cold, suddenly, and abandoned, even though he was still right there.

"I don't know what I'm doing," I said.

"You're here with me. We've wanted this for a long time, Lorraine."

I nodded. I didn't need to win anything with him now; I didn't need to ward him off. Here we were.

"We'll have Big Group tomorrow morning," he said. "Try to get it all out there. The kids who were on the camping trip will say they didn't mean it—that it was all a prank. That's what they're saying, isn't it?"

"It wasn't a prank, Elliot." I sat up, looking down at him.

Elliot looked at me with a sad expression. "They are kids, damaged kids. We will deal with it, I promise." He pulled me back down toward him. Lying beside him, nestled in his shoulder as he lay on his back, staring at the ceiling, it felt as if the rest of the lodge had disappeared. As if we were in a cabin on a big ship that had nothing to do with Sunrise Academy, or even Maine—somewhere else altogether. Maybe it was the proximity of the lake. I could hear, in the quiet pools between our sentences, the sound of the water lapping against the shore. Maybe it was because we had just made love and my body felt weightless, the way it can after sex. I was unaware of everything that lay beyond the closed door.

"I guess we have to tell them about Annie and Garrett," I murmured.

"Yeah. That's going to be tough. Some of them won't get through this. But you're right, we have to get them to talk about Annie. About Garrett. How it feels to lose them. This won't be the first death for most of them. And it certainly won't be the last. Is this your first death, Lorraine?"

I was quiet for a moment. "Sort of," I said. "I mean my grandmother died and a cousin, but this is the first person I *knew*, the first *friend*, who's died. Been killed. I can't absorb it. Do you know what happened?"

"Yeah. Or some of it." Elliot sighed. In that moment, there was only him and the story he was telling me, which was like a movie, not real life.

"Some other hikers saw Annie and Garrett with a man from Virginia who was kind of odd. That's what they said: He seemed *odd*. Someone said *seedy*. He was thin and seemed a little crazy. Anyway, they were hiking with him. They must have befriended him. You know how Annie was."

"She liked everyone," I said. "She trusted everyone."

"Yeah," Elliot said. "I guess people pass one another all the time on the trail. One gets ahead, then another one. You keep running into the same people. Anyway, a few days ago, or a week ago, maybe, nobody had seen Annie and Garrett in a while. Maybe they went off the trail? Nobody knew. And nobody saw the guy, either. The one from Virginia."

"Garrett's family was concerned because they hadn't heard from him. He was usually good about calling and sending postcards, but they hadn't heard from him in a while. They called Annie's parents, and they hadn't heard from her, either. So then they got worried, and they called the police down there—or I don't know, the forest service."

"They went in and did a search, and they found the campsite where Annie and Garrett had camped the last night they were seen. The tent was still there, but someone had taken it down and thrown it into the woods, along with some of their stuff. So they searched some more, with dogs, and they found the bodies.

"He'd buried them near there. Not very deep. The dogs found them. Garrett was shot in the head. They think the guy ate supper with them, went away, and then came back later, when they were in their tent. Garrett was quick…but Annie," Elliot's voice started to break up. Elliot, who fed on drama and was always watching with that little smile, Elliot was trying not to cry.

"Annie must have tried to talk to him. You know how she was always trying to get the kids to talk. She must have tried to reason with him."

He stopped for a moment. When he started again, his voice sounded better.

"She was stabbed. A lot. Again and again. Thirty, maybe forty times, with a knife. He must have chased her. He must have kept stabbing her and stabbing her. Maybe even after she was dead."

Elliot turned his head to look at me. His face was so close.

"I can't stop thinking about it," he said. "I don't know what to tell the kids. How much to tell them."

"Did they get the guy?"

"No," Elliot said. "That's the thing. Nobody can find him."

They did find him, of course, weeks later. He wandered out of the woods on his own. He'd run out of food and water, was half-starved, covered with bug bites, dehydrated, delusional. Gave himself up. What did it matter, anyway, if they got him or not? Annie and Garrett were still dead.

But now, because of the story Elliot told me and the way the sun had moved around to the other side of the lodge, the room felt chilly, and I was frightened, as if the man who had killed Annie and Garrett might be there, right outside the window, skulking around the lodge. Powerful, thin, and dangerous, armed with a gun and a knife.

"We should go back out," I whispered to Elliot. "Someone's going to notice we're missing."

"Yeah," Elliot said. "It's funny they haven't already. You'd think somebody would be banging on the door. Just shows how shaken up everyone is." He paused, thought a moment. "You're right, we've got to go out there. I don't want to. I just want to stay here with you. God, you're sweet, Lorraine."

"But now what happens?" I asked him. "You're married."

"Yes. And I'm very committed to my marriage. To my family."

"Then why?"

"I couldn't resist you," he said. "And with all this," he spread out his hands and I saw, again, how narrow his fingers were and how pale. He had seemed larger and more certain when he was touching me. Now, he seemed small again and his skin too white.

I wanted to feel the way I had felt before—transformed. Close to him, loved by him. But already, that feeling was fading.

"Don't you want to know what happened at Baxter?"

He was already getting up from the couch, reaching for his clothes.

"We don't have time, Lorraine. We have to get out there."

"But don't you want to know? I think they wanted to kill us."

He nodded. "They probably did."

"They're like wild animals." I was talking fast now, trying to keep Elliot in the room with me. "That's what I realized. They're like that guy who killed Annie and Garrett, only younger. I don't know people like that. Who don't have certain ways they behave."

"People who follow the rules, Lorraine?" he asked, with his little ironic smile. "But you don't follow the rules. We just made love, and I'm married. You're going to be married."

"Maybe," I said.

"Maybe," Elliot inclined his head. "But look what we just did. Don't fool yourself. We're no better than they are. We're all just animals, Lorraine, every one of us. All just animals, fighting over the same damn meat."

By the time I got home, it was late. Jake was waiting up and silently handed me a glass of wine when I got in the door.

"You hungry?" he asked.

I shook my head. I wasn't hungry.

"I'm disgusting," I said. "I need a shower."

"Go ahead," he said. He was being so nice. He was always nice. He didn't know anything.

All the way home, I'd worried about what I would say to him, if he'd find out what I'd done. It already seemed like a dream: the attack at Baxter, Annie and Garrett, the dim, weird light in the conference room, Elliot's pale, narrow body. Why had I done it? He wasn't even handsome. Jake was the one who was handsome. Elliot wasn't even that nice. But I'd been unable to stop.

Should I tell him?

If we were going to get married, shouldn't I tell him everything? Shouldn't we be all open and honest and have no secrets from one another? Didn't secrets just fester like the secrets of the children at Sunrise, with their sad stories of abuse and fear and neglect? Fear of the angry father. Fear of the furious mother. Fear of the drunken nights.

Didn't I have some of that same fear myself? Wasn't I, too, full
of secrets? I'd never, after all, told anyone, not even Jake, my real
story. I didn't even admit to myself what it had been like. Instead,
I clung to the myth of the happy Maryland childhood: my sister,
my mother, my dad when he was around, all cozy in our nice little
house. But wasn't my marriage to Jake going to be different? Weren't
we making a new life together, something pure and good?

I could imagine Elliot sneering at the word "pure." *There's no
such thing as purity,* he'd tell me. *Come on, Lorraine. You know that.*
As if I didn't really believe any of the things I wanted to believe in.
As if I knew better and just didn't want to admit the bald, cold truth.

All the way home, I'd been thinking things like this. The fields
of Trenton were bunchy and endless. One house with the shades
pulled down, a white church, and nothing else. I was tired, but I
was reluctant to get home and see Jake, because then I would have
to either tell him or not tell him.

But when I parked beside our small house with his truck out
front, I felt as if I could still be saved, could still have this life. If I
didn't let what happened seep through. If I shut it away. Closed the
conference room door and walked away down the hallway and out
of the lodge. Left Elliot lying there on the couch, the light falling
on his face through the dirty windows.

Later, in the shower, with the hot water beating down, I felt
released. I could wash off all the dirt from the mountain, the dirt
of the day. I wouldn't tell Jake, I decided. There was no reason to.
It would just hurt him, and anyway, wasn't the sex just an act of
absolution—a kind of therapy?

It really didn't matter, did it? It wasn't going to happen again. I
didn't even like Elliot. I liked Jake. I *loved* Jake—his kindness, our

house, our future, which seemed quaint and dear and impossible now. But I could still have it.

If I could just stay in the shower long enough, it would all wash away.

"You must be exhausted," Jake said, when I came downstairs.

He'd made me a grilled cheese sandwich and brought it into the living room with another glass of red wine. "You want this—or would you rather just go to bed?"

"I better eat something," I said, though I didn't want it. The sight of the sandwich on the blue plate made me too sad. He'd even cut it diagonally because he knew I would like that. He loved me so much.

I sat down. I was in my fuzzy white bathrobe, which made me feel extra clean. I was barefoot. I took a sip of the wine, and the alcohol hit me right away, pressing me down into the chair. I didn't think I could eat, but when I took a little bite of the sandwich, it tasted delicious, like it was the best sandwich ever.

Jake was in the kitchen, puttering around, wiping the counters and putting things away.

"This is so good!" I called out to him. The water was running, and I wasn't sure he could hear.

I took another bite. I felt as if I could gobble the whole thing down in a minute, then eat another one, too.

Jake came back into the room.

"How are you?" he asked, sitting down in the other chair. "Want to talk?"

I'd called him from Sunrise to tell him we'd come back early from the camping trip.

"There's a lot going on," I'd said.

Now, I told him what happened at Baxter and about Annie and Garrett.

"What?" he kept saying. His incredulity exhausted me. How could I explain everything that had happened? Just three days ago, I'd been making jokes about camping, worried about not being able to keep up on the hike, being dirty all the time, getting bug bites. I'd see a snake. Or a bear. We'd joked about it: *The Dangers of the Wilderness.* Now all of that seemed stupid and shortsighted.

When I first started talking, my voice was wooden and quiet. A matter-of-fact recitation: *Then we hiked in. Then we set up camp. Jed made pancakes.*

But when I got to the part about the girls whispering in the night, waking up to someone unzipping my tent, Shawn lunging in with a knife, I started crying.

Jake's face crumpled. He hated to see me cry.

"Oh, sweetie," he said.

I knew I had to marry him. I would never be safe if I didn't. I would never be happy.

The phone was ringing downstairs.

I got up, disoriented, and ran down to the kitchen in my night-gown to answer it. Jake had already left for work hours ago. It was almost nine.

I thought it was Elliot. "Yes?"

"Lorraine?" Kenny's voice. "Big Group at ten. Need you there."

"What?" I was all confused. "I just woke up."

"Okay. See you at ten!"

He hung up.

I stood barefoot in the kitchen, the linoleum cool under my feet. Jake had washed the dishes, and the blue plate stood in the drainer beside the sink, the wine glasses clear and completely clean.

Sunlight came in through the window. In the backyard, I could see the two large rabbits that lived there, one brown and one white with a brown streak down its back, for summer camouflage. It always seemed like a lucky omen when I saw them.

I saw the rabbits, I'd tell Jake, and he'd look up, in his mild way.

That's great, Lorraine, he'd say, and I knew he loved me, because he understood the importance of rabbits.

All I wanted to do was stay home and drink coffee out on the screened-in porch. Maybe the little boy from across the street would ride by on his bicycle. Maybe the old lady named Augusta would appear, walking briskly with her little dog. Maybe nobody would come, not even Jake, but I would know he was coming later. I wouldn't have to go anywhere, wouldn't be in a hurry. I would just drink my coffee, stay in my nightgown all day. I wanted to never go back to Sunrise. I wanted all of it to disappear. I wanted to have never met Elliot. I wanted Annie to be alive. Everything that happened to be just a story I read once and didn't like, closed the book, never looked at again.

SEVENTEEN

That morning, in Big Group, more stuff came out about what had happened at Baxter. Somehow the kids had gotten ahold of wine and some pills. The boys were plotting to attack Sage, hold him down, and stab him. Some of the girls—Erin, Contessa, and Darcy—had planned to slash my face with a razor, so they'd be sent to BHMI.

"We thought it would be better there," Contessa said sulkily when she was confronted.

This was not what I had expected. I thought Big Group would be difficult but sentimental—tears of remorse for their misbehavior on the trip, memories of Annie and Garrett—sorrowful, awkward testimonies from the residents. Instead, the schoolhouse cabin felt like the monkey house at the zoo—that same craziness and a smell that was not quite human, a sort of musk coming off the kids, even some of the staff.

I stared at the feral campers. All but Frankie, Justin, and Roy confessed, almost with pride, that they were in on the plot or had known about it.

Adam flat-out denied he was part of it. "I tried to talk them out of it," he said. "I told them they were crazy."

The others just stared at him, their expressions not even defiant. They looked bored with all the discussion, as if it were no big deal.

The kids looked the same as ever—as if nothing had happened: Frankie with her dazed, myopic expression and Adam in a clean white shirt. Contessa somehow managed to look innocent and nearly angelic with her big blue eyes and shiny blonde hair braided in two little braids, her pink hooded sweatshirt as tiny as if made for a doll.

Everyone was there: Doug and Randall and even Margo, who worked in the office, Annette the nurse, Alice the cook. We sat in a circle, each of the residents with a staff member on either side. Elliot was there, very quiet and serious. He glanced at me blankly, as if yesterday afternoon had never happened. I remembered when I had visited his house the past summer, noticed the creek out back, and said how his kids could play there when they were older. He'd said, *God, I sure hope we won't still be living in Maine.*

I was like that creek in back of his house. I was like the house itself, with the ducks on the kitchen walls and the sad little bathroom. What he would leave behind.

All the kids on the camping trip were in on the plot, except maybe Adam. They had planned to attack the same adults with whom they'd cooked hot dogs over the campfire, whose laps they'd sat in. I had thought we were giving the residents something they'd never had. That, along with the lessons, the scoldings, ICU, and the hiking—we were giving them *love* or some approximation of it. Teaching them there could be a different world. Anger that was not rage.

I myself had never experienced anger that wasn't terrifying, and the kids' attack at Baxter and my reaction, the fury I'd felt, reminded me of my childhood, took me back to that terrible time when my mother's rages seemed wordless, boundless, erupting from across the room, while I cowered by the closet door, eight years old, turning my face away.

My mother opened my bureau drawers, discovering my collection. Foreign coins my father had brought back from other countries: Tunisia, Siam, Vietnam. I'd put them in little envelopes and marked them carefully. There were special sticks and rocks I'd found in the yard and a rusty key I'd dug up in the bamboo patch in back of the Havilands' house. All carefully labeled.

What's this? she roared, pulling these precious objects out of the drawer. Disgusted, throwing them down on the floor. Hurling them in my direction. My mother's face both appalled and fascinated me. It was a face from a nightmare. Her roar was compelling. I got lost in it.

That's my hobbies, I told her weakly, trying to placate the raging beast.

Your hobby is making a mess! my mother hollered. *Your hobby is chaos!* She herself was chaos; she was a mother of chaos. And she threw it all: torn envelopes, sticks, stones, rocks, dolls, old rusty key. Anything she could find in the cluttered drawers. Anything she could get her hands on.

Later, I was sore and quiet. I had spent the afternoon cleaning my room as instructed; my mother subsided downstairs. She was in the kitchen. I could feel her presence down there. Maybe she was boiling fruit to make jam in the steamy kitchen, the air thick with the smell of boiling fruit and sugar. That sweet thick vapor rising up and her big, stained spoon.

Maybe she was ironing with her dangerous iron. The ironing board made a certain squealing creak when she unfolded it. Then she set it down, *hard!*, on the kitchen floor. Another noise that I recognized. I could track her movements downstairs.

And then she was ironing and sprinkling the clothes with the special bottle she had, with a sprinkling top. She sprinkled the clothes and picked up the iron. Steam rose like the smoke from a fire. My mother was all steam and rising heat. My mother's glasses fogged up, obscuring her eyes, until there were only blank foggy spaces where her eyes belonged.

It's all I ask of you girls! she yelled. Would she throw more things across the room? The iron itself? The potful of boiling jam? *It's all I ask.*

But then, other times, she was not that way at all. She was soft as a pillow, soft as a dream. Soft as the baby blue sky. It was early morning, the street was quiet, and we were leaving now, driving to Maine, to the Island. The whole street was gray and silent, the houses with their curtains drawn. The car already packed the night before.

Come on, girls. Gently. Gently.

Everything was whispers. My mother's voice was so kind.

My father was there, steady and quiet. We all got into the car. My sister in the back, in her nest of sleeping bags and pillows, and I up front between our parents. My father was driving, my mother silent. We were all in the car, and we were driving down the quiet street, and I slumped against my mother, and she was so soft. She put her arm around me. *Safe.*

Big Group went on and on. I couldn't concentrate. None of it felt real—the noises in the night, the knife in the tent, the silky, uneven light in the conference room—none of it existed.

I looked across the room at Elliot. He still wasn't looking at me. He was looking at the children and the hodgepodge collection of staff that worked at Sunrise, and he wore a sorrowful expression, which seemed more profound than angry. He looked at each kid, turning slowly, standing in the center of the room, staring each one down. He wasn't tall and strong like Garrett or tough and sinewy like Sage, but he had something—some wily power—they all respected.

He's smart, Contessa told me one time. *He knows things.*

He was using that now—that power. As Elliot stared at them, their boredom flickered, and there was a new look on their faces, a lost look, as if they were just children, after all, who had broken something—some toy they loved or some doll. They'd thought they could pull her head off, then put it back on—only now it wouldn't go back.

"BMHI would be better than this place," Contessa said, sulkily.

"Oh, you think so?" Evelyn asked, rising suddenly and striding over to her. "You really think so?" Evelyn's voice was loud. She was trying to do the scolding thing we'd been taught, but her heart wasn't in it. She sounded discouraged. I felt discouraged, too, and just wanted to leave. I was sick of the kids. They were all just criminals, really. No different from the person who had murdered Annie and Garrett. Just younger and not as adept. I wanted all this to be over so I could go home to my real life.

But Elliot was talking again.

Suddenly, almost involuntarily, I heard myself speak.

"What about Annie and Garrett?" I asked.

Elliot paused, looking at me sharply. "What do you want to say, Lorraine?"

I faltered, fixed with his blue-green stare. "I…uh…I think we should talk about them."

"Okay," Elliot said. "Go on."

Doug spoke up. "Lorraine's right, Elliot. We lost two of our best staff, two good friends. We need to let folks talk about that. There's a lot of hurt here. We need to grieve."

I looked at Doug gratefully. He was such a nice guy.

"I miss Annie!" Contessa said, and she started to cry. Kenny put his arm around her.

Elliot rolled his eyes. "Don't hide in that," he said sharply, looking accusingly at me. "Good distraction, Lorraine."

"It's not a distraction!" I answered wildly, not caring whether I was being therapeutic or just emotional. "They were killed! Aren't we even going to talk about it?" Hadn't he and I discussed this in the conference room just yesterday?

Elliot's eyes were steely.

I felt something shake loose inside me. I plowed on, ignoring him and Evelyn, who was watching me with amused detachment.

"Annie and Garrett are dead. We have to talk about them and what they meant to us. Of course the kids will face consequences for what they did, but that's not the most important thing going on right now."

Elliot was still standing in the middle of the room, his face impassive. When I finished, he slowly raised his hands and started clapping slowly in mock applause, which was somehow worse than annoyance or anger: it was disdain. He didn't even try to hide it.

Everyone stared at us—at him, standing in the middle of the room with his blue shirt and his little smile, and at me sitting next to Frankie, my face red, eyes starting to prick with tears. It seemed as if we would stay like that forever—him clapping, me trying not to cry—when a voice suddenly rang out.

"Cut it out, Elliot," Evelyn said, sharply.

She'd been seated off by herself. She rose up smoothly, tall and regal, and stood towering over him. She was, as always, impeccably dressed. She was wearing black jeans, and her hair was stylishly cut and expertly combed back away from her face. Her makeup was perfect.

"Lorraine's right," she said.

I am? I thought.

Evelyn turned to look at me. "The kids messed up badly on the trail. Is that such a surprise? We know you're all a bunch of hood-lums," she said, looking around at the kids, who seemed younger now, vulnerable.

"Stupid move, really," she said. "Especially you, Adam. You really fucked up."

Doug started to rise. Staff weren't supposed to swear around the residents.

Evelyn raised one long, slim-fingered hand. "Oh, can it, Doug," she said, tiredly. "As if they haven't heard it before."

Contessa giggled nervously. Shawn actually snickered.

"You all fucked up," Evelyn continued. Everyone was looking at her now, mesmerized by her height and majesty. "You had it good here: nice rooms, plenty to eat, little activities planned for you, the hikes, the swimming. What? You think you're going to get that at BMHI? At the Maine Youth Center? Well, think again. You've been safe here. Now, because of what you did, you're going to go to jail. This was the last stop, kiddos." She sounded almost pleased. "Not all of you. Some of you will get to stay, and I hope you'll take a lesson from this. But I doubt that you, Shawn," turning to regard him, "are going to be around after today. And as for you, Kurt, I wouldn't count on it."

"But that's the thing, isn't it? You're all replaceable here. There are plenty of other kids in Maine who would love to come here, take your rooms, go on camping trips, and—who knows?—maybe even complete the program, with honors. I just can't feel too sorry for you. You had your chance, and you made your choice."

"But Annie and Garrett—they didn't deserve to die."

Evelyn's voice broke. I'd never seen her sleek composure slip.

"So let's stop ranting at these losers, Elliot, and show a little respect for the people that have earned it. Your theatrics, your psycho-drama, the whole little puppeteer act—it makes me so tired."

She turned then and looked directly at him. Evelyn had never seemed so tall before or Elliot so short. He was like a crab, I thought, scuttling along the dirty ocean floor, a mangy little dog, or a rat. His hair, combed back, looked dry and lifeless, his face puffy. Elliot was always so composed; he always controlled the action, betrayed no emotion. But now, as he stared back at Evelyn, his face was a mask of hatred.

"I'm tired of you, Elliot," Evelyn continued. "In fact, I'm tired of all of you. It's been a good gig. But you know what? I can do better. It's certainly not worth dying for."

Evelyn gave a sweeping look around the room, pausing here and there, considering our faces. When she got to me, she stopped, then strode over and held out her hand. I was surprised, but I took it. Evelyn's grip was dry and firm.

"You're all right, Lorraine. But if I were you, I'd get the hell out, while you still can. You can do a lot better, too."

Then, with a last glance back at Elliot, she sailed out of the room.

EIGHTEEN

For a few minutes, nobody spoke. We were all diminished by her words, Elliot most of all. He just stood there in silence.

Then the room erupted and everyone was talking at once. The kids shouting to one another. *What's with her? We're going to the Maine Youth Center? I'm not going! I didn't do anything! You started it!*

"I want Annie!" Erin yelled. "I want her back!" And then Erin, who never cried, was crying. Some of the other girls were crying, too, and even some of the boys. It was a madhouse.

Into the hubbub came the unexpectedly deep and reassuring voice of Randall. He stood up, in his cumbersome way, and stood over us, huge and terrible in his overalls.

"Okay everybody," he boomed, "everybody just quiet down! Here's what's going to happen. Doug's going to tell us what to do, and we're going to do it. I have a feeling some of you *are* going to the Maine Youth Center, and there's nothing you can do about it. You made your bed. You knew what you were doing up there at Baxter—knew you were taking a chance. Well, here's what you get for it. That's how life works, and it's time you learned it. Maybe a little time at the Maine Youth Center will teach you that you get what you ask for. I hope so."

"The rest of you—well, Evelyn was right. You'd better be glad if you're *not* sent there, and you'd better mind your P's and Q's from now on. Do your chores, do what the staff says, and you'll get along. Here's another thing: no more smoking. Nobody, not even staff. Not in the smoking room, not anywhere, not anybody. Got that?"

Wild angry shouts rose up. They were quickly quelled.

"And no more fighting. *None.* Got it?"

"We got it, chief!" shouted Manny, but when Randall glared at him, he sank back against the wall.

"What else, Doug?" Randall looked at the director.

Doug rose from his chair. He'd been quiet, watching the action.

"Randall's right," he said. "No more smoking at Sunrise Academy. And Lorraine's right, too. And Evelyn. We're all tired. We need to get back to the lodge and get things straightened out. But before we go, I'd like us to think about Annie and Garrett. How much they meant to us. Who they were. What their deaths mean. What they have left us with."

"Do you want me—" Elliot began, but Doug waved him off.

"That's okay, Elliot," he said. "I got this."

There was Doug, tall and slender. He looked graceful instead of foolish and geeky, as he'd often seemed. I remembered hiking with him on St. Sauveur. His sweetness. His ability on the trail. How he'd asked about my life and my plans and had genuinely listened. He was like Jake, I thought: a nice man.

Later, walking up to my car after Group, after all of it, I was sad and quiet. I didn't know what I was. I felt hollow. It was too much: the emotion, the kids, the news, all of it.

Jed came up and put his arm around me, trying to comfort me. We were both just tired.

"Are you going to keep working here?" I asked, when we got to my car.

Jed shrugged. He was such a simple man.

"Sure," he said. "For now."

We stood there.

"You?"

"I don't know," I said. "It's never going to be the same."

"No."

"I mean, how are we ever going to be able to trust these kids again?"

Jed shrugged again. "I never did trust them. Did you?"

"I don't know," I said. "Sort of. I started to feel as if we were, like, I don't know, a family or something." Even as I said it, I could hear how dumb it sounded.

"It's just a job, Lorraine," Jed said quietly. "It's not your life."

He was right, even though for a while, it had seemed to be.

Justin got caught that night stealing cigarettes from the new boy, Martin, and Martin got mad and punched him. One of Justin's teeth got knocked out, and Martin was sent away.

A few days after that, Trixie ran away, but Kenny and I drove out and picked her up in Sullivan, walking across the Singing Bridge.

I held the car door open. "Get in," I told Trixie tiredly, and Trixie climbed into the backseat without a word. She wasn't sure where she was going anyway and was probably glad that we'd found her.

Everyone wanted to leave Sunrise—the staff, the residents. Whatever magic there'd been was gone.

NINETEEN

There was a memorial service for Annie and Garrett in mid-June. It was hot; there were tons of blackflies. Jake came with me, and I introduced him to some of the newer staff. The service was very long. It seemed like everybody who knew Annie or Garrett had to say something. They all had some certain memory that they wanted to share. A lot of the residents spoke, and they often began with *I just want to say*. Elliot didn't speak. He stood beside June, holding his daughter's hand. Their little girl, Josie, was all dressed up, and June was holding the baby, who cried off and on throughout the long memorial service. They looked diminished—a shabby little family from the Midwest somewhere, Kansas or Ohio. I couldn't imagine ever kissing that man.

During the service, I looked around at the staff and residents gathered beside the lake. The teachers had come, and a few counselors who no longer worked at Sunrise—Claire and Cassie—even Elizabeth showed up for the ceremony.

"Annie and I were really close," she told me, though I knew for certain that wasn't true. "I really miss her!" Tears were shining in her eyes. I could see the gold chain glittering at her throat and the tiny gold cross she wore. "We stayed in touch after I left. Did you know that? We even talked about how I could go down and meet up with them on the trail."

I didn't know what to say to that, so I said nothing.

Garrett's parents spoke and Annie's sister. She cried when she started to speak. It almost made me cry. I hoped it would make me cry, but somehow it didn't. I felt as if I were made out of wood. The lake was flat and still; the whole ceremony seemed far away. It was so hot, and the blackflies were brutal.

After the service, we all milled around, not sure what to do next. There was food inside the lodge. Alice the cook had made all kinds of cookies and brownies. There was hot coffee and iced tea, lemonade for the kids. It was really too hot to eat anything.

Elliot drifted over and stood beside Jake and me. I introduced them, but there wasn't much to say.

"You realize, don't you, that nothing's ever going to be the same?" Elliot asked me. Jake had wandered off to fetch another drink.

Elliot was standing quite close to me, but I didn't touch him. I didn't even want to.

"We're never going to go back to the way it was," he said.

Later, I thought I should have said something clever. Clever and scathing—to show that I wasn't afraid of him now and didn't desire him. But all I could do was stand there and stare at the lake.

Evelyn didn't come to the memorial service. She only came back to Sunrise one more time after that day in Big Group. Stopped in to pick up her paycheck, a jacket she'd left behind, a spare pair of shoes. I didn't speak to her. I saw her across the lodge as she came in the door. She looked different already—even taller, more stylish. She was wearing her big dark glasses, and her hair was a different color—darker, more lustrous, thicker. She had on white jeans, and her legs looked long and glamorous.

As Evelyn strode into the lodge, she raised one hand at me then went up the stairs to the office, coming down just a few minutes later with a white envelope in her hand. Her last paycheck. She was wearing red lipstick and a slight smile. I watched her walk into the staff office, take her jacket, sling it over her arm in a competent way, and pick up her extra shoes. Something about that gesture made me picture her, for the first time, as a mother of teenagers: capable, graceful, plucking old sweatshirts up off the floor, shutting a car door with her hip with her arms full of groceries.

Elliot was in his office that afternoon. He spent more time in there now. He, too, was probably getting ready to quit, working on his dissertation or even job applications. I didn't care. We were like strangers now. One time, he'd asked if I wanted to spend the night on the island with him and some of the kids. *I need female staff,* he told me. Maybe if he had said he needed *me,* I might have said yes, but probably not. Everything that had happened between us seemed unbelievable now, and I just wanted to forget it. I'd be quitting myself any day now—two more months, max.

Now Evelyn, jacket slung over her arm, rapped on Elliot's office door. I could hear that clear, competent knock from across the lodge and even, faintly, Elliot's voice from within. The door opened, and I saw him sitting at his desk. He looked up at Evelyn. I couldn't see his expression from where I stood, but I could imagine it: that little smile.

Elliot said something. Evelyn said something. Then she stepped into his office, shutting the door behind her.

I wasn't around when Evelyn left Elliot's office. I had to escort Frankie and Contessa up to the schoolhouse for a GED class. It was just a formality—neither one was any trouble; in fact, they'd both been extra affectionate and docile since the episode at Baxter—but all residents who left the lodge were being escorted *until further notice,* Doug had told us. It felt like a stupid game. What could staff actually do? We'd hired more staff in the last few weeks, but really, for all our increased numbers and all our rules, we had no power at all.

Frankie wanted to take my hand.

"You still mad, Lorraine?" she asked me.

I glanced at her without smiling. "No, just disappointed," I said, remembering how it had hurt when my dad had said that. But Frankie just looked at me; I wasn't sure she even knew what the word *disappointed* meant.

We were almost to the schoolhouse when I heard a car door slam shut.

I turned and saw Evelyn's shiny gray Volvo station wagon coming up the drive. Because of the position of the sun and its reflection on Evelyn's windshield, I couldn't see her face inside the car. I thought she might roll down her window when she came opposite us, might give one of her sardonic smiles, maybe even say something. Evelyn just drove by. As she passed, I could see her profile. I'd never seen her from that angle. Evelyn's hair was combed back, and she was, I realized, a very beautiful woman. It was only a glimpse. Evelyn did not even look at us, standing there by the schoolhouse cabin, just stared straight ahead. And then she was gone, and I could see the reflection of the trees in the back window of her car: all those leaves.

That night, two new kids, Wendy and Dean, ran away. Somebody heard they'd gone to Bangor. By the time Doug and Sage got up there, Wendy and Dean were gone.

A week or so later, another girl, Dawn, ran away and got all the way to Georgia before she was caught. It was decided she couldn't come back. She was going to live with her parents in Western Mass. *But didn't her father…?*

Yeah, somebody said. *But she wasn't safe here, either, was she?*

Everything was breaking apart. It was August already. There were new kids. I didn't bother getting to know them. All the residents were starting to look the same to me—like junior criminals. A new boy named Gene and another one, Tim, ran away, but then they got caught. A lot of the staff had already left, and more would be leaving. Jed was going to quit at the end of the month. I'd probably leave then, too. I'd applied for a job at the high school, helping out in the library. Some sort of aide or something. I wouldn't get health benefits, but Jake got them with his new job working for a local contractor.

It would be so handy, marriage. How nice it would be. The whole world was set up for people to be married. It just made sense.

One late summer evening, Doug and the new staff Marsha played guitars and sang for the kids.

Kenny quietly left the lodge and went out to sit alone on a bench near the water. I followed him out.

"That singing reminds me of Annie and Garrett," he said when I sat down. "I don't want to hear it."

He kept staring out at the water.

I didn't say anything, just sat quietly beside him. I thought about holding his hand, but I wasn't sure how he would take it. We weren't like that.

"You going to keep working here?" I asked him, after a while.

Kenny just kept staring at the water. He didn't even answer. It was like all the stuffing had gone out of him. Later, he'd be ramming around the lodge, yelling at the kids. He'd call up his wife, bark into the phone, "Come get me!" Make some crazy joke to get all the kids to laugh. But right now, he was quiet, and his silence made me feel guilty. If I'd been the one who'd been killed and it was

Annie sitting here, she would've been more authentic. She would have known what to say.

Thinking these thoughts made me resent Annie, just as I often had when she was alive. And realizing that made me feel even worse. All my thoughts just went around and around.

Finally, I got up from the bench.

"I'm going back in," I said. But Kenny just kept staring at the lake.

I spent a whole afternoon outdoors watching the kids on Reorientation—the Reos—work in the garden. They all complained endlessly, kept stopping to turn and glare at me, but I stared back stolidly. I hardly bothered learning the new kids' names. *They won't be here long,* I thought, *and neither will I.*

Everyone was mean now. The new staff Marsha quit suddenly after only three weeks on the job. She said the staff position was *a job for twelve-year-olds.* Gee, I thought, I'd say it's pretty difficult. Elliot hardly ever came out of his office.

"I'll be glad when you're through here," Erin told me one day. I didn't know if she meant that or if she really meant she was sad. I didn't care what she meant; I just wanted to be done with Sunrise.

But when I finally told Doug I was quitting, Sunrise seemed dear again. It was summertime at the lodge, and we lay on old towels by the lake in the afternoon. I could smell pine needles hot in the sun and the scent of the water.

At Group, Erin came and sat in my lap and asked me to put my arm around her.

Sorry I gave you a hard time, she told me. I couldn't tell if she was lying. I was a star now, briefly, because I was leaving and getting married. Starting my real life.

Jed was leaving, too. He and his wife were moving to New Hampshire, where he already had a job at some outdoor rec program. *Nothing like this place*, he said.

Jake and I had gotten married at the end of the summer and had found a house we could buy. It wasn't big, but the owners wanted to sell to people like us—a young couple, just starting out, who would stay in the village year round. Raise our kids in the town; send them to the local school.

I hoped I would get pregnant soon, and by the end of November, I was.

TWENTY

But things don't always turn out the way you wish they would.

Jake and I got the house we wanted and the daughter we'd hoped for, but the marriage didn't work out, and by the time Susannah was five, we'd gotten divorced. I don't want to go into all the reasons for that. To me, the question is never *Why did they get divorced?* but *How does anyone ever stay married?* The reasons a marriage breaks up are rarely simple. In our case, it probably had a lot to do with my guilt about that one dim afternoon in the conference room and the secret I carried that made Jake's steadfast, unquestioning love impossible to bear, so I put a new saddle on my life and rode on.

My year and a half at Sunrise Academy seemed like something that had happened to somebody else. My real life as a single mom had begun; it was mostly a blur: job, child, school band practice, groceries, holiday pageant, bills. Softball games on spring afternoons sitting on the bleachers with the other parents, the stay-at-home moms in their jeans. Straight from the newspaper office in my work suit and panty hose, carrying my leather pocketbook, I slid into the bleachers, exhausted, watching as the kids lost the game.

Afterwards, we would go out for pizza or get a fish sandwich at the Ocean Drive Dairy Bar, and, if Susannah didn't have too much homework, we'd drive home along the Park Loop Road, with the moonroof open and the radio on, eating ice cream cones and listening to the Humble-Yet-None-the-Less Mighty John spin the oldies. A breeze blew through the car as we passed the parking lot for the Precipice Trail. I took Susannah up there when she was nine, and she loved it. Susannah knew all the trails in Acadia as well as I did. Because it was just the two of us, we seemed almost like sisters sometimes.

"What do you think?" I asked her, displaying my outfit for my first date with David.

"You're wearing that?" Susannah asked me, aghast, looking up from the book she was reading. She was lying on the couch. Why was I going out anywhere? This was what was really fun: being home with my daughter.

"What's wrong with it? We're just going out for a hike," I said, turning this way and that. I thought I looked pretty good—the tight, tapered jeans, the green sweatshirt.

"Yeah, okay, fine," she said, dubiously.

"All right, what?"

"Well, for one thing, your hair. Plus the whole look—unless you want to do the rough-and-ready hiker-girl thing, I guess."

When I begged her, Susannah relented, sprang up from the couch, fixed my hair, and picked out a different shirt.

"A white shirt to go hiking?"

"Do you want me to help you or not?"

On a hot, sunny day in early September, when Susannah was ten and before everything went wrong, I was driving her up to Bangor. We might have been going to buy school clothes or to visit the big new Borders bookstore that had just opened out by the mall. As we approached the turnoff in Ellsworth Falls, I said, "That's the way I used to go when I worked at Sunrise Academy."

"You mean that place with the bad kids?" Susannah asked.

I laughed. "They weren't all that bad," I said, remembering afternoons at the waterfront. Annie's laughing face, her faded red bathing suit. Evelyn's long narrow legs. The yellow canoes on the water.

"Is it still there?" Susannah asked.

"Want to go look?"

We weren't in any particular hurry, and lately, I'd realized my daughter was growing up fast. She would be eleven in a few months. Soon, she'd be in high school, and then, as another mother had warned me, it would all go by much too fast. *Like a dream*, she'd said, standing in front of the elementary school, staring off at the trees.

Moments like these would be gone then. Susannah would disappear into her own life, wherever it led her. Just as I had disappeared from my family in Baltimore when I went off to college in Ohio and then moved to Maine.

I turned the wheel sharply and veered off to the right.

Susannah looked at me, surprised yet not surprised. "We're going there now?" she asked.

"Sure," I said, "why not?"

Funny, that in all the years since I'd worked there, I'd never been back even once, not since the last night I left, when Jed and I had walked up to our cars in the darkness. I'd been sure, at the time, that I'd go back. Sure that Sunrise and all of the people there would remain a part of my life, but other than running into one or two of the staff at Reny's or the Grasshopper Shop, or once at the Blue Hill Fair, I hadn't seen any of them.

Funny how things work out, Annie used to say.

Annie.

I hadn't thought—*really* thought—about Annie in years.

The road to Sunrise was familiar and relatively unchanged. The big farmhouse with the sagging barn. The beige split-level with its new-looking asphalt drive. I wondered if they had repaved it; how else could it look so black and so smooth all these years later? The barking dog in the yard—was it still the same dog? Then the field. A couple of new houses, maybe, but mostly, it all looked the same.

We came to the driveway, the one I drove down all those years ago. Was it only a dozen years? It felt like a lifetime, at least. The sign was still there, but the paint, once a lively, bright green and blue, was worn and faded. Cardboard from a twelve-pack lay on the ground at the foot of it, tall grass grown up all around. The driveway was in even worse condition than it used to be. I remembered driving there in the early morning: that feeling of expectation, that quiver of fear. It was warmer now, the air closer, and I rolled down my window. Beside me, Susannah was silent, the radio off.

Grass and weeds had grown up in the shabby field. The woods to the left seemed thicker and denser, brambly. And then there it was, shining out before us—the lake. The schoolhouse cabin, which stood on a little rise, was still there. One window was broken and patched with a piece of plywood. There were no canoes, and the lodge itself, when it came into view, looked abandoned, both smaller and larger than I remembered. One old truck in the parking area.

There was no one around.

"This is it?" Susannah asked skeptically, when I stopped the car. She looked out her open window at the flat blue lake.

"Want to get out?" I asked. "Look around? Doesn't look like anyone's here."

"You think?" asked Susannah. She opened her door and got out.

We walked toward the lodge. It was locked with a great big padlock that looked like it'd been there awhile. A plastic *No Trespassing* sign—bright orange on black—was nailed to the door.

I cupped my hands to peer in through the dusty windows. The tables were still there—those long wooden tables where the residents had eaten their meals. I could see the old Naugahyde couch, and the door to the ICU stood open. The Plexiglas smoking area was gone. After Baxter, the residents weren't allowed to smoke. Not even the Level Fours. Funny how all that jargon came right back. *Level Fours. Day Staff. The Reos.*

I couldn't remember if I'd ever told Susannah everything that happened, though I'd told her some of the funny things I remembered. Odd moments—how Kenny used to wave his arm in the air. *Case closed!* he would say. *I have spoken!*, making a big show of it to the kids' delight. I'd told her about the time Roy got scared on the Precipice Trail and the lady who always lied.

It was very quiet.

Susannah wandered down off the porch and stood on the bank, looking out at the lake, the small island, the distant shore. Beside the lodge, I could see the overgrown garden, part of the woodpile. The wood was all rotten now, dark and wet-looking.

"Can we leave now?" Susannah asked, looking back at me. "This place kind of gives me the creeps."

"Sure," I said. "Let's go."

We climbed back into the car and started up the drive. Susannah fiddled with the radio, got some old song from the sixties. She loved that stuff. I liked it, too, but now I was barely listening. I wanted to remember this moment. I was leaving Sunrise for the last time, I thought. Heading out to Route 1A and into the real world.

The Real World

TWENTY-ONE

In the evening at Caledonia, the women walk down the driveway together. The air is tranquil. It's early spring. In Maine, there may still be snow in the yard and ice in the woods; here, it's green, and the air's as soft as butter.

I have come to Caledonia, an artists' colony in Southern Virginia, to write about what happened not far from here: the murder of Annie and Garrett. I haven't told any of the other residents what I'm working on; I just say, vaguely, "a book" when anyone asks. I don't want to discuss it. I'm not even sure I want anybody to read it when it's finished. It's a private project.

I arrived last week for a one-month residency to finish the book I started a year ago, after I saw Annie and Garrett's picture in the *Bangor Daily News*. It was the same photograph they ran thirty years ago, right after the murder. They both look so young. They've stood still in time as everyone else hurried by: Annie, twenty-seven forever; Garrett, thirty, maybe, no more.

I hadn't thought about them—really thought about them—in years. It all came back in a rush: Sunrise in summer, Annie in her faded red bathing suit, the smell of the lake. Then winter, the warmth of the lodge, followed by spring: that disastrous trip up to Baxter, coming back to hear they'd been killed.

The newspaper article rehashed the whole story. There was a photograph of the man who killed them, a pale, seedy-looking man with dark hair and one of those triple Southern names killers have: Lewis Ray Bladgett. It took weeks to track him down and capture him, but he finally did go to jail. A few years ago, he'd finished serving his sentence and was released; now, he too was dead—hit by a car near his home just outside of Prineville, Virginia. I looked at his picture, at the picture of Annie and Garrett, and decided to write the book. I needed something. Maybe this was it.

That was a year ago, toward the end of winter, when I was at a pretty low point. My daughter, Susannah, was gone. I had remarried briefly, and that second marriage had ended years ago. My sister and I were estranged. My father was dead, and my mother was in a nursing home in Bangor. I was drinking too much. I was fifty-four. Not old yet, but I could see it coming, the slow train in that direction.

On cold nights, when the wind blew around my house in Northeast Harbor, rattling the windows in their casements, I would lie in bed and think about getting old. The town felt abandoned. The other houses up and down my road had all been sold to summer people. They no longer shone with lights but were silent and empty. The downtown was dead, the harbor deserted; the fishing boats were quiet, tied there in the empty night.

I still had my job at the weekly paper. I liked it all right and was good at it, but sometimes, when I was covering yet another Board of Selectmen's meeting, listening to Ralph Barnstable ask querulously *Could somebody please explain this to me?* in that way he had, or when I was taking yet another photograph of another enormous check handed over to some smiling nonprofit lady in a cardigan sweater, or when I came home and the house was so empty, I would think: *Is this it? Is this all of it?*

It wasn't all terrible. There were still the beautiful sunsets—still the mountains, the ocean, the sound of the water against the shore, and the miracle of the forest. I went into the woods as if I could find the answer there, and I walked and I walked and I walked, but sometimes, even there, I would think: *Is this it?* And sometimes, climbing one of the mountains, when there was still ice in the woods and the rocks were dark and slippery, I would imagine how it would be to fall from one of the cliffs—just fall, like the stewardess in that James Dickey poem I'd read in college. Be done with it all.

And sometimes in the morning, when I opened the *Bangor Daily News* and looked at the headlines, I thought *What year is it anyway? Who's the president? Which Bush is it now?* It all seemed the same: the wars in the Middle East, climate change and the melting icecaps, another mill closing up north—*Were there still any left to close?*—the power out due to the storm, a crack-up on I-95, grim faces of heroin dealers from New Hampshire, obituaries that might or might not be people I ever knew, and the endless weather.

But then, one morning as I read the paper, there they were: Annie and Garrett. It must have been a slow news day, because they were on the front page. Things must be pretty quiet in Iraq and Libya, Machias and Millinocket, for this decades-old murder to rate front-page status in Maine. *Killer Dies in Virginia.* And there he was: Lewis Ray Bladgett, the nondescript man who had killed Annie and Garrett, now dead himself, struck down by a car as he walked down some country road near Prineville, Virginia.

Then all those old stories about the murder: the interviews with other hikers who had seen Annie and Garrett with Bladgett on the trail. *They were very friendly. The guy seemed a little sketchy, though.* The investigation, piecing together what had happened: He'd visited them at their campsite, come back in the night, killed them both. First Garrett—a shot to the head, then Annie, killed with a knife. He dragged them into the woods, covered their bodies with leaves and brush. The dogs found them.

The article described the search for the killer. He came out of the woods weeks later and gave himself up, dehydrated, covered with bug bites, half starved. That photo of his strange, staring face. Then another, taken when he was younger, maybe a high school yearbook picture, an ordinary young boy somewhere in the South, smiling in a way that seemed sinister now, because of what he'd become.

I read the story and read it again. I went online and read everything I could find and began making notes. In the weeks that followed, I got up early and worked on my research. I wanted to tell this story. I guess, on some level, I was trying to find redemption, as if in writing Annie and Garrett's story, I could rewrite my own. I fiddled with it, made many false starts, started over. It wasn't like writing a newspaper story—it was bigger than that. Everything led to something else. When I opened one door, it led to another, then another door after that. And that door led into the woods, to a nightmare forest.

I didn't know if I was up to it. Writing about those lost people, all that lost time, made me too sad. As the rainy spring fell away and summer came, I stashed the pages to concentrate on hiking, fanatically climbing the mountains, two mountains, three. Doing them in bunches: Acadia, St. Sauveur, Valley Peak; then Cedar Swamp, Sargent, Penobscot; Triad and Pemetic; down Cadillac into the Gorge to storm up the side of Dorr. I hiked alone. I didn't want anyone with me. Anyone else would just slow me down, make me wait while they tied their shoelaces, drank water, fiddled with their backpack. I couldn't stand it. I had to be alone. And anyway, who would I hike with? All the time I was hiking, I thought about the story. It was heavy and clung to me; it would not let go.

Finally, sometime last fall, I'd started the project in earnest, getting up at four in the morning to work a few hours before starting my day at the newspaper. I managed to contact some of the staff I'd known at Sunrise. Said I was curious after all those years, wanted to compare notes. Had they seen the article in the newspaper? I didn't tell anyone what I was up to, as fearful and protective of my writing as if I were entering a brand-new love affair. It might not go well. I might have to give up on it, as I'd given up on all my other attempts at other novels over the years. Better that no one should know.

But this time, it felt different. Now, in heady bursts, I was inside the story, deeply engaged. I wasn't missing Susannah, wasn't mourning the end of my second marriage, resenting my mother, despairing over my life. It was such a relief. This was different than the kind of writing I was used to. It wasn't a local story where I needed to assemble the facts, find a catchy lede. I was writing it as a novel, so I had to climb inside the story and wander around. I had to *feel* it.

But it was hard, in Maine, in November, to conjure up the smell of the springtime forest. Maybe if I went to Virginia, I could imagine more clearly the smell of old leaves and damp bark. Intimacy with the place would give the book power, make it more real.

So I applied for a fellowship at Caledonia, the artists' colony where I'd gone once when I was in college, back when I thought I was going to be a great novelist, before life began.

I asked for a month's leave from my job to finish the project.

"Good idea," said Beverly, the new young editor at the newspaper, in her mid-thirties, with brown hair, two babies, a dog, and a husband—all on display in photographs in her office. She had taken Dobbs' job as editor after he retired. I wasn't really at ease with her, though I didn't know why. She was nice enough, very smart—she'd gone to Colby and Yale—but I just didn't like her. Her skin was so clear, so unlined! She was serene, efficient, and certain. One of those young women who will rule the world, I guess, when we angst-ridden, wrinkly vestiges of the old days are gone. We who learned to put up with things Beverly would never allow.

When she heard one of the computer geeks had sent an inappropriate e-mail joke to a new reporter, she fired him on the spot.

Dobbs would have had a talk with him, laughed privately over the e-mail, gotten him to apologize to the girl. Life would have moved on. Beverly simply fired him. That's how she was.

We were wary with one another. But I'd been there a long time by then, and she knew she needed me.

"You're valuable here," she told me, not warm, but pragmatic: a general assessing her troops. "But a break might be good for you."

She didn't say why, but I knew. I'd started to miss things. I'd be at one of the meetings I covered for the paper: a planning board, say, or town council. Someone would be droning on about ordinances or property lines or their view, and all of a sudden, I'd realize I hadn't heard anything for the last fifteen minutes—or was it longer? I'd sneak a peek at my watch. No one else noticed. They were all caught up in whatever small-town drama was currently playing out—the culverts in Pretty Marsh (inadequate) or the cruise ships (too many) or parking—and I was part of the wallpaper, really. I'd been there so long. I would come back to myself with a start, though I hadn't been asleep, just not there. And the weird thing was, I would be taking notes the whole time, writing down, in my scribbly, improvised shorthand exactly what everyone said, though it hadn't registered. Reading my notes over later, it would all be completely new to me, all unfamiliar.

"You seem a little…" Bev paused briefly. "I don't know. You seem like you could use some time off. Any particular place?" she asked brightly. She didn't really want to know what was wrong with me. It wasn't personal. She was trying to run the newspaper, get home to her "kiddos," as she always referred to them—which for some reason set my teeth on edge, that expression. She was just trying to run a business, and I was a bump in the road.

"I thought I'd go down to Virginia," I told her vaguely. I didn't want to tell her what I was really doing. *None of her business*, I thought. The truth was I didn't want to subject my secret plan to her cold-eyed scrutiny, let her see how important it had become to me. This thing that maybe could save me, could make me finally whole.

Here in Virginia, we have reached the end of the drive, where an iron grate keeps the cows from wandering into the highway, and there's a large sign on the left, a dreamy painting with blue sky and fluffy white clouds, and scrawled across it in big black letters are three words:

THE REAL WORLD

Beyond the sign, cars speed by on Route 286.

We turn and head back up the drive. The air all around us like silk.

TWENTY-TWO

A week before I left for Virginia, I located Evelyn, living in Portland with a different last name. She was Evelyn Bradford now. I called and made arrangements to visit her on the drive south.

She was gracious enough on the phone, but when I got to her apartment, I could tell she didn't want me there. She had her own life now, and I brought memories of a time she'd rather forget.

"Come in," she said, leading me into a large white room, her penthouse apartment in the Old Port.

I'd actually seen the place years before, when I was in town for a meeting of the Maine Press Association. I was representing our newspaper and felt very grown-up staying at a nice hotel, talking to editors from larger, more important Southern Maine publications. After the meeting, some of us went out to dinner, where we all got a little drunk. I remembered walking back in the chilly night, clattering over the cobblestones, excited that this could be my new life—here in Portland. One of the editors had hinted I could land a job at his paper.

"You'd be great!" he kept saying, staring across the restaurant table when the lady from Lewiston wasn't paying attention. "You ought to be down here!"

I thought he really meant it and lay in bed, still kind of drunk, thinking about how Susannah and I would move down to Portland and have an entirely different life from our life on Mount Desert Island. An urban life: going out for brunch in cool restaurants, taking the bus into Boston on weekends, having more money. I imagined the wonderful, glamorous life that we'd never live.

The next morning, I opened the curtains of my hotel room and stared out at the cobblestone streets, then looked up and saw this same penthouse apartment—an odd, square little bungalow, tacked atop one of the buildings. It had a terrace with a tiny café table and two wire-backed chairs and even, if I remembered right, a little tree. The penthouse had large windows that looked out in every direction. Whoever lived up there could see the harbor and beyond. Could watch ships come in at night and head out to sea before dawn. Still in the city, but far from the noise and chaos.

We would live there, I decided. Susannah would love it. But somehow, we never did.

I remembered that now, as I entered that same high dwelling.

"I've seen this before," I told Evelyn.

She'd already gone to sit on a white couch and was gesturing me to a chair.

Evelyn was still tall and lean and had retained that air of elegance she'd had at Sunrise Academy, and, though her hair was gray now and cropped very short, her eyes were still dark and beautiful. She was wearing gray pants and a loose, dark gray sweater, no jewelry except one large ring with a pale green oblong stone.

We sat across the coffee table, looking at one another.

"Well," she said. "You look good."

"Thanks. You look wonderful. What a great apartment."

Evelyn glanced around.

"It is nice, isn't it? I've been here eight years. I love living in Portland. You still on the Island?"

"Yes. I work for the *Ellsworth American*."

"So you're, what? Writing a story about Sunrise?"

"Yes, and what happened to Annie and Garrett," I said, trying to connect with the woman I'd known at Sunrise Academy. *I just can't talk to her,* Annie said once. *She's so grown-up.*

And now, here in her apartment, years later, Evelyn was very grown-up. She was in her seventies, living whatever kind of a life she had put together. It seemed like a good one: this beautiful penthouse overlooking the Old Port and the harbor; the spare, elegant, modern furniture; the white walls with a few large, splashy paintings.

"Did you do these?" I asked.

Evelyn glanced around at the walls.

"Yes," she said. "I've been doing some painting the last few years."

Later, after I left the apartment, I saw similar paintings in a gallery on Exchange Street. There was Evelyn's work: large, vivid paintings, abstract and colorful. But the one I found most compelling was on her wall: black, white, and gray—a violent painting of a forest with slashing trunks, broken limbs, fallen trees.

We talked about our lives since Sunrise, neither of us giving much away. Evelyn was polite, but I could tell she didn't want me there for long, so I got to the point, and asked what she remembered about Annie and Garrett. Evelyn answered my questions, filling in certain details I had forgotten.

"Why are you doing this?" Evelyn asked finally, clearly ready to end the interview. "It was such a long time ago."

"I guess it was seeing their photographs in the newspaper. Brought it all back. Maybe it's just middle age, a kind of reckoning." I gave a little laugh; she didn't.

"Ah," she said, as if middle age were something she'd tried herself once and got over—a fashion that didn't quite suit.

"You ever see any of the kids we had back then?" I asked, as I rose and pulled on my jacket. I'd closed my notebook in a gesture that seemed innocent but was calculated to elicit some final facts. Often, people revealed the most important elements of a story just as I was leaving. Maybe, once I turned off the tape recorder or put down my pen, they felt the interview was over and nothing they said really counted, and felt free to say what mattered most.

I hadn't planned to use this ploy with Evelyn; however, as I reached for my jacket, I was hoping she'd say something real. I wanted to penetrate that smooth facade and get to the slashy wilderness I saw in her painting.

"I run into Adam occasionally. Remember him?" Evelyn asked.

"The tall one?"

"Yeah. The one who didn't belong there," Evelyn said.

"That's what I always thought! What's he doing now?"

"He's a lawyer, here in town. You could talk to him," Evelyn suggested. "Wait. I might have his number."

She strode over to a small desk in the corner and flipped open her laptop. After a quick search, she scribbled something on a piece of paper.

"Here. Why don't you give him a call? I bet he'd be willing to talk about old times."

"What's he like these days?"

But Evelyn was done with me now.

"Oh, you'll find out. I'd hate to ruin the suspense."

TWENTY-THREE

"We better hurry," someone says as we start back up the hill at Caledonia. "The reading's going to start any minute."

"I'm not going," says Monica, the tall visual artist from California, and lopes off toward her studio, her canvas book bag slung over one narrow shoulder. She is working on a big project with full concentration. The rest of what goes on at Caledonia doesn't matter to Monica; the rest of us don't really matter. She is serious, and her paintings are serious: dark trees in broad landscapes, streetscapes and lonely houses.

I am jealous of Monica's concentration, though I'm getting a lot done myself. I've already gone through all of the old newspaper clippings I brought with me and the reports I pulled off the Internet. I've reread my old journals, stuff I wrote years ago about Sunrise Academy, Elliot, Jake, the lodge and the residents, that night at Baxter State Park. It makes me sad and uneasy, reading those things.

The living room is already full when we straggle in from our walk, the good couches and best seats all taken. There are only a few spindly wooden chairs left to sit in, and already, the poet stands at the podium in her tight black pants and narrow, lime-green shirt. Her black hair hangs down either side of her sharp, pretty face. She seems very confident, with her black eyes and tight clothes. She stays up late into the night and is rumored to have a terrible temper.

Daphne, whose studio is next to hers, says the poet bangs on the wall and hollers when Daphne talks on the phone, even in a whisper. *Which you're allowed to do if you're quiet*, Daphne says. The poet says her name is Cassandra, but I'm not convinced. Maybe she was a Sandy or Cassie. She's been to Yaddo and is very proud about that but never just comes out and says *I've been to Yaddo*, just makes little mentions: *In Saratoga this. Saratoga that.*

I will never go to Yaddo. If I reach my own private pinnacle of success, my book will be for sale at the Walmart checkout—the writer people disdain but can't put down. That would be okay with me, but here at Caledonia, popular success feels like a lesser dream.

I listen to one or two poems, which Cassandra reads in a hushed voice, as if every word were holy.

When the next poet gets up to read, I slip out.

It's too early to go to bed, but I don't really feel like working. Maybe I'll just go back to my studio and lie down. Every studio is equipped with a narrow bed, so that we weary residents can nap between bouts of creative endeavor. I feel like an imposter here.

There is no one else on the path. All the other residents are either at the reading or in their studios, working. Maybe some of them are already in their rooms, talking quietly on their cell phones to their husbands or lovers back home. *I'm having a really good time,* they are saying. *I'm getting so much done.*

Who would I call? There is no one.

My studio is at the very back of the barn, not nestled snugly among the others but off by itself, at the end. Back here, the lights fall away, and this part of the campus is very dark. Beyond, there are only some clumps of bushes, an old fence, and then the back road.

I keep my studio unlocked so I don't have to fumble for my key. It's always dark when I arrive: early morning before sunrise, after supper when the sun is down. Tonight, when I go in and switch on the light, the room is exactly as I left it: desk under the window, bed by the far wall, big reading chair with a lamp on a little table.

I'm too tired to work, so I lie down on the narrow daybed and pull up the coverlet, which is old and worn. How many writers have spread out under this same pink coverlet, thinking about their work? Thinking of the story, the poem; the crises and disappointments that fuel their work: dreams they once had, lovers they've left, regrets and desires. They have lain here trying to figure out how to turn that mush of experience into a work of art, how to make the sad, ordinary events of their lives extraordinary and meaningful on the page.

I hope there are no lice in the pink coverlet.

After a little while, I turn off the light by the bed. I might as well sleep here; I don't feel like walking all the way back to my room in the residence hall. On another night, I might be frightened, alone in the studio, far back in the barn. It's dark outside the windows, and the room itself is dark. It's so quiet, except for the occasional rushing sound of cars on the back road. I've heard there are wild dogs back there, some chained outside lonely houses, some roaming free.

I wake sometime in the night, confused by my dreams. A little girl climbed into my lap and put her arms around my neck. We were somewhere outside at a picnic table. One of those old wooden ones with dark stains. The little girl was so affectionate; I hugged her close.

I love you so much, Susannah, I said in my dream.

It was a good dream. Not like other dreams I've had about my daughter. The one where I'm screaming, the one where I sound like my mother. Not like the many dreams where Susannah is lost and I am searching for her in some dark landscape, some ruined forest where the trees grow too close together, and the ground is soft and wet.

This dream's like a promise, an omen. But when I wake, the picnic table and the smiling child are gone. There is only the darkness and silence.

Further back, on the road that runs behind Caledonia, I hear a car start up, then drive off.

TWENTY-FOUR

Adam's office was in one of the newer buildings in downtown Portland, not far from the public library. I'd imagined a dark, dirty place on a side street, a list of names by the door—some typed, others printed, some scratched out with a ballpoint pen. Many things could have happened to Adam in the last thirty years. But wouldn't Evelyn have warned me?

I remembered her light, mocking smile. *Oh, you'll find out. I'd hate to ruin the suspense.*

It's unlikely I'll ever see her again—her beautiful apartment, long legs, smooth hair. The wild paintings in the living room and the view from her penthouse window. The large ferny plant in the corner that's almost a tree. Photographs of her children—the ones she acquired when she married Bradford, maybe her own—those two dark spindly adolescents I met one time at Doug's Shop 'n Save a million years ago in Ellsworth. *This is Lorraine,* Evelyn told them as they stared at me in their rangy, storky way, bored and contemptuous, while Susannah clung to my hand.

Susannah will never be like that, I remember thinking. But then, of course, she was. And then some.

I'd called the number Evelyn gave me, expecting it to ring and ring, imagining Adam as a teenager, lounging at his desk in a shabby office, tall and handsome in his cocky way. But of course, he was older now, too. He'd been one of the oldest residents at Sunrise Academy, just waiting to *turn eighteen and get out of this fucking place.* He must be nearly fifty.

"Smith and Wesson," a secretary's voice said smoothly.

Was that really what she said?

"What?"

The secretary reeled it off again. I'd heard it wrong. Some long name that sounded like a typical law firm; must be the right place.

"Is Adam King there?"

"May I tell him who's calling?"

"Lorraine Sunrise," I said, thinking the outlandish name would get his attention. It made me sound like a Native American or a seventies hippie. Well, maybe that's what I was.

"One moment, Ms. Sunrise," the secretary replied.

I thought it highly unlikely that I would actually speak to Adam, let alone see him, on such short notice, but there was his voice on the phone. Older and deeper, yet still recognizable, even now, after thirty years.

"Is this really Lorraine, my favorite staff at Sunrise Academy?"

I laughed. "It is—though I don't know about your favorite."

"Oh my God! I was just thinking about you. This is unbelievable."

His voice sounded young, warm, confident—or did I just want one of those lost children to have grown up right? There were such terrible stories over the years: the picture of Shawn getting shot in the stomach on the front page of the *Bangor Daily News*, mouth open in an *oh* of surprise and pain; Nita's hoarse, whiskey voice on the phone; somebody yelling at Frankie in the background to *Get off, for Christ's sake, the baby's crying!* And, of course, what had happened to Annie and Garrett.

All the people I'd known at Sunrise seemed doomed. Maybe I'd been doomed, too, by my association with them.

But Adam. That tall, handsome boy who'd never belonged there. Who'd grabbed Kurt when he threw rocks at me by the lake. Who had possibly saved my life that night up in Baxter. A lawyer now. Adam King. Maybe he was all right.

"How are you?" I asked.

"Just great, now that I'm talking to you," he said. "Listen, where are you?"

"I'm actually in downtown Portland." I didn't want to tell him I was right outside his office building. That seemed a little creepy. "I'm on my way to Virginia and stopped off in Portland. I've just been to see Evelyn. Remember her?"

"Sure."

His voice sounded different now, guarded. Or was I just imagining that?

"I ran into her—when was it, maybe a year ago? She looked great."

"She's living in the Old Port," I told him, "in a penthouse apartment."

Adam chuckled. "Yeah, she would be. She was always kind of, I don't know—glamorous."

"That's exactly what I always thought. I was a little afraid of her."

"Really?" Adam laughed. "I never thought you were afraid of anything, Lorraine."

The way he said my name. His voice. It brought it all back: those long days by the waterfront, the still, hot air of summer. The inside of the lodge cool and dim. Elliot watching it all from his office.

I was so young.

"So, you're looking up old residents?"

"A few," I said. "I'm a reporter—"

"Uh-oh," Adam said, teasing.

"No, this isn't for my paper. I'm taking a break. But I'm thinking of writing something about what happened back then."

"At Sunrise?"

"To Annie and Garrett."

"Oh." Adam's voice had changed again. "Yeah. I don't know what I can tell you. I've kind of tried to put that away."

What was it Elliot always said about Adam? That he didn't like to deal with anything. With whatever landed him at Sunrise or the mystery of his father. *We haven't even scratched the surface*, Elliot used to say. *He's got secrets, but he'll never tell.*

But as a reporter, I was used to people claiming they didn't want to talk, then spilling all the beans. Most people will tell you everything, if you wait long enough. *Just shut up and listen*, Dobbs used to say, and it worked.

"I guess I tried to forget it, too," I said, "but it's always been lurking in the background. Now, I'm trying to face what happened, so I can be done with it."

"Yeah, I get that," Adam said.

"I thought you might help me remember how it was back then at Sunrise."

"Oh, how it was…" Adam's voice sounded faraway, as if he had turned away from the phone and was looking out a window in his office. A wide window that looked out over the tops of the buildings, out to the ocean beyond.

"Well, I'd be happy to help if I can, for old times' sake. And I'd love to see you. Are you in town for a while?"

"I'm leaving this afternoon. I can come back another time, or we could talk by phone."

"No, listen, I could use a break. Want to have lunch? I just have to clear my desk and make a few calls. I could meet you at one-thirty at The Possum."

"That sounds great," I said. "It'll be good to see you."

Actually, it would be weird to see Adam after all this time, to expose my weathered face to his scrutiny. The last time he saw me, I was twenty-four, my hair long and wavy. My big toothy smile, junk-store dresses, and faded blue jeans. Now, I was a middle-aged woman with a wrinkled face and short hair dyed a generic reddish-brown. I wore sensible Maine clothes: black pants and a sturdy jacket, and I felt lumpy and frumpy as I walked around the Old Port for the next hour, killing time until lunch at The Possum. Whatever that referred to. I definitely wasn't going to order meat.

As I wandered through the little shops, I pulled spring clothes from racks of shimmering fabric, letting myself imagine that I would buy a dress or maybe a new linen shirt—that bright blue one—to transform myself into a younger, hipper version of myself. As if by buying a shirt, a skirt, or a whole new outfit, I could undo the work of years. All of my past could be erased: the marriages that didn't work out, the loss of Susannah, my essential loneliness—as if by putting on other clothes, my entire history would disappear, and I'd have a better life to show Adam: *Look what I've become.*

Maybe a new sweater would help.

But now it was time. Regretfully, I left the shop. I would go as I was. It didn't matter anyway, did it? He was probably married.

"No, actually, I'm divorced," Adam said.

"Same," I said.

We were at a back table in a hip downtown restaurant with saffron-colored walls and a tattooed waitress. In the dim lighting, he looked remarkably the same, although when we'd met outside on the street, I could see he'd aged. He looked older than I did, I thought, but you always think that.

He still had that mop of thick hair, mostly gray now, and his face was lined. He looked like he'd had a hard life: lots of smoking and drinking, though I guessed he did not drink now. *Gave it up*, he would tell me later. He was taller than I remembered, broad-shouldered but thin, and his good suit hung loosely on him.

On the sidewalk outside the restaurant, he'd flashed a big grin when he saw me.

"Lorraine!" he grabbed me close in a hug, held me out at arm's length.

"You look terrific!" he told me. "Exactly the same."

"Thanks, Adam." *Still charming*, I thought.

"Shall we go in?" he asked, opening the door for me, and I remembered his old-fashioned courtesy. It was noticeable at Sunrise because the other kids had no manners at all—*raised like wolves*—but Adam was always polite.

Now, sitting opposite him in the restaurant clatter, I felt surprisingly relaxed.

"Children?" I asked. I knew from my own experience that this question was not always welcome.

Adam smiled. "One son, Justin. He's seventeen, just finishing high school. Graduating at the top of his class. Lives with his mother in Falmouth, but I see him a lot. How about you?"

"I have a daughter. She's in California."

That's what I always say. There was more, but I wasn't going to tell him my personal anguish. This was about Sunrise Academy. About Annie. A story that began thirty years ago when I first drove down that bumpy driveway and walked into the lodge.

I didn't want to talk about what had happened since then. There was too much to tell, and not tell, and I was more interested in the boy he had been than the man he'd become. Sitting here in this dim, golden restaurant, amid the gentle hubbub of other people's conversations, his face kept changing. Now he looked like the teenager I knew all those years ago, then like a man I'd never met before and was not particularly drawn to. There was something a little louche about him, corrupt. It made me wonder if he would ask me for something by the end of the meal. Money? Sex? I reminded myself that I was a reporter. I knew how to do an interview.

"Can we talk about Sunrise?" I asked, taking out my notebook.

"Why don't you tell me, first, what you hope to accomplish?" he countered.

"Oh, you *are* a lawyer," I said lightly.

"Well, that's what I do, Lorraine." He leaned forward. "So what are you doing here? What do you want?"

"I guess I want to resolve some unanswered questions. To understand what happened back then."

"To Annie and Garrett?"

"Yeah, they're a big part of it. There's a bigger story, too, and that's what intrigues me. How people get like that. The man who killed Annie and Garrett but also those kids at Sunrise. How do people get lost? Can they ever find their way back? That place made a big impression on me because of what happened. I'd never been around people like that."

"Yeah," he said. "You seemed kind of scared at first. I felt sorry for you. I thought they'd eat you alive, the kids, and the counselors, too. You were almost a kid yourself. How old were you, anyway?"

"Early twenties. I had just finished college. Twenty-three when I started working there."

"Yeah? Well, you looked about seventeen," Adam said. "You realize all the guys were making bets on who'd nail you first. Only that wasn't quite how we put it." He laughed.

I felt uncomfortable, as if we were back in that other time, when he was the confident teenager and I the frightened young staff. The boys in the lodge, down by the waterfront, nudging each other as I walked by, in my shorts, in my bathing suit. Aware of them, trying not to be. Trying not to notice their hairy legs, their maleness.

"Well, you were a bunch of teenage boys, and it was a pretty unhealthy place."

"Yeah, but you were hot. Not that you aren't now."

This wasn't what I wanted from him, this clumsy flirtation. Was it all a facade: the good suit, the nice manners, this hip, moody restaurant? Was he, in the end, just a jerk?

"Anyway," I said briskly, taking up my pen. "I don't have any real agenda. I didn't even plan to interview you. But when Evelyn mentioned that you were just down the street—"

"You figured you might as well," Adam finished for me. "Okay, I'll see what I can dredge up. But I'm warning you, I haven't thought about that place in a very long time."

I didn't believe him. He'd thought about it plenty—that's why he was willing to see me on such short notice. He was curious, but he was playing me; I wasn't going to get much out of him. I'd ask a few questions, just for show, and in another forty-five minutes, I'd be back on the road, driving south to Virginia. This would all be behind me, only an anecdote.

"Okay. Let's talk about what you do remember," I said. "How long were you at Sunrise, anyway?"

"I was there a couple of years, then aged out. Elliot wouldn't ever let me say I'd completed the program. *You're still holding back,*" he said in Elliot's voice.

I laughed.

"That's exactly what he sounded like," I said. Adam was always a good mimic. He grinned at me and was again the boy I remembered. I might get something out of him after all.

"I want to hear your memories of Sunrise," I told him, "and what's happened to you since then. What have you been doing all these years? How did you go from Sunrise to becoming a lawyer, living here?" I waved my arm around the small restaurant with its amber walls, as if it were Portland itself.

"You want to hear the story of my life?" he asked, half mocking. "Well, I don't have any big plans at the office this afternoon, although I do work pretty hard. I know," he said, reading my expression. "You remember how I always tried to get out of chores. These days, actually, I'm known as the partner who works too much."

Adam laughed easily. He kept seeming younger and younger, or maybe I was just getting used to his nearly fifty-year-old face.

"I'll tell you what's happened to me, but you have to tell me your story, too. Deal?"

He stuck his hand across the table, and I shook it.

"Deal," I said. I didn't mean it. I'd never tell him the truth.

We wound up spending the rest of the afternoon at that little table. Between bites of sandwiches and, later, sips of strong coffee, Adam told me his history: about returning to York, how strange it had felt to be back at high school, where he needed an extra year in order to graduate.

"Let's face it, Sunrise wasn't big on academics."

"Was it hard going home?" I remembered his nervous mother with her cupcakes at the Christmas party, the burly stepfather who never quite looked you in the eye.

"It was okay," he said, shrugging. "I was just glad not to be in a dorm with a bunch of smelly teenage boys. That was a pretty unhygienic crowd, you know."

"I can imagine," I said.

"Can you?" he asked. "I always felt like the staff didn't really know what went on at Sunrise. Maybe Kenny or Randall, but most of the staff didn't get it. It was like there was this whole secret society—*The*

Land of the Residents," he intoned dramatically, like Rod Serling. "A lot of stuff went on late at night, when the staff was sleeping."

I was itching to take up my pen, but I was afraid it would deter him, so I tried to commit his words to memory.

"That last summer was crazy," Adam said. "I mean, not just Annie and Garrett—after that. It was like everything fell apart. Nobody was in charge. And people kept leaving. Remember?"

"Oh yeah," I said. "I was one of them. I couldn't wait to get out of there. I was getting married."

"That's right!" he said. "I remember that guy. You married him?"

"Yeah."

"But it didn't work out?"

"No, not really."

"Ah," Adam said. "Well, we'll get back to that."

He ordered more coffee. "You want some?"

I nodded, though I never drank coffee in the afternoon anymore. I'd forgotten how much fun it was—this buzz. I felt great—jazzed up, exuberant.

"I'm going to regret this tonight, when I can't get to sleep," I said, even though I loved the caffeinated hum. After the weariness of winter and my shrunken, lonely life, here I was, sitting in a cool restaurant in downtown Portland with a somewhat attractive man, drinking too much coffee and talking about myself. It felt wonderful: the sideways flirting, the conversations around us, the slam and clatter of the restaurant kitchen. I felt a shimmer of hope, of possibilities. Maybe this could be the moment when everything changed, the way sometimes you turn a corner and everything's entirely different on the other side of the block. This could be it: this afternoon, this unexpected reunion. His story, my story—or some approximation of it. Our lives and lies unspooling around us in this downtown restaurant with the tattooed waitresses and the saffron walls.

"Want anything else?" the waitress asked.

"Can we just sit here?" I asked her. "We're catching up on the last thirty years."

She shrugged. "I guess so. We don't close until ten. Later, if we get a crowd."

"Perfect," Adam said, smiling up at her, and she smiled back.

Oh yes. Still charming.

He looked back at me. "So…where was I?"

"You went back to York."

"Yeah, my last year in high school was pretty great. I was older than everybody and way more experienced. I played it up, of course. I would let things drop—little things—about Sunrise. Made it sound like I'd been in jail—which it wasn't, really. It actually wasn't that bad. For some of the kids there, it was pretty nice."

"Doug Ritter used to say it was the nicest place some of them had ever lived."

"Yeah," Adam said, considering. "I bet that's true. He was smart about some things, Doug. I wonder what ever happened to him. Anyway, I did okay. I played sports: basketball, baseball. Had this terrific girlfriend, Nicole Wallace. I was kind of a star, I guess. It was great."

I could imagine Adam, tall and handsome, older than the others, with a romantic, dangerous story to tell. Maybe even mentioning the murder. How glamorous and daring he would have seemed to the soft, upper-class high school students in Southern Maine.

He'd graduated at the head of his class; spoken at graduation, telling his tale of redemption; and gone on to the University of Southern Maine. *My mom was hoping I'd go to an Ivy League school, but my track record was pretty funky.* He'd transferred to BU after a couple of years and went on to law school.

"Then you came back here?"

"Yeah. My dad got sick, and I wanted to patch things up with him."

"What was that like?"

"It was tough."

He paused, then went on. After he'd moved back to Maine, Adam decided he liked the quieter pace, the proximity to nature.

I wasn't sure he was telling the truth. It seemed like a story you'd want to be true but wasn't. He'd gotten married and had a son, Justin, but the marriage, he said, "didn't take."

"That's it, really. That's my life," Adam said. "I've been with this firm for twenty years. Justin's in high school. He and I go camping every summer. Travel some."

There was more, but he wasn't going to tell me. *You'll never get him to talk*, Elliot used to say. Maybe I would.

"Okay, let's talk about that camping trip."

"Which one? You mean up at Baxter?"

Stalling, I thought.

Adam sighed. "I was afraid you were going to ask about that."

He paused for a moment and then continued, as if thinking out loud. This seemed rehearsed, as if he'd figured out what to say back at his office, maybe after we got off the phone.

"That was pretty bad. I don't really remember the whole thing. Maybe I've blocked it. But I think some of the kids just wanted to see how far they could take it. They wanted to scare you and Jed and—what was that guy's name? *Sage*. They didn't like Sage. They liked you. In fact, if it makes you feel any better, there was quite an argument about what they would do to you. The girls didn't want to involve you at all. But there was one guy…"

"Kurt?"

"Yeah. That guy. He was crazy."

"I always thought he wasn't that bright," I said.

"Yeah, well, maybe. I don't really remember."

"What *do* you remember, Adam? It never really got untangled, what happened up there. Help me figure it out."

I could remember all of it: the sounds in the night, the ripping noise when someone unzipped my tent. Two boys struggling by firelight on the pounded-down dirt of the campsite. Jed's wounded arm and the blood. Trudging down the mountain path next morning at dawn. The long drive back to Sunrise in the silent van.

"We never really figured out what happened up there," I said, "and then, when we got back to the lodge, we got the news about Garrett and Annie."

"That was the same day?"

I looked at him, shocked.

"I can't believe you don't remember that." The two events were so closely linked in my mind.

He shrugged. "Well, it was a long time ago. I guess we didn't think what happened in Baxter was that big of a deal. I mean, we were always getting in trouble, back then. Stuff was always happening. Always some big crisis—some drama. But if you're right about the timing, the whole episode must have been eclipsed by their deaths. I guess people sort of forgot about it."

"But some of the kids got sent to jail, to the Maine Youth Center," I said.

I couldn't believe he'd forgotten what happened that night.

"Yeah." But he seemed impatient with me now, with the whole conversation. He'd *closed down*, Elliot would have said.

And I was tired of him, too, tired of the whole business. Tired of trying to figure out what probably had no bearing on the present. Or did that one night in Baxter, and what came after, set the course for the rest of my life?

In any event, I wouldn't get any more out of Adam. I remembered, from the old days, his Teflon surface. He was probably a very successful lawyer: cool, smart, and opaque. Giving nothing away.

Adam put his black credit card on the table and said, quietly, "Let's get out of here."

"I'm just going to the ladies' room," I said. As an act of faith, I left my pocketbook behind and walked down the narrow corridor.

I looked at my face in the bathroom mirror, relieved to see that I looked all right. Good, in fact. Cheeks flushed, eyes shining. I looked younger, prettier. Caffeine, I thought, and a man's attention. I combed my hair with my fingers, washed my hands and face.

"Okay," I told myself briskly, "in another fifteen minutes, you'll be driving on 95."

When I came out, Adam was standing by our table. Now that I was used to this older version, he looked more attractive. Tall and fit with his flop of gray hair, his handsome face, and his crooked, familiar smile.

"Ready?" he asked me.

When we got outside, I turned and put out my hand. "Thanks, Adam."

"That's it? You didn't exactly fulfill your part of the deal, Lorraine. You never told me your story."

"Maybe some other time. I've got to get back on the road. Here," I said, taking a business card from my pocket. "If you think of anything else, you can call or send me an e-mail."

"And you have my number."

Suddenly, I didn't want to go. If he'd said just one thing, made any gesture, I would have stayed. If he'd looked at his watch, said, *It's six o'clock. I'm not going back to work anyway; let's go get a drink*, it might have been different. We might have walked around Portland together. We might have told our real, whole stories to one another. He might have told me about his father, why he'd been in prison. I might have told him everything—or almost everything. I would never tell anyone about my daughter.

Then, to my surprise, he put his arms around me in a hug that went on a little longer than it should have, until, at last, he pulled back.

"Wow," Adam said, his voice hoarse.

We stared at each other.

"I have to go," I said, though I didn't want to.

"Let's stay in touch when you're in Virginia."

I knew it was time to turn and walk away, to go back to the parking garage and retrieve my car. Even so, I wanted to keep talking to Adam, this new Adam, who had just emerged when we were parting.

But I was fifty-four, not twenty-four, and I knew better than to believe in anything, so I turned and walked away from him without looking back.

TWENTY-FIVE

Adam   April 1, 2011 4:27 a.m.
To: Lorraine
Re: here in Virginia

Got your message that you arrived. Sorry I've been
so long getting back to you. Sounds like a beautiful
place, Caledonia. You must be settled in by now.
Have you had a chance to explore the area? I'll bet
it's nice now, just starting to be spring. We've got
another snowstorm coming. It was really great to
see you, Lorraine.

    Adam

Lorriane   April 1, 2011 4:29 a.m.
To: Adam
Re: here in Virginia

What are you doing up at this hour?

Adam   April 1, 2011 4:33 a.m.
To: Lorraine
Re: here in Virginia

I could ask you the same thing. Me? I couldn't sleep.
Too many thoughts.

Lorraine   April 1, 2011 4:52 a.m.
To: Adam
Re: here in Virginia

This is when I get up, even at home. I like to start
working when it's still dark. It makes what I do seem
secret and private. Here in Virginia, I like to get out to
the studio before anyone else is up. We have studios
in a big old barn about a quarter of a mile from the
residence hall where we sleep. Mine's #9, at the very
back, near the road that runs behind Caledonia. I
was here before—I think I told you—a million years
ago, when I was in college, and it's amazing how
little it's changed. Same old barn with the studios,
same residence hall. I love it here. It seems luxurious
to write all day, walk in the woods or along the back
road, and just let my mind float around.

Lorraine   April 1, 2011 4:59 a.m.
To: Adam
Re: here in Virginia

Sounds like a great place, Lorraine. Maybe I'll see
it someday.

My hands hover over the keyboard. I'm not sure what to say. This early-morning exchange feels exciting but also invasive, as if he were peering in the window. Did I say too much? Is he politely ending the conversation or asking for more?

What does he want with me, anyway? His messages are almost flirtatious—or at least, as if we were friends, which we're not. I'm not sure what I want with him.

I click shut the program, close my laptop. *That's enough.*

But I can't shut down the feeling inside myself, an excitement bubbling up like a spring.

Outside, it's just getting light. I'll go for a walk on the back road, a country road through the rural southland. Clear my head, focus on the story.

Lorraine   April 5, 2011 8:23 p.m.
To: Adam
spring

Really beautiful here and not as cold. Had a great hike at a place called Calvary Falls, near the Appalachian Trail. Already seeing signs of spring.

    Lorraine

Adam   April 5, 2011 8:27 p.m.
To: Lorraine
Re: spring

That sounds really nice. Still cold here. Not even a whisper of spring.

Remember those hikes we used to take at Sunrise?
That time Roy got scared on the Precipice Trail?
Spending some time with my son this weekend.
Maybe a day hike in the White Mountains. We'll see.

Adam

I think about how it could be—if Adam and I became friends at this stage in our lives, both of us middle-aged. Sadder and wiser—all that. I think about visiting him in Portland. Dinners at The Possum, which could be *our place*. Those amber walls.

I'd have to meet his son, Justin. He wouldn't like me at first, wouldn't trust me, *this new woman Dad's seeing*, I imagine him saying scornfully to his friends. *She's old!* he might say. But then he'd get to know me, and I would charm him. I used to be charming, didn't I?

It could happen. Might happen. He's writing me, anyway, and I can tell he's interested.

I usually stay off the Internet while I'm working—or trying to work. It's too tempting to check my messages, and I could easily find myself wandering down the aisles of Zappos or Amazon—those long, winding, endless labyrinths.

But tonight, I keep logging on, to see if Adam has written, to feel that little glimmer of anticipation, then delight, if he has. I keep my replies brief and friendly, and he does the same, both of us circling around that embrace on the sidewalk, that moment.

I try to concentrate. I'm writing the book as a novel but anchoring it in the truth. Weird how the parts I make up seem truer than the things I remember. I think I've managed to re-create the feel of Sunrise Academy. To describe Annie and Garrett, those days by the lake. Now, I am trying to pull it together and make it a story. It's kind of like kneading bread. Trying to get the whole messy lump to pull together, to achieve its own springy unity, its own bouncy life.

You have to start with the body, my friend Alan's always telling me. He's read my attempts at novels over the years. Alan is kind, yet persistent. He teaches English at University of Maine Orono and is well versed in literary traditions, which either makes him an expert or a curmudgeon stuck in the past—I'm not sure which.

I haven't told Alan about this one, but I know what he'd say: *Begin with the body.*

But why should I play by the rules? The reader will know what's coming. It's inevitable, right from the start. In stories like this—any story, really—it's always the same. The girl is lost.

It's three in the morning, and I can't sleep. Adam hasn't written in almost a week. I lie in my bed in the residence hall, ruminating on my humiliation. It was all my imagination—that he would want me. That anyone would. I'm *old*, a grotesque cartoon of myself—that bright, daring girl so spendthrift with her power, her youth. It was my sword in the world, but I only thrashed it wildly, throwing my charms away on men who didn't matter.

Like Elliot. How brave and daring I'd felt with him and then, afterwards, how terrible.

Was that when everything turned? Was that the one slip that poisoned my life? That stupid, disastrous whim?

I can't imagine Caledonia without Adam's e-mails. In just a few days, he's become the center. A glimmer of something possible. Thinking maybe I'd stop off in Portland to see him on my way home; wondering if we would touch. The possibility of romance, the welcome oblivion of desire—and now it's all gone.

I still have a week before I get back in my little blue car and drive north, closing the distance between us, up over the Blue Ridge

Mountains, back across West Virginia, Pennsylvania, Massachusetts, heading back up into Maine. The little spring leaves shrinking back into buds, the buds tightening, squeezing back into the black branches of the trees as I go north. My yard will still be patchy with splotches of snow, which could last, I know, right into May.

I can't just lie here, thinking about my return to my barren life. I might as well get up and work.

Quietly, I creep out of bed and pull on my clothes, grab my laptop, and quietly, quietly, go down the hall in darkness, past rooms full of fellow writers and artists, all sleeping.

Outside, the night air is eerily foggy, the campus vast and still. I walk quickly down the dark road to my studio, past the white blur of the cottage that houses the office, then past the silent fields. The studio barn is a large dark shape in the darkness. The mist is cool against my face. I walk quickly; it's much too quiet. All the way past the studios to my own at the very back. No cars on the road beyond, no sound but my breathing.

I'm glad, again, that I don't lock the studio. That I don't have to fumble for my key in the darkness, can just open the door and go in.

I work through the night until morning comes, quiet and dim. When I stand up from the desk, my back's stiff, and my eyes are blurry. Adam still hasn't written.

As I walk down the gravel road toward the residence hall, the whole place seems abandoned.

"Seems like everybody's disappeared this morning, doesn't it?"

His voice sounds as old as a cellar. It's Angus, the hoary old poet, with his brown cardigan sweater buttoned against the damp chill. Usually, I avoid him: his sparkly dark eyes under those monstrous eyebrows, his insinuating, too-familiar manner, as if he wants to connect in some way that feels, because of his pubic-hair beard and startling eyebrows, obscene. His fingernails are long and yellow; his beard is stained and yellowish, too, around his mouth. I don't like to look at his teeth. I never sit with him in the dining room where he holds court, having fashioned himself as the keeper of Caledonian history, the teller of ancient tales, where gales of laughter rise up at his impudent, irreverent memories of brighter days.

Remember how it was back then? As if we all were as old as he is. How old is he anyway? Sixty-seven? Seventy-six? Eighty-two?

The younger residents probably think I'm old, too. Those young women with their buoyant bodies, shiny hair, and perfect skin. Do they even see me at all, or am I merely, dismissably, old?

At least Angus has had the foresight to create a persona for himself: the wise old jester, the sage.

Aww, I think he's cute!

He knows everybody!

With his stories about Bly and Ginsberg, Corso and Snyder, the Black Mountain poets.

Did you ever meet Richie Feldman? The young poets ask him reverently.

Yeah, sure. We drove across the country together, way back. It was pretty wild. He shakes his head. *Good times. Good times.*

"Hey there," Angus says now, moving toward me. "Give an old guy a hug, will ya? Looks like you could use one yourself."

He's too close; I can smell him.

"I've got to go," I say suddenly, backing away.

I turn and run down the drive, right past the residence hall, out to the parking lot, into my car.

I just have to drive, I think. I just have to get out of here.

And then I am rumbling down the driveway, bumping over the bars that prevent the cows from escaping. But I am escaping. Turn right when I get to the highway—toward Prineville, the city that I've been avoiding, my destination at last.

TWENTY-SIX

Prineville is a once-thriving railway crossroads with a "revitalized" downtown of brick buildings, narrow streets, and tall, shady trees. There's a river, an old-fashioned train depot, and a farmers' market on Saturday mornings. The town's a postcard of Americana. There's even a green park with a white gazebo for band concerts on summer evenings.

It's not far from where Annie and Garrett were killed on the Appalachian Trail thirty years ago. Garrett had been hiking more than a month when Annie flew down to meet him. They came off the trail here in Prineville and sent their final postcard to Annie's sister: *Spending the night in Prineville. Tomorrow we'll get back on the trail.*

The historical museum is small and full of pre–Civil War exhibitions from Prineville's heyday as a crossing for rail cars loaded with cotton, livestock, and slaves. There are beautiful old photographs of long-lost splendor, when these brick streets were new: horse-drawn carriages, ladies with parasols, and a local boy who made good, the nationally known television evangelist who founded the tall steepled church that tolls the hour with, I suspect, a recording of a bell.

There's a house tour that leaves every two hours. I pick up a shiny trifold brochure, considering whether to go. The tour costs twelve dollars, which seems like a lot. Still, it might be something I could do with my afternoon.

"How long does the tour take?" I ask the uniformed man at the desk.

"Oh, we don't run the tour till May," he tells me. "But you can use the map on the back—there, see?—and walk around yourself."

I'm entranced by his accent and am content to listen as the man in the museum tells the history of Prineville: the railroad, the war, the revitalization effort, and their native son, the successful Baptist minister.

"Been mighty generous to this town. We are blessed to have him."

"Is he still living?"

Wasn't there some scandal surrounding him? Child porn…a mistress? Misappropriated funds that got funneled into a private account and spent on, what, exactly? Frilly tuxedos? Stretch limo? His wife's high-heeled shoes? I honestly can't remember.

"Well, no, he's no longer with us, physically," the man says, smiling gently. "But in spirit, he will always be among us, right here in Prineville."

"Can I ask you something?"

"Well, sure," he says, in his kind voice with a mild accent.

"There was a murder near here, about thirty years ago."

"Well, now, I don't remember anything about that."

"A young man, Lewis Ray Bladgett. He grew up near Prineville, I think. In Cedarville, actually. He killed two people—a man and a woman who were hiking on the Appalachian Trail."

"You don't say. Really?" The man looks at me, unperturbed. "Might have been, maybe. But, like I said, I don't remember anything like that. Not that I can recall." He makes a great show of tidying up his brochures. "Got to get back to business, I s'pose. You have yourself a nice day, dear."

I've been dismissed.

It still isn't raining when I leave the museum. Perhaps it will stay dreamy and foggy all day, and the rain will hold off until night.

I walk around Prineville, wandering up one street and down another in the downtown historic district. Beyond the beltway, there's a confusion of new roads and four-lane highways, sweeping off-ramps and the graceless sprawl of strip malls and big-box stores. Here in the shabby, genteel heart of Prineville, it's like we're in another time. The houses are large and formal, with curved drives and wide verandas, stained-glass windows, towers, and sleeping porches, cupolas, curlicue trim.

The side streets are not as prosperous. One hulking house has been divided into several dwellings. Upstairs, a window stands open, and a pink curtain hangs, dispirited, over the sill. A yellow Big Wheel trike lies on its side in the yard, an old couch on the porch. Street after street of mismatched, abandoned houses, three-decker wooden apartment buildings with torn screens and rickety steps. Someone looking out of a window; a man with a scary-looking dog on a leash; two boys in a dirt yard. A bad smell hangs in the air.

I walk down the next street. Here, the sidewalks aren't brick but decrepit cement, the slabs slanting unevenly this way and that. One large knobby tree shoves up the sidewalk with big brown roots that pour out, humped and scaly, like the knuckly fingers of old people, like my mother's hands.

Now, the fog is lifting, and a hot strong sun slants down. The air is heavy, the heat impossible, Southern. There's no heat like this in Maine.

I'm beginning to place them here: the characters in my book. The boy Lewis Ray with his aimless, haphazard life. Annie and Garrett, in love and on leave from the trail. Spending their second-to-last night together, then going back into the woods.

I know what I have to do next. Locate the trailhead and walk down the trail to the campsite where Annie and Garrett were killed. I have to experience it firsthand, to feel and smell it: the damp woods, the dark path, the charred wood and ashes, the dead fire.

I have to make it real to myself, so I can make it real on the page.

But if I don't hurry now, I'll miss supper, which is served at six o'clock sharp, so that all the artists who like to pretend they are Europeans, not from Michigan or Ohio, complain: *Why do we have to eat so early?* But I don't care because I'm from Maine, where you can eat at five o'clock, if you want, and it's not weird at all.

Back at Caledonia, I have just enough time before supper to check my e-mail and am delighted to find a message from Adam.

Adam   April 10, 2011 4:58 p.m.
To: Lorraine
Checking in

How's it going down there?

I answer him right away.

Lorraine   April 10, 2011 5:47 p.m.
To: Adam
Re: Checking in

Figuring things out. I've decided to go to the campsite where it happened. Creepy but necessary. It's not far from here. Might even go down there tomorrow.

There's no answer, though I wait at my desk in the quiet studio. He must have left work for the day.

I wake early the next morning to the persistent *ding ding ding* of my alarm clock, shut it off, and turn on the light, eyes scrunched shut against the glare. I can lie here a moment—no longer, or I'll go back to sleep.

I have to get the book finished. Less than a week left at Caledonia. After that? I don't know.

My life in Maine seems like it belongs to some other person. I cannot imagine going back to it. I know everything that will happen: the slow, swollen spring, then the sullen, unwilling summer crowded with tourists and summer residents, then the end of summer, then fall. Nothing any different except that I'll keep getting older. I will visit my mother in the nursing home, take her to Sunday brunch. When the time comes, I'll sit by my mother's bedside, take her hand in mine, and say things to fill up the hours. And who will hold my hand when my time comes? Who will wait with me for my final departure?

I can't think about that now. There is only this, the task I have set myself: to finish the book. I don't know if it's important or not, this story I'm trying to tell. But at least it's something outside of my head. Something that I can focus on.

I pull on my clothes, grab my laptop, and go out into the chilly air. It's still dark, and the campus is silent. The light from my flashlight jounces; the black hedge seems to lurch. I walk quickly past the administration building, between the two quiet fields, and approach the dark hulk of the studio barn.

In the shadowy distance across the damp grass, my studio waits, far from all others. It's so dark around me, so quiet. No sound from the silent back road.

Every time I approach my studio like this, before dawn, I have the same thought: *What if someone is in there?* The disgruntled old poet, enraged by my rebuff, waiting for me in the dark. Or some random nut, like the one who killed Annie and Garrett. It's never locked; anyone could get in.

And now, when I open the door, I know this is the time.

He's here.

TWENTY-SEVEN

He's sitting in the big reading chair. I see his shape in the dark. My heart leaps.

"Who is it?"

"An old friend."

I shine my flashlight on him, and, for a moment, he looks exactly the way he used to look at Sunrise—that handsome boy.

"I thought you might need some company," Adam says.

"What?"

"Well, you're going into the woods to find their campsite, right?" He's smoking a cigarette.

"You can't smoke in here," I say, automatically, and he laughs as if we were back at Sunrise. *What are you going to do about it?*

"I got thinking about you going out there all alone. It's not really safe, is it?" Adam says. "So I thought I'd drive down and go with you. Only took about ten hours to get here."

"Ten hours?" I say, still trying to absorb the fact that he's here.

"Drove fast," he says. "Hey, and I brought some camping supplies—did I mention I camp with my son? Up at Baxter, sometimes. Out west, when we get a chance. One of those useful skills I picked up at Sunrise."

He's completely relaxed, just an old friend on a visit, sitting in the reading chair, legs crossed comfortably, the way any man would sit after a long drive.

I'm still trying to get my bearings.

"How long have you been here?"

"Oh, not long, just a couple of hours. Drove most of the night. I'm pretty tired."

But he doesn't look tired. In the golden lamplight, he looks like the teenager I once knew: the preppy prince. Like one of those St. Paul's boys I knew growing up, taller than anyone else, entitled and bold.

"Yeah, I could use a nap," he says, eyeing the daybed.

"You're not even supposed to be here."

He shrugs. "Who's going to care? It's not like I'm going to be traipsing around the campus. Nobody has to know I'm here. They won't even see my car. I parked down the road at the church, walked over."

"In the dark?"

"Yeah. I had a flashlight." He holds up a flashlight a policeman would carry, businesslike and official, matte black. "Why don't I take a nap, while you get some work done? Then we can drive down. Hike into the woods, for your investigation of the past."

He's got it all planned. I can barely keep up, like he's rushed into the room and grabbed my hand and is running away down the road, pulling me along.

He smiles. "You look a little dazed, Lorraine. Go get some coffee. I'll stretch out here on the bed."

By the time I get back with two mugs of hot coffee, Adam's asleep. He's taken his shoes off, pulled up the pink coverlet, and is lying on his side, long legs folded up, his face peaceful. It feels weirdly normal, having him here, though I don't quite trust him.

The coffee kicks in, and I'm sharper. It's getting light now.

How did he know where to come? I must have told him my studio was at the back. I guess I did. All those e-mails back and forth. Did I tell him I never lock the door? I might have. I try to remember that dreamy early-morning correspondence.

Tell me more, he would write. *What's it like there?*

I look at the man in my bed. Who is he, anyway? Some guy I hardly know.

But I have to get to work. I open my computer and glide into the story and then the rest of it—chair, shoes on the floor, man in the bed—all of that recedes, and I'm deep into my work by the time the sun shines in the window, filling the room with warm light. When I look up from my laptop, it's as if I were waking from a dream, a memory of Susannah's infancy, those peaceful afternoons when we napped together, sun warming the bed where we lay.

Adam is still asleep when I quietly leave the studio. I'll take a shower, have breakfast, and bring something back for him. He's come all this way, so why not? We'll go into the woods together, just like he said, and discover the rest of the story.

It will be an adventure. We'll be provisioned with camping supplies and food to eat on the way. I'll let him drive, and this time, I'll be the one with an arm slung negligently on the open window of the door.

Does Adam remember the day we drove north with Erin, looking for that runaway girl? Does he remember the hot dogs and potato chips on the stained picnic table, the cars going by on Route 2, and the windblown couple in the red convertible with the out-of-state plates?

That memory is more distinct, in some ways, than the years in between—those early memories of Sunrise in summer and the noisy crowd by the lake. The time Kurt threw a rock at me, and Adam came to my rescue and grabbed me when I almost fell.

And that other time at Baxter, Adam was there again. Has it always been Adam? Always there to save me? Now he's here; can he save me again?

He wakes as I come in the door.

"How long did I sleep?" he asks, sitting up.

"A few hours. It's almost eleven."

"Great."

He's alert already and cheerful. Is he ever in a bad mood? Even on that terrible morning at Baxter, he wasn't glum. *Oh come on,* I remember him saying. *Let's just walk down and get it over with.*

"Is there someplace I can take a shower?"

"There's a bathroom across the lawn in the other part of the barn, and I brought you a towel."

I hand him a blue towel and a bar of soap. I've brought food as well: a banana, a bottle of water, an energy bar.

"Thanks, Lorraine. You're the best." Already, he's fresh as a daisy. "I'll be right back!"

He springs up, plucking the towel from my hands, and, to my surprise, kisses me briefly on the cheek as he heads out the studio door.

I put my hand to my face. I'm sure it means nothing.

An hour later, we're on the road heading south. It's warm, and the damp of the past few days makes the air feel soft and springlike.

Adam's driving. We've taken his car: a big black SUV full of camping equipment he brought from Maine: two backpacks, two sleeping bags, an ax, two small tents.

"I figured you're not quite ready to share a tent with me," he said, smiling.

He's thought of everything.

Now, sitting beside him in his comfortable car, with a map of Virginia spread out on my lap, I feel as if we're on vacation together instead of investigating a decades-old murder.

Adam glances over. "You okay?"

Would it be odd to say that I'm happy? Instead, I ask, "Do you remember that time we drove north to look for Starr?"

"Sure. You and Erin and me. We stopped at some little roadside gas station, didn't we? Have a picnic or something?"

"Hot dogs," I say.

"That's right. Erin really hated you," he says.

"I thought after that day she kind of lightened up."

"Yeah, not really." Adam laughs. "She really had it in for you. She was scary. She would do anything!"

"Really?" I say, thinking how Erin had seemed to soften after our trip up north and even accept me. "She was Level Four, wasn't she? She always followed the rules."

Adam shakes his head, smiling. "Oh, she had you fooled. She fooled everybody. She was the worst of us all."

He continues smiling as he drives. The windows are open, and the breeze lifts his hair, as if someone were lightly brushing a hand through it. He looks serene and handsome.

I alternate between feeling completely at ease with him—the old friend, almost a cousin—and edgy. What am I doing, going into the woods with some man I don't even know?

We stop at the Super Walmart for food and bug spray.

"I'll go in," he says. "I know what we need. You can stay in the car."

As I watch him cross the broad parking lot, I think how good it feels to be in this big black car, to be with this competent man, to be on this expedition, to have a purpose. I'm not going to worry about hidden motives. Anyway, I've got protection. Along with bananas and yogurt, I also borrowed a knife from the Caledonia kitchen and slid it safely in my backpack when Adam wasn't looking. It's not like I think anything bad is going to happen. But just in case.

Back on the road, we drive past the green farmlands of Virginia and the mountains off to the right. We pass a couple of shopping centers, the Goodwill, a gas station, and a Dairy Queen. I remember taking the Sunrise Academy kids for ice cream on hot summer days. How they seemed like children sometimes. Where are they now?

"Did you ever see any of them after you left, the kids from Sunrise?"

"Not really, no," he says.

I'm not sure that's the truth. He must have looked some of them up.

"Never?"

He frowns slightly. "Let me think. I have run into a couple of them. Actually, come to think of it, I nearly had one as a client. Remember Manny?"

"From Lewiston–Auburn?"

He smiles. "Yeah. He called me up one time. I thought he wanted me to represent him. Figured it'd be something sketchy, and I don't really handle criminal cases, mostly real estate, business deals, a few divorces. I keep it pretty clean."

"What was he like? When was it?"

Adam shrugs in his easy way. "I don't know—a few years ago? Honestly, he didn't sound good. Kind of down and out. He'd been living in Lewiston since he left Sunrise. Never finished school. Got into some kind of jobs program, I guess. He wasn't real swift, you know."

I remember Manny's handsome face: quiet, watching. That little smile.

"I always thought he was kind of bright."

"Oh no," Adam says. "Dumb as rocks. Anyway, he called me up, wanted to come see me. I told him sure, come ahead. I expected him to look the same, only older. He was entirely changed. I would never have known him."

I picture Manny standing at the corner of the lodge in a plaid shirt. Quiet and self-contained. I picture him leaning against the wall, all alone. Why was he even there? But then I remember: Manny had stabbed another boy at a foster home.

But he had it coming to him, Manny had said earnestly in Group. *I mean, he was really bad. And anyway, I didn't kill him. I didn't even hurt him that bad.*

How could I have forgotten that? I'd even told Jake about it when I got home. How it struck me, the way he'd said it, as if stabbing someone were just an ordinary thing that anybody would do.

"Yeah, he'd gotten really fat," Adam says. "He looked terrible. Smoked all the time. Missing teeth."

Oh, yes, I know the look.

"You okay?" Adam asks, glancing over.

"So what did he want?"

"Who, Manny?" Adam shrugs. "Oh, you know, the usual. Said he wanted to find out what I'd been doing all these years. I thought he'd probably gotten into trouble and needed some legal help, but that wasn't it. He didn't even know I was a lawyer. He just wanted money."

"And he thought you'd give it to him?"

I try to picture the sleek office where Adam spends his days and Manny, old and flabby, in a hoodie sweatshirt and dirty, outsized white sneakers, coming to see his old friend. But were they even friends, back then? Who was Adam friends with, really?

After some desultory conversation, Manny finally getting around to it: *Think you could help me out?*

"You didn't give him any money, did you?"

Adam shrugs. "Oh, sure. I gave him something. I didn't want any trouble."

"What do you mean, trouble?"

"Oh, you know, making a scene," Adam says, then changes the subject, quickly. "Look, I think we turn here."

He twists the wheel, and we turn onto a narrow dirt road. On one side is forest and on the other some farmer's grassy field. We bump over ruts.

"Won't this hurt your car?"

"It's a Ford," he says, as if that explains everything.

The road curves left; he's driving more slowly now.

"Think this is the right way?"

"Pretty sure. Hope so."

Adam never seems to lose his good nature. I remember his equilibrium as a boy: his handsome face and good manners. What Elliot used to say about him: *Oh, he's smooth.*

"You ever think about Elliot?"

Adam, concentrating on navigating the bumpy road, doesn't look at me.

"No, not much."

Then, without glancing over, he asks casually, "You ever sleep with him?"

I'm shocked at the question. "Why do you ask?"

Adam laughs. "We always wondered. Some of the residents even put bets on it. I didn't," Adam adds quickly, "but others did. Shawn. Kurt and Manny. They were all hot for you. That long curly hair! Those little dresses! A lot of nighttime activity took place because of you. You and—what was her name? That teacher with the big shoes?"

"Layla. Really?"

"Oh yeah."

He laughs like we'll both think it's funny. "We thought about you—the women, anyway. Some of the men. We liked Garrett and Kenny. The rest of them, mostly, were idiots. We thought we were smarter than all of you."

All this time, he's been driving deeper and deeper into the forest. The road is narrower here and deeply rutted. It is taking a long time to drive in, and it will take a long time to drive out.

"Where do you think the trailhead is?" I ask him to change the subject. I'm uncomfortable with this conversation. Adam seems different now, saying these things.

"I have no idea, Lorraine. I've never been here before."

Only, why do I think that he *has* been here, maybe years ago, sometime between college and law school, driving alone in late spring?

"This make you uncomfortable? All this talk about Sunrise, how we thought about you?"

"I guess so. A little."

"You were always so transparent," Adam says fondly. "You weren't tough enough to work there. You weren't like Evelyn. You couldn't handle yourself. That's probably what made you so hot. Your, I don't know—vulnerability. Come on, you can tell me. You and Elliot—you guys ever do it?"

"No," I say, staring down at my hands, certain he'll know that I'm lying.

But he only says, "Jeez. Too bad for old Elliot! He sure wanted to. He was always watching you. Must have killed him."

"I was engaged, you know," I say primly.

Adam laughs again. "Yeah. But Sunrise was like its own little world, wasn't it? Everything else seemed unreal when you were there."

"Elliot was married. What makes you think he had affairs?"

"Oh, you could just see it," Adam says. "He was one of those little guys who always want to feel bigger. He was fucking Evelyn—and this other one, Claire, before that. We all knew it. It was almost like he wanted us to know. Another head trick to control us."

I don't like that he said *fucking Evelyn*. It makes Adam seem coarse. The car feels claustrophobic, and I feel queasy.

We're deep in the woods now, the road just a narrow track. The trees are closing in around us, and the woods look tangled, dirty, unkempt, the ground mossy and dank. It will be hard to move through this forest because it's so thick.

At last, we come to a clearing with a small gravel parking area and a rusty blue pickup that looks like it's been there for years. There's just space for the SUV, and Adam pulls in.

"Well, here we are. There's the trailhead."

And, sure enough, there's a log post and a dirt trail leading into the damp, dark forest.

By the time we've gotten our packs out of the car, I wish I'd never come. There are tons of mosquitoes and blackflies. I spray myself all over with Cutter's, closing my eyes tight and spraying the cool poison right into my face.

"You think you got enough of that stuff on you?" Adam laughs.

I open my eyes, and he's right beside me, tightening the straps of his pack. He's carrying the tents and food; all I've got is my sleeping bag, a change of clothes, and the knife I slipped into my rolled-up clothes in my backpack. It's a big knife, with a long, sharp blade, used for carving meat. I felt foolish taking it, but I'm glad, now, I have it.

TWENTY-EIGHT

After a while, the trail opens up, and we are walking along a pleasant forest path, broad enough that we can walk side by side, which makes me more comfortable. I didn't like having him behind me, watching, appraising.

"This is nice," I say, to break the silence between us.

Adam says nothing, but I hear his tread. The backpack must be heavy even though he doesn't complain. He was always a good hiker, even as a teenager. Never sweaty or bitching like the other, ill-equipped kids with their cheap sneakers and tight black jeans. Adam always had proper hiking clothes. Good leather boots, the right kind of gear.

"Did you hike with your family when you were a kid?" I ask.

"Some," he says.

We walk on in silence. I am getting used to the cadence and begin to feel the quiet elation I always experience in the woods: the strength of my legs, the fine, clean force of endeavor.

I imagine Annie, with Garrett behind her. Imagine what it was like. It was spring. She was twenty-seven, with only a few days left before she would fly back to Maine. They'd been off-trail and had spent the night in Prineville, where they got a room in a roadside motel with a hollow plywood door and a small TV on a battered bureau. Little packaged soaps in the bathroom and a tin-walled shower that made a sound like a Chinese gong when you hit the side of it, which Annie did, first by accident, then again to amuse Garrett. *Bong!* There was a questionable, cheap brown rug on the floor and an ugly maroon bedspread. But for all that, it was romantic—to be alone together and off the trail, no chance of anyone stopping by to share a meal or talk. She took a long hot shower, then Garrett did, and they made love on the double bed in that Prineville motel with the sound of the cars going by.

It sounds like a river, she said, lifting her head to look at him as he lay beside her, both of them dazed and content.

His eyes were so close and so blue. His face—dear and familiar. *I love you.*

I love you, too. But I'm starving, he might have said.

They both would have been starving—all that hiking and sex, and they both always liked to eat. I remember Annie standing in the kitchen in her rumpled blue oxford shirt, big wooden spoon in her hand, saying exuberantly, *Wait'll you taste this! Don't you just love good food?*

I remember Annie and Garrett sitting at the long table in the lodge, both of them eating huge helpings at supper and neither one feeling, as I always felt, that they shouldn't eat this or that. Annie just laughing and saying, *Oh, you look fine, Lorraine. Don't worry about calories! Eat! Enjoy! It's good!*

And then, a million years ago, on a dim quiet springtime evening, they were walking down the highway together hand in hand in Prineville, Virginia, their hair still wet from the shower. Neither realizing it was their last full night on Earth.

What would Prineville have been like in those days? A busier, more prosperous place. No Walmart, back then, just a diner, a drugstore, a five-and-dime, an IGA. A hardware store and a clothing store with a mannequin in the window wearing an Easter dress. Annie might have stopped and looked at the dress, then turned away, laughing.

What? Garrett would ask.

That dress, Annie might have said. *I could never get away with it. Can't you picture Lorraine wearing it, maybe? Or Layla?*

Sure, Garrett might have answered, not really interested, playing along. He would have done anything for her. They had not yet had time to tire of one another. They were still so new in their love. They had not decided to marry, had not yet begun to bicker. Neither one felt stifled, suffocated, or resentful. They were just in love.

I think you'd look nice in it, too, he might have said, putting his arm around her.

They would have gone into the diner then and sat in a booth and eaten big platefuls of food, then walked back up the highway to spend the last full night of their lives in a real bed, holding one another, waking early before sunrise to make love one more time, before they pulled on their hiking clothes, shouldered their packs, and headed back onto the trail.

Adam's behind me again. He's very quiet. I remember how easily, naturally, he always moved through the woods.

"What are you thinking?" he asks me.

"Oh, odds and ends," I say. "Actually, I was trying to imagine what it was like to be Annie walking here. Do you think she was scared, like she had some kind of premonition?"

"I doubt it. I bet it came as a total surprise. When you're young, you don't think bad things will happen, unless you've had a pretty terrible childhood. And then you expect it all the time."

"Did you have a terrible childhood?"

"Pretty terrible. You?"

"Not terrible, exactly," I say. "But I had a difficult mother."

I don't want to tell him about my mother's rages or my own rages when Susannah was young. The guilty memories that bunch together, repeat, and come back to haunt me, deep in the night, when I can't sleep.

"It's complicated," I say.

"It's always complicated," Adam says. "And it's always completely simple."

"That sounds like something Elliot would say."

"It *is* something Elliot said. I got it from him. I was listening, you know, back then. I was watching."

What does he mean, he was watching? How much did he see?

"What are you doing here, Lorraine?" he asks me. "What are you trying to find?"

How can I explain how it felt when I saw their faces again in the newspaper? How it all came back to me. It seemed as if, after Annie and Garrett were killed and the kids attacked us at Baxter, nothing really went right. Oh, maybe at first. I left Sunrise, I got married, and we had Susannah. But the marriage ended, and then things went wrong with Susannah.

But I don't want to tell him all that, so I only say, "I don't know. I guess I needed a project. Seemed like it had all the elements of a good story."

"Is that it? I thought maybe you were investigating. Trying to find out what really happened that night up in Baxter. You are kind of nosy, aren't you?" Adam asks, his voice suddenly cold, and the woods seem ominous again, even though it's just the same: sunlight coming down through the trees, uneven splotches of light on the forest floor. Quiet path turning this way and that, random big rocks and leaves.

Who is this man, anyway? Why did he suddenly appear at Caledonia with his backpack and tents? His story seems rickety, fabricated out of old bedsheets and sticks in the backyard. And I fell for it, as I've always fallen for what any man told me. Whenever I've been stuck in a bad place, some man's come along, and he's been nice and he seems intelligent, and he happens to have a tent, and I think: *Oh! This is the one!* and go into the woods with him, and I've always been wrong, except maybe way back, with Jake. Then he was the one who chose badly.

I'm walking more slowly now, and my pack feels heavy. I'm no longer imagining Annie and Garrett. No longer summoning images and re-creating their story in my head. I am back with my old anxieties churning around inside, my inabilities and my failings. My marriages and my daughter, my dead-end job. All the regrets that still plague me after all the miles I've walked, trying to shake them. All that meditation! That fucking yoga! All that massage and craniosacral therapy, all the potions and lotions. None of it's worked—*really* worked.

"You okay, Lorraine?" Adam's voice brings me back to the moment. "You're slowing down. Want to stop and rest? Take a drink of water?"

"I'm okay," I say, though I'm not.

We walk on, the silence between us heavy. I struggle to redirect my thinking, to concentrate on the woods around me. Concentrate on the forward movement. Concentrate on the story.

"How much farther, you think, to the campsite?"

"I don't know," Adam says. "But we'll find it. It was number twenty-one."

"Don't you think it's weird we haven't passed anyone?"

"Yeah, I don't know. You can go a long time on the AT and not see a soul. And then you'll pass, like, three or four groups in a row." Adam paused. "What happened with your daughter?" he asked me. "You don't talk much about her."

"Well, there's not much to tell. Things got kind of bad when she was a teenager, and I couldn't handle it. I finally sent her to a residential treatment center when she was fifteen."

I don't know what I expected, but I'm taken aback when Adam laughs.

"Kind of ironic, isn't it? How'd that work out for her?"

"She wasn't there very long," I say. "She ran away."

"She did, eh? Good for her! How long before they found her?"

"They didn't."

Adam looks at me sharply. "But she came home eventually, right?"

I shake my head. I can't speak. I can't talk about Susannah.

I think he will put his hand on my arm, say something kind. He's a parent, after all. He must know what this costs me. Instead, he laughs again, harshly: a short, hard laugh like a bark.

"Karma's a bitch, isn't it?" Adam chuckles. Then, seeing my face, looks down. "Aw, come on Lorraine, what happened to her?"

I shrug and walk on.

By the time we reach the campsite, it's not dark, but the light has changed.

"Number twenty-one," I say, taking off my backpack.

There's a small clearing in the thick forest and a wooden platform, dark with damp. Down a narrow path, a small outhouse.

At first, the place seems too ordinary to hold so much history.

Then I see the logs arranged around a charred fire pit, imagine two people sitting there companionably, talking about their future.

I can feel it, then, what I came for. Can almost see Annie smiling, her crinkly eyes, and Garrett's face, his long hair. Can imagine them sitting there, looking up as Lewis Ray Bladgett emerged from the woods.

Well, Lewis Ray! Annie would have said, as if they were old friends, though they'd just met that afternoon. She would have offered him something to eat, maybe given him a beer. They might have bought beer in town, before heading back to the trail. They would have walked the same path Adam and I just walked, talking or not talking. In love with one another, as certain of their future together as they were of the path that stretched before them, over mountains and hills, all the way to Katahdin.

Lewis Ray would have been shy and a little awkward. Garrett would have preferred to be alone with Annie—irrepressible Annie, who never left anyone out, not even Lewis Ray. Not even me. Garrett might have rolled his eyes at Annie's latest stray, even though her generosity of spirit was one of the things he loved most about her. Lewis Ray might have stood in the shadows, unwilling to enter their circle of light, but Annie would have known how to coax him, and he would've finally edged in to sit awkwardly on a log near the fire.

Annie would have carried the conversation. *I can talk to a post,* she used to say, laughing.

That's when the other party went by. The couple from New Hampshire who saw them at the fireside that night, then camped farther down the trail: too far to hear the gunshot, to hear Annie's screams. Who walked on the next morning, away from the place where Annie and Garrett lay, littered with leaves and twigs from the forest floor.

"Well, I better get going," Lewis Ray might have said, after a while. "Thanks for your hospitality."

Or did he just leave abruptly, knowing he'd be back later?

"What are you thinking about?"

Adam already has one of the tents up. I am still standing by the wooden platform, staring into the darkening forest.

"Annie and Garrett."

"Ah."

Adam puts up the second tent, moving deftly. He doesn't seem tired, though I'm exhausted—and he had the heavier pack. He must be in really good shape.

I want to absorb my impressions, but I ought to help.

"What can I do?" I ask.

"You could find some kindling. And bring over some of those logs."

Later, when we've eaten our supper, we sit by the campfire; the heat feels good against the evening's chill.

I'm quiet, trying to recapture the story. Adam is quiet, too. He seems moody. Our earlier camaraderie has faded, and, I think again, *I don't even know this man.*

"We still haven't seen anyone else," I say. It is making me edgy.

"Well, it's early in the season," he says. "We'll probably pass someone when we head out tomorrow."

We're hiking back out in the morning. I should have enough by then to wrap up the novel, and Adam will go back to Portland. To whomever is waiting for him there. If there is someone.

"Did you tell anybody where you were going?"

Adam is quiet for a moment, staring into the fire.

"Who would I tell?" he says, finally. "I don't have a lot of friends. My son's pretty busy these days. I get along with the people at work, but we're not close or anything."

I imagine his sad life—that he lives in some very nice apartment, but all by himself. Dates women he's not particularly interested in. Goes to work, stays late. Eats in restaurants.

Beyond the small circle of firelight the forest is dark and endless. I hear something, some animal, maybe, moving stealthily through the thick trees. A silence, and then it begins again, almost as if the forest itself is moving, closing in on this place with its history of terror, old screams.

We sit in silence, then Adam says softly, "You haven't changed much, have you, Lorraine? You're still pretty trusting. I mean, you don't know me—not really. You've just taken my word for it—the whole story."

At first, I think he's kidding.

"I mean, how do you know that's my car, even? I could have rented it—or stolen it—for all you know. And nobody knows we're together. Nobody back home in Maine even knows I'm here. And you didn't tell anybody, did you?"

He looks at me, his eyes glinting.

Suddenly, I'm afraid of him; I can't speak.

"By the time they figure it out at Caledonia—if they do—and someone comes looking for you, it will be too late. I'll be long gone."

Now, I am frozen, terrified, my heart pounding.

He's still regarding me calmly, as if we were having an ordinary conversation.

What the hell was I thinking coming out here with him? Had I learned nothing?

"I could be psychotic, you know. It could all be a string of lies—everything I've told you. Could have come down here to make sure you don't put anything in that book that I don't want there. I mean, what do you really remember about that night up at Baxter? We don't need you digging around in the past. And you haven't exactly been honest with me, either, have you, Lorraine?"

In the flickering light from the fire, his face looks misshapen.

"I mean, what's the story with your daughter? Is she dead? Is that why you clammed up back there?"

I force myself to answer.

"She's not dead. I just haven't seen her in a while. She's in California." But I don't actually know if that is the truth. It's what I'm used to telling people.

"California?" he scoffs. "Yeah, right! Let's face it, Lorraine, neither one of us has had any luck with our lives. If anything happened to us out here, the world wouldn't miss us. And you wouldn't miss this, would you?" He indicates the dark woods, the small patch of light by the fire. "Wouldn't it be a relief, Lorraine? To just get it over with? Your whole shitty life? You're not happy. You've got a dead-end job. Your daughter won't speak to you—if she's even alive. You don't have anyone close to you, if you ever did. Sounds like you can't stand your mother, and now you're saddled with her. It wouldn't be so bad, would it—to just be done?"

I've stopped breathing.

Then, he smiles at me.

"Got you thinking, didn't I?" He picks up a rock and throws it, suddenly, into the fire, and a spray of sparks fly up. The sudden move makes me flinch, and he laughs.

"Ah, I'm just fucking with you, Lorraine. Hey—no," he turns and looks at me closely. "You didn't believe me, did you?" He's still laughing, ruefully now. "Ah, I'm sorry. I scared you. I took it too far. I was just kidding. Come on. You always were gullible."

I don't know what to believe. Maybe he was only joking, but everything he said rang true.

"Very funny," I manage, finally, with a crimped sort of smile.

"Ah," Adam says again, putting his arm around me. "I was just kidding around."

"Yeah," I say stiffly.

"You're really tired," he says, his arm still around me. "You okay?" he asks, looking into my face. His arm slides down toward my hips, gently brushing past my waist, my hips.

"Wow," he says softly. "You look just the same, Lorraine. You look like a young girl in the firelight. Just like I remember you."

His voice is tender, but I don't trust him. He leans in, trying to kiss me. I pull away. "Aww, come on," he says. He tightens his grip around me and pulls me toward him, and then he is kissing me roughly and fumbling at my breast.

"Stop it!" I shove him away and manage to stand. "Get off of me."

"Ah, don't be like that!"

I snatch up the flashlight, reassured by its heft, and go down the narrow path to the outhouse. The door doesn't shut right, and even though Adam is far away, still sitting by the fire, I hold the door closed with one hand.

After I'm done getting ready for bed, I head back to the platform lit by the dying fire. I don't look around at the forest; it's too big and too dark. I just want to get in my tent and go to sleep and leave in the morning. Once we get back to Caledonia, Adam can go on his way.

I can see him, silhouetted, still sitting by the fire, but from this angle, I can't see his face. In the dim light, I can't even see the color of his hair. He could be anyone.

"Good night, Lorraine," he calls softly. "No hard feelings."

I crawl into my tent, remembering how I lay with my head at the far end that night at Baxter. How that saved me. I pull my nightgown out of my pack, because I can't bear the thought of sleeping in my dirty hiking clothes. Tomorrow, when I get back to Caledonia, I'll have a nice hot shower. I'll think about that as I go to sleep, imagine the sound of the water, the feel of it on my body, my upturned face.

As I unroll the nightgown, it feels weird, heavy and hard: something in it. And then I remember the knife that's rolled up inside.

It seems silly now. And yet, when I've wriggled into my nightgown and burrowed down into the sleeping bag, I put the knife on the cool floor of the tent, close by me, just in case.

Somehow, finally, I fall asleep, and then I am dreaming. I'm Annie at this same campsite on the Appalachian Trail, a half day's journey from Prineville.

In my dream, there is someone beside me. Someone I love who is warm and dark in the night. We've made love, and now I am tired. The forest is quiet around us, and I am savoring, in my dream, that lovely silence: the silence of the forest, the silence of love.

Oh this, I think in my dream.

We're asleep beside one another. I love him so much. *Garrett!* His name in my mind, his body beside me. We've zipped our two sleeping bags together to make one whole. We are united, asleep in the forest like children.

Something—a noise outside the tent. A rustling sound. I poke Garrett.

What is it? he whispers.

An animal?

He sits up first. So he's the one who is shot when the tent is torn open, and the bullet flies in.

I scream. I clutch him. I scream. Then someone is grabbing me, pulling me out. It's that man. What's his name?

Lewis Ray! I say. *Lewis Ray!* Because that's what you do when somebody's crazy. You say their name. *Stop it*, you say, *Lewis Ray.*

But then he's thumping at me with something hard. Thud! And it hurts. It's a knife.

I look down. I am bleeding. *I'm bleeding.* He is stabbing me, stabbing me!

I try to pull away, try to reason—I think I can reason with him, but he's stabbing at me in the dark. This cannot be real. *He shot Garrett!* I don't believe any of this, as he stabs and he stabs. I try to escape but feel myself getting weaker. Try to escape.

But then I am sliding down.

Far away, I hear someone panting. A serious sound, like a dog. *You!* he shouts. *You made me do it!*

He is sobbing. I want to reach out. *No, it's okay*, I should say. I should tell him that I understand. How unhappy he is and how broken. I should tell him. But I'm sliding down. Sliding down into the forest. I look up and see all the trees. Hear him sobbing, but he's far away; the trees are far away and fading, their branches only dark shapes. Fading branches against the night sky. The sound of his sobbing. The sound I am making, which is something animal now, a kind of moaning. I feel it ebbing away.

All this, I think.

Now sleep.

And the forest, so dark a moment ago, is golden and full of light.

Something like peace washes over me as I wake, or half wake, from my dream.

She's gone, but I hear her voice. Annie's gone, but she's left a legacy: a blessing, a kind of release. My half-awake thoughts are jumbled, but at the corner of my mind, there's something that feels like hope. I'm lying here, clinging to the dream, to that feeling of peace—when I hear something outside the tent.

And just like that, I'm awake and rigid. Alert.

Somebody's moving around out there. There's a muffled, shuffling sound.

Is this what Annie heard in the night?

More sounds.

Adam's just going to pee, I tell myself.

He pauses just outside my tent, waiting there. In the long silence, I reach out stealthily. I am aware I have the cold knife in my hand. Slowly, not making a sound, I rise until I am sitting, facing the door of my tent. I can't hear him anymore outside, in the dark, but I can feel him.

I sit quietly waiting, the darkness a solid thing.

Am I imagining this? Is he gone? Was he never out there to begin with?

No sound from outside the tent. Is he there? Can he hear my heart pounding?

Then, with a sudden movement, he unzips my tent, rips open the flap, and leans in. There's no light. I can't see his face, only the dark outline of his body against the night sky. It's just like that night at Baxter, but this time, I'm ready, and I am the one with the knife. He says my name; I'm already moving. I launch myself at him and strike.

After

Coming out of the forest next morning, it does not seem as far.

That's always the way, my dad used to say. *It's always shorter on the way back.*

How I loved my father! Waited for him to come home every time when he'd been away, until he never came home again.

So many thoughts were going around in my head all morning, while I cleaned up the campsite. It's easier than you might think, to drag a body into the forest, dig a hole, and bury it, cover the dirt with leaves.

The tents and the sleeping bags—they were harder. So bulky! I didn't want to carry it all out myself. I'm just not that strong.

I even ate a little, a couple of energy bars, and I drank some water. No sense carrying water out of the forest; I poured the rest into the ground.

Now I'm almost back to the road. His car will be there, and I've got the keys. I'll take it partway and then leave it.

I've already thought this through. There's nothing to connect me with him. He was right about that. He didn't tell anyone where he was going, and nobody at Caledonia ever knew he was there. We kept it a secret.

No one knows what I'm writing about, and when it's published, I'll make sure it's under a different name. I can resume my life, such as it is.

It doesn't matter anyway. Nothing matters now. Everything that matters happened a long time ago.

Yesterday, we passed no one. We were the only ones on the trail the whole way. Now, coming back, again, no one. *Lucky*, I think. I've been lucky. No one will ever know.

It must not be very far now. I've been walking so long. The woods feel friendly, mostly, but I keep thinking I hear someone behind me, the way Adam was behind me yesterday, getting me to tell him things I never tell anyone. Still, I didn't tell him my biggest secrets, did I? I kept those close.

Can't shake the feeling that someone's behind me. I keep looking over my shoulder, but there's only the trail and the trees.

The path seems completely different; it always does, doesn't it, when you're going in a different direction? I don't remember that fallen log, that enormous boulder. But this is the right path; I know it by those white blazes. It's very well marked.

I spot something up ahead, where the trail curves off to the right. Something—or someone?—half hidden beyond the trees. I can't tell who it is, but I know by the shape it's a woman. At first, I think it's Annie.

Annie! I say, raising my hand in greeting.

But, then, when she smiles back, I see that it isn't Annie. How could it be? Annie's dead.

Who is it then? Someone dangerous—someone else that I have to get rid of?

No, now I see who it is.

Susannah, of course. It's my daughter.

My own lost girl, come back at last.

I pick up my pace and then I begin to run to embrace my daughter, but the forest swallows her up again and my outstretched arms find only the empty trees.

THE END

ACKNOWLEDGMENTS

Thanks to Rosa Mayer, Mary Sherman Willis, and Genevieve Morgan for their encouragement and good advice.

Photo by Katherine Emery Photography.

ABOUT THE AUTHOR

Martha Tod Dudman lives in Maine and is the author of *Dawn; Expecting to Fly, Black Olives,* and *Augusta, Gone,* which was adapted as an award-winning film.